A THRILLER THAT EXPOSES THE SOVIETS' STEEL FIST INSIDE GLASNOST'S VELVET GLOVE

"A VERY FINE ESPIONAGE THRILLER . . . THE BEST PICTURE OF LIFE IN MOSCOW SINCE *GORKY PARK* . . . Sebastian is such a good storyteller no one is likely to put this book aside until he has finished it."
—Ralph Graves, author of *Autumn*

"A NAIL-BITING, HARE-AND-HOUNDS STORY . . . for all the old-fashioned quality of its picture of the Soviet Union, *The Spy in Question* is so modern as to undermine the very assumptions of the espionage thriller."
—*The Washington Post*

"ALMOST EVERY PAGE OF HIS NOVEL IS EN-LIVENED BY ATMOSPHERIC OBSERVATIONS. . . . The plot . . . is one of those mirror-maze constructions which if shown in a diagram would be worth hanging on the wall just for the intricacy of the design."
—*Newsday*

"FAST-MOVING   ermer BBC correspondent exp   985 on
charges of spyi   *iews*

"ADROITLY PLO   LING
CONCLUSION."
—*Publish   Weekly*

Tim Sebastian

THE SPY IN QUESTION

A DELL BOOK

For Caroline

ACKNOWLEDGMENTS

Warm thanks should go to Anne McDermid, Peter Ginsberg, and Robert Mecoy for their tireless advice and encouragement. My thanks also to Larry D'Anna and Jimmy Warner.

Tallinn, Soviet Estonia
JUNE 1968

She had been six. Just six years old when the first of the textbook tragedies arrived. Quite old enough to cry textbook tears. Remember?

An elder brother, blessed with a will and vitality that had transformed the little family from the aimless to the inspired, had gone to war and been killed, they said. The records were confused and they didn't know how, they said.

But Father had returned. And returned again in the fifties, this time from prison, his head shaved and his spirit broken. Remember?

And they had lived quietly in a state-decreed area of nine square feet per person, while outside the window the drills and excavators built communism.

The fifties had helped dull the pain, but they

hadn't done much for the hatred. Hatred of friends, even of herself. And for a long time, it seemed, there was no one to help, to soothe, or to share. Remember?

The lucky few found others who had walked similar roads, sat up nights and cried with the frustration of it all. Ira Nikolayeva had found such people.

And she remembered them all as the clock chimed discordantly in the square.

◆

The third hour of night. *Tri Chasa Nochi.* The hour when you die unnoticed, in silence. There was darkness across three time zones. One half of the Soviet Empire asleep, watched over by the other.

A yellow patrol car had drawn up soundlessly in the middle of the main square, its front windows wound down, lights doused. The two-way radio spat intermittently, breaking the peace of the Baltic city. There was one hour to go before the state decreed official sunrise in the Estonian Republic.

The two officers sat in the car without moving, the peaked caps pushed high on their foreheads. Around them the well-ordered tedium of Soviet provincial life weighed heavily. To look at, they seemed halfway between the living and the dead.

Ira watched from a window on the third floor. The car couldn't have been better positioned. She buttoned her cardigan against the summer breeze.

On the bed beside her the man was asleep, a single sheet across him. He had been rough with her and inexperienced. Hours earlier, before falling asleep, he had whispered, "My name is Dmitry." But she had already known that. Now there was just the waiting.

At 3:40 the explosion shattered the glass of the apartment building's main door, ripping the iron frame from its hinges and slamming it into the road.

"Ten, eleven, twelve . . ." Ira could hear herself counting. Where the hell were they?

And then the militia were running toward the entrance, a dozen of them out of nowhere. Lights and cars appeared from neighboring streets. People were hurrying into the square, thick smoke drifting over them.

Ira peered out. The militia had begun shouting wildly. They were confused, frightened. One of them was herding a family into the street, the children wrapped in blankets, the men in striped pajamas. A fat woman with a hair net was screaming incoherently about an air raid.

"Jesus. Mother of God." Dmitry had started awake. A Communist with Christ on his lips. Ira shivered. He fumbled for the light but the power had failed. It didn't take much. The wiring and the circuits were weak. On his knees beside the bed, he hunted for his shoes. Someone knocked on the door.

"Don't come out." It was the caretaker, desperate to take charge. "It's only the first floor. Stay where you are and someone will be around soon."

Dmitry stood up and leaned out of the window. As an afterthought he turned back to Ira. "Are you all right?"

She had begun to stalk Dmitry two weeks earlier. She had felt his life's pulse, watched his movements, assessed his friends. He lived way outside her world. He was Party, twenty-four years old and climbing. Tall, fair-haired, square-shouldered, he came straight out of a worker's poster.

A smiler, Ira had concluded. A *ganzer macher*, someone had muttered in Yiddish—a big shot. One day, they felt certain, Dmitry would fulfill their dreams. As the saying went, "He would go to Moscow and see a tram."

Ira had watched him flit from meeting to meeting, caught the anxious encounters in the corridors of the Party institute, noted the well-dressed figures from the Regional Committee who courted him. Dmitry was cutting political teeth. They had been right. He was the one to take.

On the last two Wednesdays she had blustered her way into the discotheque at the workers' hostel where he lived. It hadn't been difficult. The bouncers had orders to admit all single women and exclude all single men except for Party members. They were different. They had first choice.

Ira had worn the tightest blouse she could find. It accentuated her bosom, marked her out from the shapeless, sagging figures around her. In the corner the Party organizers had stood around in a group, morose and carping. They weren't pleased with the turnout—underage schoolgirls and overage clowns— some caked in makeup, their lipstick smeared over tooth and chin.

They had all noticed the brunette with the boyish haircut and the beckoning eyes. But protocol demanded that Dmitry have the first try.

For an hour Ira had danced to his tune, ruffled her fingers through the short hair on the back of his neck and swayed just an inch too close. As she made for the door he had followed. She had only to reel him in like a prize trout and Dmitry Kalyagin was out of the water, lying on his back—beached.

◆

"What's going on?" He slammed his fists on the windowsill. "What are they playing at? Bastards, scum. Something must be done about it." It was the age-old Russian intention. When in doubt, just do something.

Ira tried to smile. "They'll be here in a minute, the militia. Then we can go."

Every two nights she had changed apartments, moved from city center to suburb and back again. A slim brunette with faded jeans and only a spare T-shirt to carry. She wasn't beautiful, the nose and mouth too large for the elfin face. But she had something. They all said that.

"When you do it," Anatol had told her, "rope him in, screw him, and then let him sleep. We'll manage the rest." Dear Anatol, she thought bitterly. Just the essentials.

They both heard the footsteps on the landing and the lights came on.

"Comrade Kalyagin, open the door." There were two of them, in high black boots and breeches. They looked like traffic police but then they *all* looked like traffic police. Two paces behind them the caretaker was on tiptoe, trying to see into the room.

"You are Kalyagin, Dmitry Ivanovich?" asked the senior of the two.

"Of course, come in." They shuffled into the room, barring the caretaker, looking around them, officious but uncertain.

"You heard the noise. A most regrettable incident."

"How did it happen?" asked Dmitry.

"The proper authorities are investigating. It's fortunate no one was hurt. A report will be prepared." They won't ever say it, thought Ira. They'll never admit to a bomb. But Dmitry had known it instantly.

"Who are you?" The senior officer had turned to her. He took his notebook from an inside pocket. She knew what was coming.

"Documents."

She passed him the red internal passport. He copied the details.

"You're from Riga."

She nodded. His look took in the bed and the open window behind her.

"Perhaps you saw something from up here? Anything at all?" He looked hard at Dmitry. "And you?"

"Nothing."

"You have been here all evening?"

"We returned after midnight," said Dmitry. "A few minutes after."

The militiaman handed back the little book to Ira

and saluted. As the door closed she turned to face Dmitry.

"Sit down," she said, "I have something to say to you."

◆

And she had said it.

It was strange how Dmitry had reacted. She had talked more fluently than she'd expected. How she was the daughter of a Jewish refusenik, how her papers were forged, how her friends had organized the bombing as a small demonstration, how the police now had a record of the two of them together. How easy it had been.

She had talked for just over three minutes, reminding him that in the closed, sanitized world of the Party, the merest hint of their liaison could finish him. The Party sought the pure in heart, whiter than Arctic snow. No time for sins, still less for confessions. He'd have one shot at it—and only the perfect arrived.

All it needed, she said, was a phone call—price two kopecks—and Dmitry would be off the ladder for good. Go on bastard, try me! But he hadn't, just sat there like a small boy, his candy taken by a bully. And then just as she was leaving each had made a promise. She in silence and he in a soft low whisper, every word clearly audible. It was Thursday and neither forgot their promise.

Downstairs again, she picked her way through the broken glass, taking in the scarred plaster in the hallway, the troughs in the ceiling. Nothing excessive, they had said. Just a few fireworks. Communists like fireworks.

On the street the militia were standing around in groups. An ancient fire engine was parked on the pavement. Dust and debris littered the square. No one looked at Ira as she emerged. She crossed the square quickly, heading for the station.

Chapter 1

DECEMBER 4, 1990

James Dawling, convicted traitor and prison inmate, used to get his mail the way everyone else did. It would come opened, with the stamp of the prison censor on the envelope and a blue pencil squiggle on the letter itself.

After a few months he had even begun to recognize the censors' initials, and when one of the sets disappeared for a few weeks, and he discovered the man had retired, Dawling sent a note thanking him for his kindness and attention.

The letter never arrived because none of Dawling's ever did. That was the rule.

And yet, since the summer, he had been surprised to find that communications to him were arriving by a different route, not through the censor, and with no address or signature. One had been pushed under the door of his cell, another beneath his tool kit in the carpentry room. They were odd, he thought, but quite instructive.

So instructive, in fact, that when the "Nanny," as he called him, paid a visit, Dawling knew exactly what to say.

"Morning, Stuart." The man was shown into the visitors' room.

"Morning, James. How's it going? Only another fifteen years and you'll see the back of this place!"

Dawling smiled forgivingly. He knew their ways, knew their strokes. The acid was never far from the surface. They would hate him till the day he died. This one especially. The standard ex-colonial, he was tall, stiff-necked, mustache turning to gray. For use with the low-graders. Fit, but with a brain like a potted plant. Dawling took in the suntan and smelled the after-shave, instantly resenting both.

"What's the lesson today?" he asked, flicking a speck of dust from the arm of his prison uniform. A thin figure, oddly fastidious. Stuart lowered himself into the chair opposite.

"I thought we might go back to the summer of '82, just a few weeks before you . . . er . . . left the embassy in Moscow. You'd been there about two years as I understand it. That sound right?" The eyebrows rose rhetorically. "After all, that was your heyday, wasn't it? First secretary, good prospects. Must be some pleasant memories from that time?"

Dawling hung his head, crestfallen. Stuart could

see he was balding rapidly. It made him look almost babylike, with his scrubbed pink complexion. "But we did that last month," he complained. "Can't we do my other favorite bit? I mean, when the KGB approached me." The voice mimicked that of a small child. It was the ritual foreplay. Dawling would never give of himself without it.

"Tell you what," replied Stuart, "ten minutes on the approach and then we'll look at that summer in Moscow."

"Thank you." Dawling beamed at him. The atmosphere seemed to settle. They lit their cigarettes and chatted like old friends. Dawling chatted.

Stuart fixed a smile on his face and leaned back. He was tired of the visits. Traitors were boring, the job was boring, and he couldn't see the point of it. Dawling had been questioned months ago. In the unkind clutches of the interrogators he had admitted fifteen years of assorted treachery. And for that they had broken him, his self-respect, his arrogance. So why go on? he thought. But London insisted on the meetings, infrequent, irregular, unexpected. One day, went the theory, he would sell his soul for some peace. But not this day.

After an hour Stuart got up to leave and Dawling chose his moment.

"Of course," he murmured, almost to himself, "you've still got your big-time sleeper in Russia, your own Moscow mole"—the voice was suddenly mocking—"so why bother with me?"

Stuart turned around sharply, his guard down. "What are you talking about?"

"Oh, come on. It's obvious, isn't it? You've still got the big boy in there. Some high official you turned before my time. Best one ever, I shouldn't wonder. I mean he may have gone to ground for a year or two, which was why I couldn't finger him. But he's still there, dreaming of England, isn't he?" He smiled suddenly. "Unless, of course, you're having doubts about him. Eh?"

Stuart shook his head pityingly. "Give it up, James. Save it for the Christmas play. You'll get quite a few laughs with that one."

A few miles from the prison Stuart looked for a phone booth, dialed a London number, and gave a detailed account of the way he'd spent his morning. By the time he reached home the classified signal was in Moscow. The one person authorized to read it acted immediately.

Chapter 2

DECEMBER 5

Moscow.

It was an emergency contact, absurdly amateur, and it broke all the rules. Parker could feel the blood rushing to his head. He knew the symptoms. He'd trained to deal with them, watched for them. But fear will have its way.

On the other side of the restaurant a party of patrons were looking across. Had the waitress pointed him out? Do you stay or run? And in this city of nine million cold-hearted Slavs, where do you hide? Fifteen hours by road to a friendly border.

Parker steadied himself and made a conscious effort to relax. Put your hands on the table, slow the breathing down, ease the lines in the forehead. It was working. Gradually his body began feeding him the signals.

"I say, George, did you not hear me?" It was one of the secretaries on the opposite side of the table. "I was asking whether you felt like bridge this weekend. We've still got a game to play off."

"Sure, that's fine. Sorry . . . can't hear a thing with all this racket going on." Parker gestured at the singer, whining her heart out into the microphone at the other end of the room. Thank God for her. At least he hadn't had to talk much that evening. Just get on with chewing the shashlik. He didn't like embassy parties, least of all when they took an outing to a Moscow restaurant. They always stuck out so much. It went against all his training.

He tried to spot the waitress who had handed him the note. Did she know what she'd done? Was she one of Sasha's free-lances? Christ, the whole thing stank.

"George, will you rescue me from this creature?" Mary Cross was grinning at him, two places down on his right. Harrison, from the consulate, was leering inanely down the front of her dress. Parker smiled back at his assistant. "Don't worry about Harrison," he told her, "he's no threat to the female sex, at least that's what his wife told me." There was a general guffaw along the table.

Parker began to wish they had invited the wives that evening. But at least, if anything went wrong, Suzy was out of it. They'd get her out. They'd always promised that.

He waited twenty minutes before leaving. The rest
of the party seemed too drunk to notice. Just as well
they'd been seated in the corner. The quarantine
table, Parker reflected. Minimal risk of infection for
the local population. He pushed his way through the
dancing couples and gypsies and headed for the
door.

As he approached he could hear shouting on the
street. Two or three uniformed militia were struggling with some drunks. Patrons were jeering.
Parker thought nothing of it. A fistfight was often the
end to a beautiful Moscow evening. He pushed past
the doorman and turned right. And then someone
screamed. He looked around to see a militiaman on
the ground. Two people had pinned his arms and a
third was kicking his face. Suddenly everyone
seemed to dive in.

As he turned away Parker found himself staring
straight into the eyes of a young man. The contact
must have lasted less than a second. For by the time
Parker had registered it the man had gone, brushing
him lightly on the sleeve.

He got into his car and felt his coat pocket. Inside
was a thin envelope, rough paper, made in the
U.S.S.R. Bloody Sasha. What a cocky bastard he'd
become. Hell of a way to organize a drop!

◆

When he arrived at the embassy the lights were
out. The Soviet guards on the gate barely stirred. But
because it was Parker's car they phoned the time

over to the Foreign Residents section at KGB headquarters.

Jenkins let him in, his shirttail hanging out from
under an ancient acrylic cardigan. He scampered
quickly back to the front desk. On a small hotplate
below the emblem of the Crown, he began heating
his soup.

The embassy looked grander by night. Dark pictures hung from dark paneled walls. The twentieth
century seemed not to have impinged. A former ambassador had once described the building as a large
and overexpensive cocktail cabinet. But Parker
knew better.

At his desk he read the message. Just once. No
need to dissect it. How quickly it had all been set in
motion—London's request for a search on Kalyagin,
a signal to Sasha, Sasha's report. And now he had it.
The proof. Should he pass it on tonight? Parker decided to wait. After all this time a few more hours
would make no difference.

London could read it in the morning. They would
sit around drinking their tepid tea on the sixth floor
and congratulating themselves. The Moscow source
was alive and well. The three-year hibernation was
over. Parker had found him, Parker had checked. No
need for concern after all. Now what about lunch?

Parker locked the note in his safe. On impulse he
dialed Mary Cross's number. No one answered. He
left it ringing for about five minutes and then dialed
again. Just to make sure.

Outside, Moscow had died. Only the Kremlin

floodlights hinted at life, burning on through the night while the guards kept watch on the Lenin mausoleum. As if someone might steal it in the dark hours before morning.

◆

It was nearly 1 A.M. before he arrived home—the gaunt, yellow-ocher rectangle on the ring road that the foreigners call "Sad Sam." It had been Sad Sam all right for the German POWs who completed it in the early fifties, long after most other countries had shipped their prisoners home. The real name of the building is Sadovo-Samotyechnaya. And like a real ghetto, there is only one way in.

The tiny enclave is home to more than fifty families who watch each other and gossip, much as the Russians do beyond its walls. "The Great Divide" is a nine-foot fence that the local children climb for a glimpse of the decadent West—the Volvos, the Finnish kitchen equipment, American children playing baseball. A place for everyone and everyone in their place. The way the Russians like it.

Suzy was asleep, tired out by their three-year-old son, Steven. The boy had established mastery over her by his sixth month and never let go. Parker adored him, the more so because he hadn't wanted children. While Suzy fussed over shoe sizes and snowsuits, he would luxuriate in the boy's company, his gift of mimicry, his command of language, his make-believe world devoid of intrigue or sin. Parker felt cleansed through his contact with the boy.

He slept well. The security of the city felt seduc-

tive. Nobody would attack you, rob you, or harm you
in any way, unless they were meant to. Moscow
never changed. Nothing was left to chance. Parker
could afford to sleep well.

Chapter 3

DECEMBER 6

He saw the ambassador immediately after lunch. Unlike other embassy staff, Parker had the right of instant access.

The old man got up from his desk. "I suppose we'd better adjourn . . . mmm?" He pulled his walking stick to him and hobbled up the wide staircase, leading the way. "Come along." He gestured toward a door cut in the paneling. "Let's open up shop."

Parker unlocked the door with a plastic card. This was the "cage"—a room within a room, built on struts, made of special concrete. The construction materials had been flown in from London under diplomatic bond. Only British workmen had been allowed to touch them.

The two men passed through an air lock. Parker

pressed a switch and the outer wall filled with the noise of jumbled voices—a recording mixed many times over. A final guard against electronic eavesdropping.

They sat on hard wooden chairs, their legs folded uncomfortably beneath a trestle table. Sir David White, one year away from retirement, outwardly doddering, his long gray hair permanently awry, fumbled for his glasses. "Tell me what you have." Parker gave him about half of it and left out the names. He didn't want the old fellow dropping dead from fright.

Mary Cross noted that the cage was in use. As Parker's assistant, she was the only other diplomat with a key. After twenty minutes she tried the door but the override had been activated from inside. The room was impenetrable. It looked like a long session. She would have to find out the score later on. She was good at that.

Ms. Cross, as she wrote her name, was, at twenty-four, the youngest diplomat in the embassy. Most of the staff liked her. The men enjoyed the slim waist and the swell of the hips. They wondered who kept her warm during the long Moscow winter.

In summer she had done all that was expected of her—thrown the right number of cocktail parties, struggled with the ambassador on the dance floor, and tanned herself on weekend trips to the Bay of Joys. There had even been a nighttime topless dip in the Moscow River with a few of the junior staff. But no one got near enough to satisfy their curiosity. The

Russian drivers called her "Lebyodushka"—Little Swan—although she was a brunette, with a wide mouth and an upturned nose.

Looking at her ready and welcoming smile, it was possible to forget that Mary Cross had wide and varied experience—three years at Lady Margaret Hall, Oxford, and a year's postgraduate study at the University of Bucharest in Romania.

"Why Romania?" the Foreign Office had asked at the first interview.

"I wanted to broaden my horizons," she told them without a hint of a smile.

And because the British still love the unusual and eccentric, and Romania seemed more enterprising than secretarial college, they had accepted it and asked no further questions.

Mary saw Parker dash past the office door. She got up quickly and followed him into the corridor.

"Problems?"

"No, everything's fine." He was handing his keys to the security guard, hurrying to the door.

"Good time last night?" he asked.

"Oh, I just went straight home to bed." But she said it to herself. Parker had gone.

◆

Her answer, she reflected later, had been only partly untrue. She had not gone home, but she had certainly gone to bed.

Mary sighed. That was the problem. For the man she had joined in that bed wasn't just the citizen of a non-NATO country—first rule broken—but he even worked for a non-NATO embassy. Cardinal sin. Automatic excommunication.

And it shouldn't have happened.

She fought the Saab into gear and nosed it out along the Morisa Teresa Embankment. Lunch at home today. An afternoon off. Not a moment too soon.

He, of course, had planned it all sometime ago. She'd known that, and even compensated for it. Made sure they never went home together, stayed too long together, avoided long looks, and held hands. Kept it all, well, sort of friendly.

And then she'd let down her guard, just once, gone back to his apartment, let those Balkan hands run all over her, let her good intentions float out the window, over Dmitrovskoye Avenue, and dive into the Moscow River.

Did they know? Of course *they* would know. The Russians listened to everything. But could she keep it quiet, keep him quiet, get the relationship back on the rails before it did her damage?

Inside the apartment, she poured a gin and tonic and settled back on the sofa.

I'll write to Mother, she thought, and realized she was worried. She often thought of her mother when things got tough.

Darkness came suddenly in the early afternoon. The streets were crowded. Only "the Capitalist" was working—the giant snow-clearing machine, so named for its grasping hands.

The minister was slumped in the back of the old Volga, which twisted and skidded through the rush-hour traffic. He leaned forward to the driver.

"Please turn down the heater." There was no response.

"I said turn down the heating." The bullet head and the beige cap moved a fraction.

"The switch is broken." And then with bad grace: "I'm sorry, Comrade Minister."

Sorry, he thought. Maybe that was something. In the old days the drivers would break the cars up for the hell of it. Now they were sorry and the cars broke down by themselves. God, there was a long way to go!

By the time they reached the compound the savage heat had made the minister feel sick. The driver missed nothing.

"Something wrong, Comrade?" He came around and opened the passenger door.

"I'm sick, what of it?"

"Good night then."

The driver banged the car into gear and lurched off across the parking lot. The minister stood for a moment, inhaling the icy air as the taillights disappeared toward the Lenin Hills.

Minister Kalyagin was still tall and fair. The twenty-year climb from Estonia hadn't changed that. But the figure had gone. The endless Party lunches, where the few gorged themselves on behalf of the many, had pushed his belly well over his belt. Still, he comforted himself, only dogs went for bones.

He turned around and saw that the militia had already opened the main door. They were standing awkwardly, wondering when to salute. Get a move on! Soviet officials don't hang around on street corners.

The phone was ringing as he entered the apartment.

"Comrade Minister, good evening. I'm glad I found you." It was Perminev from Protocol. Kalyagin called him "Ishaika"—sniffer dog. A true child of the Soviet system, a bureaucrat of indeterminate status and level. You never knew if he was above or below you. And, most likely, neither did he.

"You got home all right? Someone said you weren't feeling well."

Someone. They always used that word. Kalyagin's mind registered a small question mark.

"I'm fine," he said. "I'll go to bed early. Maybe I ate something. Thank you for calling. It's not serious."

He made his way to the sitting room, turning on lights as he went. They had installed an elaborate glass chandelier, made in Czechoslovakia. In the current climate of stringency he'd been lucky to get it. The new general secretary had ordered cutbacks all around.

The apartment held few personal possessions. Cream walls, a brown sideboard, parquet floors. At least he had his own stereo. A Sony from the Central Committee store. His secretary had come over especially to look at it. He flipped it on as he crossed the room.

Kalyagin sank into an armchair and looked about him like a patient in a doctor's waiting room. He had just begun to enjoy the Mozart when he heard a car honking outside. Six stories below it blared out into the Moscow chill and then stopped abruptly.

◆

Perminev disliked the Protocol section. "Ass wiping," he called it. Some of the ministers from the outlying republics could barely fasten their own trousers. If a car didn't take them, they would be utterly stranded. They couldn't manage the buses, they couldn't find the metro, and they wouldn't even have five kopecks for a ticket. Some, he thought bitterly, hadn't walked on a city street, ridden a tram, or suffered a chance encounter with anyone for decades. This one, though, was different.

He glanced down at the blue file. This Estonian, Kalyagin, was a cut above the rest. Perminev tapped his pen on the desk. What was it that stood out about the man? He flicked through the pages. Yes, that was it . . . "likes walking." Well, the Estonian was going to have to settle for going by car. For life.

Perminev closed the file and locked his desk. He hurried out of the office and down the corridor, signing the personnel register beside the elevator. . . . A neat little man, his colleagues thought. A shade too thin, some said. Ferret-like, thick black hair greased back. He turned few heads along the corridor.

◆

The minister switched off the Mozart and went into the kitchen. In the refrigerator was the polyeth-

ylene-packaged meal from the Central Committee
store. There were fresh vegetables in a pot on the
stove. He could exert himself and turn on the gas or
have one of the staff maids on twenty-four-hour duty
come up and do it for him. Or anything else for that
matter. That was freedom of choice.

The sound of the horn had excited and unsettled
him. An old Morse signal that came to life and died
away again with only his recognition. A mental trigger. He had learned it both awake and asleep. He'd
hear it in a crowd or a graveyard. "If they played it at
your funeral," someone had once told him, "you'd sit
up and take notice."

He looked at his watch. Four-fifteen Moscow time.
Three hours ahead of London. After all these years
London was activating him, pressing his button. Suddenly he realized he was shaking. They wanted a
status report, a health check, they called it. Across
the thousands of miles of Europe and western Russia
a hand was knocking at his door.

Kalyagin reached out to the wall where a cockroach was ambling leisurely across but thought better of it. Reprieved, the insect crawled behind a pho-
tograph of the Kremlin.

A memory flashed at him from his childhood. He
must have been fifteen at the time, for he was visiting
his mother in the Tallinn hospital, where she had
spent so many of her final years. He recalled seeing a
cockroach heading toward her and without thinking
he'd picked up a newspaper to kill it. But the old lady

was quicker. "Don't do that," she had told him. "It's company."

◆

Perminev had not eaten since lunch. He was desperate to get home. Fat chance. They always kept him waiting and apologized with total insincerity. He hated it but made a mental note to try the same tactic on his own people.

"Come!" A door had opened from the inner office and a general stood there in full uniform. Inside there were two more officers. Perminev was shown to a low wooden chair while his hosts remained at their desk, status confirmed. It was a big room, barely lit by the single bulb in the middle with the cheap lampshade. He sat down under one of Lenin's angrier portraits.

"This is your final report?" The oldest of the three gestured toward Perminev's blue file.

"Yes, I think it's all there."

"Think?" The man pursed his lips. "No qualifications?"

Perminev sensed a trapdoor opening in front of him—an oubliette with a long drop down. Too late to turn back. "All the details are correct." The senior officer took off his glasses, looked at Perminev, and cocked an eyebrow at his two colleagues. Far below them the central heating coughed terminally.

"In that case," said the officer, "he will be summoned in the morning." He fixed Perminev with a stare. "On your final recommendation. Good night, Comrade."

Not until he got to the bottom of the hill did Perminev look back at the building he'd left. It was one of those beautiful Moscow nights, streaked with red. He looked hard at the Lubyanka. Perhaps people were right. If you stood on the roof, you might indeed see all the way to Siberia.

◆

The general wished his lieutenant good night and remained alone with his personal assistant.

"That's one problem less," he said, "which of course leaves us with another." He yawned and shut his eyes. "Our chairman says there's a leak. He can hear it. Like air from a tire. He wants us to shake a few trees, see what falls to the ground."

The assistant looked eager. "Where shall I start?"

"I have started," said the general. "Matter of fact, I started in England. No reason. Just a thought."

"You mean Dawling," the assistant inquired.

The general stared straight ahead and yawned a second time.

◆

Parker left his car by the Intourist Hotel where it would excite no attention. Across the road the thermometer showed the temperature sliding. Soon the slush would be frozen. In the streetlights the people were little more than shadows.

By the time he reached the Sadko Cafe, Parker was shaking from the cold.

He hadn't wanted to meet there, right on Pushkinskaya. Much too near the Kremlin. The center of Moscow was said to be full of informers and watchers, some paid, others hopeful of payment. Sasha was already there. As he caught sight of Parker he ordered coffee and cocktails, Russian style.

"The bartender is a friend." The boy was reassuring. An odd face, thought Parker. The East written clearly into the features, the slant of the eyes, the flattish nose. A wide face, pale and sickly but not unpleasant. He remembered him saying that he'd come to Moscow from Central Asia to get a little civilization. Perhaps he'd believed it was sold across shop counters.

A waitress brought the drinks—milky, sweet concoctions made up of Vietnamese gin, Cuban brandy, and Syrian grape juice. Soviet foreign policy in a glass.

The boy chewed his straw.

"Did you make the signal?" Parker took off his glasses. They had fogged up in the dry heat of the cafe. He cleaned them on a napkin. "We need to know more."

"The contact has been made by now. You know it won't be easy the next time. It'll get more and more difficult. Like calling God and expecting an answer."

At the next table two girls began to laugh. Parker looked around sharply. They were reading the future from coffee grounds. They giggled again.

"What news do you have?" he asked the boy. "Have you got a job?"

"Got it yesterday. Sort of unofficial. A friend of mine works at the Bolshoi. He arranged it. Helping out, loading, that sort of thing. I was worried it might damage my hands and then who will bring honor on my poor country?" He snorted with laughter.

"When can you get the reply for me?"

"You'll have it tomorrow."

"Good. I'm going to leave now. You stay here for a while."

The boy looked hurt. "Of course. I know that. By the way, I'm playing tonight." He smiled bashfully. "It's a competition against France. We will win, of course."

And then he looked at Parker and the face was serious. "So now you know my plans. Tonight I work for Russia and tomorrow against it. I won't ask you yours."

◆

Parker eased himself gratefully into the cold air. The masses surrounded him, pushing, striving. The Gadarene instinct alive and well.

He worried about Sasha. The boy was high-strung, artistic, moody. Not right for the game. And yet he had what London had been gracious enough to call "commitment"—the desire to sell out his country because he no longer believed in it. They liked that type. It was one-way traffic and no obligations. No carping or histrionics. The man was a find.

Parker recalled the first time they had met. An extraordinary evening. He and an embassy colleague had been talking to a singer at the National Hotel. They had half expected to be propositioned and they were. But the invitation was unusual. "Come to an artistic salon," the girl had said. The salon was a rickety tumbledown flat near the zoo. There'd been no front door.

Through the smoking joss sticks Parker had made out a dozen or so people, sitting on the floor, leaning against the walls. Most were in their twenties or seventies. The middle generation was absent.

Mugs of coffee had been distributed and the performance began. An out-of-work and unpublished poet recited rhyming couplets, two girls assaulted violins in the name of music, and a bearded Central Asian did instant sketches in chalk. Alternative Moscow. In the middle of an awful and endless ballad Parker had turned around to find Sasha, bored and frustrated and looking for conversation.

He had talked about Soviet life and compared it unfavorably with his dreams. And as the violins screeched on they had agreed to meet and talk again, as much to escape the salon as to cement a relationship. Parker was to escort the boy across the narrow border between the normal and the secret. But on the night of their first meeting he had few expectations. Sasha, by contrast, was congratulating himself on a job well done.

◆

Kalyagin switched out his light soon after ten. He had encoded the message from memory. The key was an English nursery rhyme, known to hundreds of thousands of children the world over. So simple, so like the British. You had only to reverse the order of the lines according to the day of the week and you were there. Add some mental arithmetic and a harmless verse became a tool of espionage.

He had planned to spend the evening drinking. Why not? As long as you didn't get pissed in public, no one said anything. Not that you could get pissed in public these days. None of the ministries served vodka, and since the new general secretary had arrived the Kremlin was dry for the first time in history. It was disgusting. The man had come to power on a sea of mineral water.

But tonight . . . well, tonight he'd heard the signal and the drinking was out. Kalyagin knew he needed a clear head.

In bed he recalled the many and varied uses of alcohol in the Soviet system. Back in Tallinn in the late sixties there had been two of them running for the chairmanship of the district cell. God, he'd wanted that job . . . no, not wanted . . . he'd needed that job. The first big leap up the ladder.

But Ouspensky had been the favorite. He'd been screwing the daughter of a Central Committee man —an ugly cow—even mentioned something about marrying her and she had gone all gooey and tiptoed off to Daddy, who'd promised to fix it.

But Kalyagin had had his own friends. Be nice to Ouspensky, they told him. Take him out for a drink, somewhere really public. Give him a real dose. Shaft him.

Ouspensky had been so grateful for the invitation. Probably desperate for a night away from Daddy's girl. He had really wanted to let his hair down. They had gone to the Mira Hotel, where all the foreign tourists stayed, and by eleven Ouspensky was heading for trouble. He had gotten into a heated argument with some Finns who were just as drunk as he was. Then he had thrown a bottle at them, then another, and the militia had stepped in, hacking at anything that moved, and Ouspensky was out of the race.

Next day Kalyagin had gotten up to denounce him at the local Party meeting. But he could have saved himself the trouble. They already knew.

Later, Ouspensky had been quite philosophical about it. "It doesn't really matter," he told his colleagues. "It only matters if you care."

It had been a good lesson, and since that day Kalyagin had tried not to care too much about anything. And yet you had to hold on to something. In the darkness he put out his hand to the bedside table, feeling under the clock for the thin strip of paper. It was there all right, on one side a series of numbers, listed in two vertical columns. The "health check." The report on his vital signs. Stable and improving by the day.

Chapter 4

DECEMBER 7

Zina Potapova was probably rated one of the least important people in Moscow. She belonged to the Services Department of the Council of Ministers. Years earlier they had passed her an eight-page contract that held out the prospect of a new apron and slippers every year and life imprisonment or death if she opened her mouth about anything she saw. She had signed.

On the whole, Potapova had pleased her employers. She had completed the statutory one year's probation and the KGB had declared her clean. The one nagging doubt about her father's death in one of Stalin's labor camps was ignored. After all, everyone knew someone who had died in the camps. No one was that clean.

But Potapova, lean, stooped, and unsmiling, was not quite so ready to forget her father. And when her sister gave a birthday party about a year after she signed her contract and they had tripped back down Memory Lane, sung a few of the camp songs and cried their eyes out into the vodka glasses, it had all come out. The hatred, the bitterness, the resentment.

By chance a British teacher had been among the guests, and what he had heard he did not keep to himself.

It was the start of a long road for Potapova that led on a freezing December morning to the government compound and to Minister Kalyagin's flat on the sixth floor.

Perminev arrived barely half an hour after her. In the elevator he had been careful to muss his hair and pull his tie off center. He wanted to create the impression of last-minute urgency. It all helped increase the pressure.

"When did you get the call?" Kalyagin appeared angry.

"Just forty minutes ago. You have been asked for eight-thirty exactly. Entry by the Borovitsky Gate. We have to hurry."

The minister relaxed visibly, but his heartbeat had quickened. This was it. He had known it for days. He, Dmitry Kalyagin, was on his way.

Perminev helped him with his coat. Kalyagin turned around to face him. His expression betrayed nothing. There would be no smile, no sharing of the occasion, not with this creature, least of all with this one.

But even he hadn't expected the car. Gone was the aging Volga. In its place a shining snub-nosed Zil, plush, exclusive—unattainable.

To Westerners the car was a straight copy of a six-ties American sedan. To Russians it meant power in their hands. A thought not lost on Dmitry Kalyagin.

◆

Zina Potapova cleaned Kalyagin's rooms assidu-ously, called up the laundry service and ordered pressing for one of the minister's suits. Despite her inner bitterness, she had that age-old Russian con-cern for what was right. Things had to be done *kak sleduyet*—the way they should be. Ministers had to be properly dressed, cleaners were supposed to clean. Jobs were there to be done. And if you didn't work, you didn't eat.

Deep down, of course, she knew it was not quite like that. If you didn't work, they came and got you and made you. She knew it, but she preferred not to think of it.

In three years they would retire Potapova and that would be the end of it. If she lived that long. She hadn't spent her life preparing for old age, wasn't part of the Soviet quest for mastery over the human body. And she had never believed that communism helped you live longer.

Potapova noticed that some of her friends went into the hospital with one illness and came out with another. She had concluded long ago that they would not take her there or anywhere else.

That attitude probably explained why she went to the minister's bedroom with no feeling of trepidation, lifted the alarm clock, and peeled off the strip of paper as if it were a price tag.

She slipped off her left shoe and placed the paper facedown under her ankle stocking. Just an extra precaution, she thought. Not that Potapova considered that sort of thing necessary. She was simply doing as she had been told.

She passed out of the building and was duly logged by the militiaman at the gate, the caretaker in the hall, and plainclothes security in the parking lot. Just as she had been on entry. Zina Potapova knew none of this. At the time her sole concerns were to deliver the message and get to the shops. The rumors said a consignment of tomatoes would arrive at her local *gastronom* early that afternoon. She wanted to join the line at the front not the end. Of course, she thought, the rumors could always be wrong.

◆

The bowers and scrapers had left the room and the general secretary faced Kalyagin across the desk. Between them two bottles of mineral water. Kalyagin tried to catch his breath from the dash upstairs. Quickly he took in the bank of colored telephones on the man's left, a row of television sets, a flag, no Lenin! In front of him the desk was bare. No files, no homework, no records. Just the two of them. The bald head rose in greeting.

"I've admired your work." It was a friendly voice, almost melodic. The lilt of the provinces. So deceptive. "You did well to raise production figures. I'm speaking here of microtechnology. It's what we need. You know how far we lag behind the capitalist countries?" The left eyebrow lifted quizzically.

"Indeed." It was Kalyagin's first word since he had sat down.

"Anyway, your ideas, your results have been impressive. I hope there'll be more successes. Considerably more"—the mouth turned down with evident distaste—"than those achieved by some of your colleagues."

Kalyagin became aware that he was not supposed to speak. The general secretary enjoyed monologues. God knew he was eloquent enough. From the boondocks to Moscow in just eight years. That was eloquence!

He sat back in his chair. Kalyagin could see tiredness in the eyes. "I was going to lecture you, my friend. Partly because you're there, I'm here, and this is the room for lectures. Always has been. But what would be the point? You know our weaknesses and inefficiency—even"—the eyes held steady—"our corruption."

Kalyagin swallowed. The official textbook was being rewritten before his eyes. Others may have thought it. Only this one said it. Along the Embankment he could hear a police siren wailing.

You couldn't help being impressed by this man, even though he had an easy act to follow. Brezhnev had spent his last years falling asleep, Chernenko had arrived with one foot already in the Kremlin wall. After those two the only way was up.

"You know I've taken certain measures already. It's a beginning. Nothing more." The general secretary got up from the desk and went over to Kalyagin. The move caught him off guard. A real *muzhik*, he thought, a big fellow and so sure of himself.

"You're still young, aren't you?"

"Each day a little older, Comrade General Secretary." Idiot! Stupid thing to say!

The leader seemed to agree. He nodded. "I intend to make this a young country. We should be young, in our movements, our energies. Uh? Too many grandmothers around here, praying to ghosts, moaning into their beards. Too many of them hiding crucifixes under their pillows and reading Lenin in the library."

He gripped Kalyagin's shoulder, guiding him to the door. "You're to be a candidate member of the Politburo. The Central Committee will vote on it this afternoon. The announcement is about to be made. I congratulate you."

Kalyagin tried to check his pulse, but he could feel the surge through his body, the excitement. Don't just grin, speak!

"I'm honored, Comrade General Secretary. What can I say? I will do my utmost to serve you." How easy it was to find the clichés. But then you grew up with them, fed on them, recited them, learned the liturgy of the faith.

The general secretary's hand tightened on his shoulder and Kalyagin sensed the strength.

"I have no doubt of that," he said. "No doubt at all."

As if by a signal, the door to the outer office opened and two members of the Secretariat appeared. Kalyagin felt their presence, one each side, close, discreet. These were professionals.

Outside was bright sunshine, the snow crisp underfoot, the Zil's engine already running. Across the wide square Kalyagin could see the heads of the tourists being shepherded around the Kremlin churches. Odd, he thought, how the Cross still dominated the rulers of All the Russias.

◆

It took Zina Potapova under twenty minutes to reach the Kazansky station. She had taken the metro, which, like the snow clearing, never failed. She blended well with the midmorning crowd. A black canvas shopping bag in her hand. A shapeless woolen hat on her head. Her feet were housed in thin plastic shoes that had turned her toes into icicles. So what? she thought. They make summer shoes in winter and winter shoes in summer. Even *Pravda* wrote about that. But it didn't change anything.

The station was a seething mass of humanity. A scene of almost biblical confusion. But the majority were going nowhere. In the great, grand halls they sat listless, lolling asleep on benches. A few lay on the stone floor, children asleep on mothers, boxes and bags strewn around them. To Potapova, who had read of such things, it seemed a little like purgatory, the sorting house between heaven and hell.

She headed for the women's lavatory, little more than a series of troughs, evil-smelling, overflowing with human wastes. It wasn't a place to stay and no one took notice of anything. Normal inhibitions were suspended. Behind a swaying cubicle door Potapova removed her left shoe and salvaged the paper from the minister's flat. She placed it in the bottom of a plastic shopping bag and folded it in her hand.

The instructions were simple enough. Stand in the line at the station's pharmacy and look sick. Not difficult, thought Potapova, who was strong as an ox but suffered from congenital Soviet hypochondria.

She barely felt the bag taken from her, barely heard the "Excuse me" that accompanied it, and saw no more than the back of a dark raincoat and a rabbit-skin hat. Sighing with relief, she relinquished her place to a teenage girl who couldn't stop sneezing. "You should try herbs," she told the girl. "Better than all this medicine."

Potapova made it to the *gastronom.* She lined up for an hour and a half for the tomatoes but could afford only a quarter kilo. When she got home she found most of them were bad. And for that as much as for anything else she sat in her thirty square meters of state-rented accommodation and wept soundlessly.

◆

The message reached Parker three hours later but he didn't read it until he was inside the embassy. The ambassador's wife was holding a bridge competition. In the front hall she could be heard calling out lists of names. There were oohs and ahs from the gaggle of diplomatic spouses around her and much frantic excitement. Wherever they went, thought Parker, England went with them. He pushed impatiently through the little crowd.

"I say . . ." someone shouted after him.

But he ignored it.

A hand gripped his elbow and held it. Parker turned angrily.

"What the . . . ?"

It was Harrison from the consulate. Bright Harrison, handsome Harrison, said the women.

"I say, George. Got a minute, have you?"

"Sorry, Kevin, got a couple of things on right now."

"Oh, anything I could help with?" The tall athletic figure leaned against the banister. Harrison was a climber, thought Parker. Anxious to get on, make the grade, switch from consulate to chancery. That's what he said.

Parker shook his head. "Uh-uh. Another time, maybe. Okay?"

The quick smile in response, facial skin stretched. "Sure, George, catch you later."

Thirty minutes later Parker had translated the dispatch and encoded it. The prefix was the top NATO classification—Cosmic. Not even the signals clerk would know what it contained.

Parker handed it over and watched the message typed into the computer. As soon as it was entered the transmitters would be programmed for "spectrum spread" signals. In essence it meant that the message was chopped into tiny component parts, each fed out at a different frequency. Only in London could the receivers decipher the program code and reassemble the segments—electronic shorthand, just a shimmer in the atmosphere.

It was quite possible the Russians would intercept it, but they wouldn't break the code. And if they ever did, George Parker hoped sincerely he would be somewhere else, well outside the Soviet Union.

He made his way downstairs again. Standing beside the reception desk, Harrison waved. He was dressed in an orange shirt and green striped tie and it struck Parker that the man couldn't have gone to a very good school, although he hated himself for thinking it.

◆

Mary Cross counted twenty-four hours and felt better. Nothing had been said at the embassy. She believed she'd gotten away with it.

It was good that Lazarevic hadn't called to crow about his conquest. Maybe they could settle back into the old ways. The occasional lunch at the National and the three pecks on the cheek—three because Lazarevic made a point of saying that God loved the Trinity. Three it would be from now on.

She had written to Mother. Dear Mum, what a winter, see you in January, so busy here. No details. And she had placed the letter carefully in her handbag and taken it over to the Swiss Embassy, where her friend Gudrun worked. Gudrun would mail it when she reached Geneva.

Of course the letter could have gone in the British diplomatic pouch, but you never knew—someone might have asked a question. Why was she writing to her mother in the Hungarian capital of Budapest instead of in London, where the lady was supposed to live? What was she doing there, how long had she been there? The questions could become endless.

Mary looked at herself in her bedroom mirror and smiled. She liked what she saw. The questions wouldn't really have worried her. Mother had met a Hungarian businessman, married again, decided she liked Budapest after all. Gone to live there. Legitimate enough. Romantic even. Innocent. But the Foreign Office wouldn't have believed it. They wouldn't have believed it at all.

Mary Cross pouted at herself in the mirror and decided to put on some clothes.

◆

So Dmitry Kalyagin was no longer a minister from Estonia. He could now take his seat in the inner sanctum and taste power. Real power. They had brought him back to his apartment and suggested, oh so carefully, that he might like to get ready to move. If Comrade Kalyagin wished it, of course. If Comrade Kalyagin had no objection, an apartment had just been refurnished on Kutuzovsky Prospekt at the express wishes of the Comrade General Secretary. As Comrade Kalyagin was no doubt aware, it was customary for members of the Politburo to reside there.

No compulsions, of course. And if he felt strongly about it . . .

When he pulled up, the building staff had all been there, lined up outside, Perminev among them, their breath billowing out over the parking lot. Such amazing deference, such respect. Kalyagin could scarcely believe it. And then he had looked closely into their eyes and he'd seen it. They had looked away after a few seconds. There was no devotion in those eyes, no love, no revolutionary fervor. Kalyagin saw only one thing. Fear.

He had dismissed them brusquely, the maids, the clerks, the security men and drivers. He didn't want to see that look any longer.

And yet Dmitry Kalyagin was the right man to move up the hierarchy. A generation earlier and he wouldn't have made it. He would have been too much of a threat, too quick, too full of the ideas and concepts that no one had wanted. Those were the Brezhnev years, when the Party and the apparatus had seemed to stand still.

Dmitry recalled how senior officials had actually slept during meetings of the Supreme Soviet. No one cared that the Western television cameras showed them slouched over the tables snoring. The very sessions designed to show the world their competence.

Kalyagin remembered that friends of Grybkin, the ambassador in London, had told stories of such pictures on the BBC. People had just laughed. No one was going to be thrown out for sleeping. Who, they all asked, would be left?

For years the Kremlin had been putting out the comforting message . . . keep it quiet, don't rock the boat, and the fun will go on and on.

Even Leonid Ilyich had gotten to the stage where he'd sign most things that were put in front of him. Why not? At his age he wanted friends, not enemies. Who wanted to go with a knife in the back when you could have the full show in Red Square and your children would keep their perks? Never mind that the country was going down the drain. That wasn't the point.

But the push for change had begun in the late seventies. They had all seen the old man stumbling down the steps in Vienna, catching hold of Jimmy Carter—of all people—for support. And they had felt ashamed.

Kalyagin recalled a visit by a senior figure in the Tallinn *Raikom* who had talked disparagingly of the old women in the Kremlin. It had seemed pretty daring at the time. The man had watched Dmitry closely for his reaction. And when he had smiled and begun laughing, the man arranged another meeting, and then several more. And finally a trip to Moscow.

Looking back, thought Kalyagin, the general secretary's offensive had been in the making for many years. First the move from the provinces to Moscow. No one had taken much notice of the stocky fellow with mud on his boots—a reference to his first job as a tractor driver. But under the patronage of Brezhnev he had gone to work in the middle and senior echelons, building a power base.

The man seemed to want the impossible—a smooth transition from the old crowd with their war medals and snapshots of Lenin to the new dynamic generation. In a country that traditionally relied on death or treachery to change its leaders, that was asking a lot.

Of course, he reflected, the new leader had fooled them all, especially the Western press. The idiot correspondents who drove their Mercedes and Volvos around Moscow had marveled at how the man had rocketed to power. Not a bit of it. The transfer of power had been the best planned and most smoothly executed of any in Soviet history. And he had been part of it.

Kalyagin looked around the apartment, fresh evidence of his new power. All the space he wanted. Anything he wanted. He had only to order and the limitless resources of the Mother of Socialist States would provide. Perhaps a pornographic film from Denmark, a soccer ball from Britain, a baseball glove from New York, a French suit. He smiled, his mind toying with the possibilities. What a long way he'd come!

But he hadn't come alone. The girl from the flat in Tallinn had come with him. Not always the same girl, in fact, mostly, not even a girl at all. But they had all used her name for identification. Ira—the password. He never knew when they would come. In the early days the visits were infrequent. At first he had dreaded them. They were bloodsuckers, squeezing

him for information, gossip, wanting him to put a
word here or there.

And then they would leave him alone and after a
few weeks he would feel unwanted, abandoned. Had
he not given them what they wanted? Did they value
him no longer?

Dmitry began to need both his lives—the normal
and the safe, the secret and the hazardous. The one
held meaning only when it touched the other.

He had risen gradually and then with unexpected
speed. At each level he was tested and given access to
the next. He learned local politics and the quarrels
with Moscow. He watched the scramble to be noticed, the ambitions of youths—the most dangerous
of them all.

By the mid-seventies Kalyagin had acquired the
winning touch. They all said so.

And yet the information came to him with painful
slowness. Everything from the center, for only the
center was trusted. For years he passed on reports
about local defense . . . where were the weak
points, who were the men to watch. The battle psy-
chology, the chain of command . . . who made decisions and who could change them. Later came the
confidential reports to the Central Committee, and
Kalyagin had moved from people to policies.

He could never go too fast. They told him that.
Keep it slow and steady, but keep it. You're alone out
there, the only one we have. If you're worried, duck
out. Stay silent for a month, a year, or three years,

and he had. However long it takes, they had said. But stay in there.

In the late seventies he had come into his own. He had befriended an arms negotiator. The one with a daughter in Tallinn, the one with ambition for his daughter, who wanted a place at the School of Foreign Languages. And Kalyagin held the key.

That had been simple. And the man had never known of the hook in his neck, never even suspected. But it wasn't until the early eighties that Dmitry knew he had scored.

He alone had told the West that Moscow would break the arms talks over Cruise and Pershing deployments in Europe. He alone had told them how long Moscow would stay away and what would be the next target when they finally returned to the table.

After that he had gone to ground, played for some lower stakes. An attempted coup in Iran, pressure on Nicaragua, rapprochement with China. The West had known in advance and made its own arrangements. And the Kremlin had chalked up the failures to experience.

Kalyagin went into the bedroom, took off his shirt, and looked in the mirror. It was only then that he allowed himself a smile. After all, he had something to be proud of, whichever way you looked at it. Maybe tomorrow he would organize a treat. One of the "safe" girls from the pool—half escort, half secretary. *"Sekretutki,"* they called them. And then he frowned, trying to focus his eyes on the mirror. What was that on his shoulder? Dmitry Kalyagin turned abruptly away and the smile left him. For where the general secretary had gripped him a small dark bruise was just beginning to appear.

◆

Perminev hadn't waited for his treat. He had driven straight to the new Trade Center on the Embankment, just past the headquarters of the Russian Federation. A squat, gray building that carried no outside identification. Like most things in Moscow, if you didn't know about it, you weren't supposed to be there.

He had slouched past the fat old doorman, paid to obstruct and upset even the best clients, past the trees growing out of concrete, the fountains, and the giant clock and headed for the open glass elevators.

These days he had gotten used to the place. But it had been a shock the first time. The center could have been in London or even New York. A shopping plaza where sparrows flew around unfettered and half-dressed whores adorned the catwalks. Mother Russia seemed represented only by the female bundle sweeping the floors, hair restrained by a handkerchief.

He had sat on the terrace drinking coffee, watching the foreign businessmen complaining about the service. The waiters were at their worst, dodging between the tables and mouthing "Just a minute" as they brushed past the angry clientele.

Behind him an American was being taken for the ultimate ride. The young brunette at his side had already secured a pile of presents in shopping bags and, with one hand on the man's knee, was going for the jugular . . . marriage. Perminev noted that she had worked hard on herself. Over a magnificent body she had flung a black three-quarter-length gown with slits everywhere. She had contrived to look more undressed than dressed. Her makeup was faultless.

It wasn't until Perminev got up to leave that he realized where he had seen her before. Department 4, KGB, on Dzherzhinsky Square. She had looked just as good in her uniform.

But tonight was his turn. An hour after arriving Perminev believed himself in paradise. Below him was one of the softest, best-sprung beds he had ever slept in. Above him a slim Georgian girl called Nona, who whispered one moment and shouted the next and seemed to have no normal speech in between.

She belonged to Department 4's colorful group of state servants, half on the payroll, half off it. She was allowed to keep 40 percent of the foreign currency she received and for that would pass on all information gained at bedtime.

To her Perminev was an extra. She just did as she was told.

After three or four years most of the girls found a Westerner who wanted to "save" them and were led off to the Palace of Weddings with an exit visa waiting by the door.

Not a bad deal, thought Perminev, stroking the girl's hair. After all, they weren't much use for long.

Their looks went, their brains got addled. Why not
let the West worry about them?

For the moment Perminev had no worries. Some
of the day's congratulations had rubbed off on him.
He had a patron in high office—a man whom he
might one day bend or even supplant. It had happened plenty of times before.

He looked out the window and across to the smoking factory chimneys and the slogans about electric
power. Yes, Comrade Dmitry Kalyagin might yet be
able to assist his faithful servant.

◆

Ira Nikolayeva had slept badly. No longer the attractive girl who "had something," no longer healthy
or slim, she had slept alone. When she awoke it was
dark and she was sitting on the sofa. No sign of a
moon, just the lights in the neighboring buildings
and beyond. As far as the eye could see there was row
after row of dormitory buildings that made up the
microregion of Chertanovo. A friend had told her,
"It's just like New York really, only we're more secure."

The room had grown cold and her joints had stiff-
ened. She shuffled to the bathroom for the tablets,
tying her long gray hair with a rubber band. Of
course the pills were useless. But you had to fight,
didn't you? They all said that.

Nikolayeva tiptoed past her daughter's room and
on impulse turned back and pushed open the door.
She suddenly remembered Lena was at Pioneer
camp and wouldn't be back till the morning.

Putting on the light, she flinched slightly at the bear garden that faced her. On the walls were the teenage collages, the souvenirs from holidays in Yalta and Odessa. The postcards, the theater programs, the letters and school certificates—together they made up the logbook of a Soviet adolescent. Everything named after Lenin—everywhere. The schools, the boardinghouses, the theaters, the parks. Everywhere the same compulsion to live in a dead man's shadow. Nikolayeva leaned against the doorframe and let the memories come.

She saw Lena as a baby with the thinnest of wispy blond hair. She lifted her up, seeing the pink lines on her cheeks made by the pillow. The child was struggling to wake into the world, baby tears rolling down onto her nightdress.

There had been a hurried party, way out in the suburbs of Yugo-Zapadnaya, and as always with Russians, there was a little verse, or a story, or a truism to fit the occasion. But this one had stuck. An old woman, someone's aunt, had leaned over the squealing child and recited it:

"When you are born *you* cry and everyone else laughs. Try to live so that when you die *you* laugh and everyone else cries."

She closed the door and went back to the living room. It doubled as a bedroom but the sheets were in the cupboard and she was too tired to make up the couch. The television news bulletin *Time* was half over and she reached across to turn it off. And then she saw the face she had not seen for decades and had

hoped never to see again. It came at her out of the
screen like a blast of cold wind from the Baltic, taking
away her breath.

Nikolayeva gulped fast and slumped back into a
chair. The days and the distances seemed to melt
away in her mind.

She shook her head and tried to clear the memory.
What had they said? Jesus Christ, what had he done
that he should appear on the Soviet news—the most
important half hour of propaganda in the Communist world. Something about the Politburo?

And even though she fought it, she could see the
little room in Tallinn, could feel the hands and the
rough blankets, could sense the shame and the feeling of degradation, the sudden loss of all the things
her mother had taught her and she had heeded.

She looked up, her cheeks wet with tears. On the
screen the face had gone and the talk was of tractors.

Chapter 5

DECEMBER 8

Lena arrived well before dawn. The internal charter had dropped the party of students into Domody-edovo airport on the outskirts of Moscow soon after 3 A.M.

Fog had been closing in and the temperature hovered around minus thirty. There would be no more flights into Moscow until the afternoon.

She had brought the day's chill with her. Niko-layeva felt the cold cheek and ruffled the long brown hair. Everyone said the girl looked like her mother. But then no one had seen or heard of the father.

They sat at the small table in the kitchen, Niko-layeva in her dressing gown, the girl still in her knee-length boots, the kettle steaming, the air clammy.

"I've brought you something, Mama. Look, open

it." Lena took a small parcel wrapped in rough gray paper from her bag. Inside was a lump of soft white cheese. A tear appeared in Nikolayeva's right eye.

"I don't know if I should. . . . What would Marina Alexandrovna say? She told me not to eat this. . . . She said it was not good for my blood. You shouldn't have bought it." But she was smiling all the same, gripping Lena's hand.

"Mama, we'll have it for breakfast. No, sit still. I'll make it."

The girl was flushed, full of the trip, the friends, the parties, and the clothes. Tonight she would tell Sasha about it. Sasha would want to know all the details. She had bought a present for Sasha. She knew he would love it. Sasha, Sasha, Sasha. Nikolayeva read the signs. Sasha was a lucky man. In his case, she considered, far too lucky.

Lena put the cheese in front of her mother. To Nikolayeva it looked so good. How hungry she felt. She reached out to cut a piece and without warning a wave of nausea passed through her. She turned away, retching violently onto the floor, felt her daughter's hand on her forehead, the sweat breaking out. Her body shuddered. Suddenly she felt cold. Lena was crying quietly, gathering up the cheese in its paper, throwing it in the garbage.

"I'm so sorry, Mama," she kept saying. "So sorry."

Nikolayeva shut her eyes, once again exhausted by the sickness. She had wanted the cheese so badly. Too badly. In another life she would have fallen on it and devoured the final morsel. In this life a hand kept reaching out, taking away the pleasure, injecting the pain. But there was just a little business to complete. Then she'd be on her way.

◆

By midafternoon the sickness had gone. Niko-layeva could smile again and think about ignoring Marina Alexandrovna's instructions. The sun had risen unexpectedly in a blue sky. The best of the Russian climate was outside her window. Nikolayeva felt the stirring of her old determination. At first the face on the television had made her feel horror, re-vulsion. Now there was resolve. The more she thought about it, the more she had to know for cer-tain. Could she have been mistaken after all this time? I'm just a silly old fool, she told herself. But she knew she wasn't.

She waved good-bye to Lena just after 3:30, put on two pullovers, a hat, and boots and slipped into the courtyard. Please let there be a bus!

It dropped her an hour later on the Garden Ring beside the Puppet Theater. The streetlights had come on and it was getting dark. Nikolayeva missed the turning once. So many years had passed since she'd taken the route. But then she saw it—a shabby red-brick building, always in danger of being con-demned, never anyone to take the decision.

She recognized the creaks on the bare wooden stairs. Only the graffiti was new. Around the corner was the door. She didn't even need to look at the number. But as she rang the bell she could feel her-self fainting, falling, and she tried to breathe but couldn't, tried to scream but nothing happened. The excitement and the weakness took their toll.

Anatol found her on the doorstep, picked up the bundle, shocked by the lightness of it, and carried her inside. It wasn't until he was back in his own room that he recognized her.

He had always stayed on the inside. For Anatol had a face you couldn't hide, couldn't lose. He was kneeling beside the couch. Even so he towered over her with his thick black beard, the hooked nose, the polished dome of a scalp.

Coming around, Nikolayeva recalled every blemish, every mole, every centimeter of that remarkable face. For Anatol had plotted with them, fed them, and hidden them all. And in those days Soviet Russia knew no greater sacrifices.

What was it he had said to her, all those years ago in Tallinn? "Next year in Jerusalem." The same as Scharansky had shouted out in court when they sentenced him. The same as they always said when they saw off their friends and their comrades to the West or the camps.

Nikolayeva could read much of her own life in the lines on Anatol's face. So much joint suffering. She remembered the sad little gatherings at the Leningradsky station and the airport. A Jew being seen off by fellow Jews. His last possessions in makeshift cardboard boxes tied with string. Everything else sold or given away. In his pockets some photos of relatives never seen, an address or two, a phone number. On his back his last Soviet suit.

Sometimes the guards at Immigration would abuse such people, call them scum and traitors, push them roughly onto the plane. Customs officials would make them turn out their pockets, undo everything, call over the plainclothes KGB to read their letters, check their photos—all in the national interest. Petty gestures born of sullen insolence. Soviet Russia would slam its door behind them, preferably with their fingers caught in it.

It had been different when they were sent to the camps. The friends and relations would stand each day outside the court, being photographed by the KGB, their identity papers constantly under scrutiny. If they saw the prisoner truck, they would yell out loudly as it went past, "We are with you."

Nikolayeva looked up, trying to read the expression in Anatol's eyes.

"Why have you come?" He didn't say it unkindly but she had forgotten how direct he could be.

"I needed to see you," she implored. "I wanted to talk."

"Was it so important? You knew the rules when we closed the network. No further contact. Everything finished."

"I know, Anatol." She put out her hand to touch his. "But I saw something. I was upset. To me it is still important."

He got to his feet. "I'll make tea."

◆

She watched him busying himself behind the hanging beads. They did little to hide the tiny kitchenette with the kettle and the electric hot plate. Anatol was washing cups in the sink. Why had he never married? Or perhaps he had. No one had ever asked him because that wasn't encouraged. They knew him simply as Anatol, which wasn't his real name. But they knew they could trust him. Nothing else mattered.

"I know why you're here." He had pushed his way through the beads again and pulled up a chair. The tea was on the floor. "So you saw him too. I was right, wasn't I? I knew he was the one.

"You should feel proud." Anatol turned away, reluctant to hold her eyes.

"I feel disgusted." Nikolayeva sat bolt upright on the sofa. "How can you talk of pride? You know what I did because you told me to do it. And you sit there now and talk of pride."

Anatol saw the flushed cheeks, felt the anger. "It was the only way," he whispered. "We both agreed that at the time. And what has happened since has only justified what you did. Can't you see that? Can't you see the value of what you did?"

"I disgusted myself, shamed myself . . . for what? For a people I have never seen and never shall see. For a plan that has brought me nothing and taken away what I had. Do you have any idea how much I hated you for asking me to do it? Because you didn't seem to care, did you? To you it was just part of the job. 'Duty' you called it."

Steady, she thought. She could feel the sickness

rising again. Almost any change of emotion seemed to bring it to the surface.

"You shouldn't talk like that," he told her. "It was a long time ago. You . . . both of us . . . we have to forget. It's not for us anymore. We're finished." Anatol wiped his forehead.

"Yes, and who finished us?" Nikolayeva looked up angrily. "The whole network shattered when the British closed it down. Only they forgot to tell two of our couriers in time and so you had to arrange an accident for them because they knew what had happened . . . that I burned Dmitry Kalyagin when he was nothing. I turned him and now he's on his way to the top. Estonia first, then the Politburo. My prize, Anatol, my ugly little prize."

"I can do nothing about history. Tell me what you want and then you must leave."

The giant has aged, thought Nikolayeva. And I with him. Outside, the wind was gusting violently. From the apartment below Nikolayeva could hear music. Comfy tunes from Moscow radio. Happy hour for the workers. She glanced at her watch. Six o'clock and all was right with Russia.

Anatol pulled himself up in his chair. "My dear"— he smiled—"let us talk about the future and not the past."

Nikolayeva saw that behind the smile his eyes were watching her carefully, trying to read her thoughts, gauge her reactions. Oh, Anatol, I know you so well, she thought.

"You want the future? Then let's talk about my daughter." She turned to face him.

◆

"You want to eat?"

"No."

They had been sitting for almost two hours, much of that time spent in silence. For they had come to subjects and names that were never mentioned aloud and never could be. Each name activated a built-in alarm. Each knew what and who the other meant. It was a sad reunion. Nikolayeva found a man without purpose. "You've lost your fire, Anatol, your energy. What have you done? What do you do?"

He shrugged. "I have returned to my old ways." He pointed to the clocks on the mantelpiece. "I mend them."

"You're a fool marking time for a future that you don't have. Look at me, look." She pointed at her face. "I'm dying and I'd rather be doing that than mending clocks. I still have my contacts—I'm not forgotten."

"You should leave now. You've stayed too long. Who knows if they still check me. Who knows if someone saw you in the corridor and started asking questions."

"You're a coward, Anatol." Nikolayeva stood up. "A coward and an idiot. Me, I still have things to do." She laughed softly to herself. "My little minister . . . such a big bird in the Kremlin . . . much fatter than he used to be. He used to fancy himself with the girls, that's why we got him, isn't it? Well, it's time this big bird came down to earth." Her voice was almost a whisper but it filled the little room.

Anatol came over and touched her shoulder.

"Leave me alone. Don't touch me. . . ."

"You don't understand, Ira. He's on our side really. He gives them what they want, but he works with us. How can you, of all people, forget?"

"I forget nothing." Nikolayeva spat on the floor. "Nothing."

◆

Anatol watched her from the window. He could hear his heart in his temples. In the old days he could cope with it, control it. But he had lost the habit. Nikolayeva was dangerous, he knew that. She had the power to wreck her old operation—long after she had given it up, passed it on. Her mind should have given up along with her body, but it hadn't.

Years had passed since he had thought of anything secret, years when the nervous tic in his eye had disappeared, when his throat could relax, when shadows became just shadows again and sleep came without vodka. All the defenses that he'd built so carefully began to disintegrate. Anatol knew he would not sleep that night.

Chapter 6

DECEMBER 9

By dawn he had decided. He pulled on his shapeless black coat and the brown fur hat, closing the door quietly, taking care not to bang it. The street had begun to fill up. They were all early risers in Moscow —something to do with the transport.

Nobody saw him as he passed the synagogue. It was the only one that still worked in the city—so many dreams and fears, he thought, all under one roof. Anatol's family had lived in the area since the thirties, long before it became scruffy and overcrowded. He had walked the street ten thousand times, clinging to his father's arm, swept along by a strength he had never possessed.

He found Kolya at the beer bar at the top of the hill. It was closed but the old man always shuffled round the area until eleven o'clock—the hour of the wolf—when the bars opened. Anatol wanted advice but Kolya was evasive.

"Do what you think is best." Kolya's eyes were fixed on the pavement.

"And what is that?" asked Anatol.

"It's complicated."

"That's why I came to you. Just as I did so many years ago. Why do you refuse to help now?"

"I am no longer in a state where I can help you." Kolya looked at Anatol, his mouth open, eyes narrowed. He was much shorter, but he, too, had a beard. Somehow he wore his Jewish faith like a protest flag. His eyes were large and the mottled, lined face drooped like an elephant's.

"I cannot make the decision on my own." Anatol returned the stare.

"You have to. There is no one to ask anymore. They've all gone . . . all the old ones. And the young people . . . they don't talk to me."

A militia van rolled past them, spattering slush onto the pavement. Anatol watched until it was out of sight.

"I feel I'm alone," he said.

"In this, my friend, you are. And may God find you at the end of it."

◆

Nikolayeva slept well into that morning. She awoke with her strength and her hatred renewed. In her mind Anatol had become "the idiot watchmaker." She shrugged to herself. He should stay in his basket like an old dog. No use to anyone. But Kalyagin, that was a different matter.

She got out of bed, cold feet on cold floor. Lena had left for her classes, but she'd be back midafternoon. Today was special. They were going to a party at Marina Alexandrovna's and Lena was bringing Sasha. She must try to look her best. But her thoughts went back to Kalyagin. How many years was it? Fool! I have only to look at my daughter. The exact day, the exact hour are stamped on her forehead.

Kalyagin. She whispered the name to herself over and over again, remembering the times she had hated him for being there—and, in the years that followed, for being absent.

After that first night she had never again let him touch her. Not once. But even as she had walked out of that bombed apartment building she knew the damage that had been done to her.

In all, maybe, they had met a dozen times. And then she had refused to go. For he had seen the tiny bulge in her belly, seen the light in her eyes. She recalled the smile of smug satisfaction, as if he was looking into her future and seeing the suffering to come.

And then he was gone. Gone when she needed comfort after the birth, gone when she might have shared the joy of the child, gone when the decisions had to be made and the money found.

All by herself Nikolayeva had appeased the state in all its daily bureaucratic machinations—trade unions, teachers, doctors, the militia. She had faced them all.

Kalyagin, she muttered again. It was time to finish it.

She sat at the kitchen table and watched the children playing in the snow. The grandmothers stood around in groups, gossiping. It was their job to look after the infants while the mothers worked. That was the importance of the family unit, they were told. Truly, thought Nikolayeva, the state had taken care of everything.

And yet it hadn't been like that in her case. Nothing had smoothed her path. From the first prenatal interview the barrage of questions had been ceaseless. Who was the father? Why don't you know? What did he do? Why won't you say? Why, why, why? At every stage it had been the same. Parent meeting or workers' committee.

Nikolayeva had lost count of those miserable confrontations. But she had not forgotten the sense of anger and shame. How dare they judge me, she had thought. Pig-faced careerists, cloaking themselves in moral righteousness from nine to five, then screwing each other silly when they left the office.

Nikolayeva dressed in a hurry and went outside. No one greeted her. She tripped once on the ice and almost fell but nothing would deflect her. Someone, she decided, would have to pay for all those years . . . for *that* night and for the thousands of days that had followed.

The first telephone had been vandalized but the second was working. She dialed just two digits. A woman's voice answered.

"Zero two, militia."

"Please connect me with Internal Security."

"I'm sorry that is not possible. What is your business?"

Nikolayeva had expected the answer. "No" rarely meant no in the Soviet Union. It just meant you had to try a little harder. It opened the bidding.

"It is possible and you will do it—that is, if you value your career and wish to pursue it."

"*Zhditye!*—Wait!"

The woman officer on Zubovsky Boulevard pressed two buttons beside her. The first switched in her supervisor, the second began the "snoop" recording.

"What is your name?"

She hesitated only a moment. "Nikolayevna, Ira Dimitriyevna.

"What matter do you wish to discuss?"

Nikolayeva stood freezing in the phone booth with its cracked windowpanes, and the words tumbled out. Betrayal. Deception. And the story of an agent a step away from absolute power. She could sense the tension on the line.

When she was satisfied she had said enough, she replaced the receiver and wandered home. There had been ample time for the militia to trace the call, but she knew that would not help them. Not yet at least. She felt so light, her head clear of sickness, no pain in her joints. Today was a golden day. A gift from God.

Nikolayeva had forgotten that it was Thursday—

and she had kept an old promise. Kalyagin would die
as surely as if she herself had pulled the trigger.

◆

The tape of the call was forwarded to the Moscow
section of the KGB behind the Lubyanka. A major
stamped "Further Action" on the transcript but
didn't know where to send it. One thing struck him
as odd. It wasn't like the usual denunciation, which,
God knows, they encouraged as part of the natural
workings of Internal Security. No, this was too specific. Too detailed, and too near the top. He decided
to feed it to the computers.

◆

Anatol waited until darkness to move. From the
cupboard in his bedroom he took an old walking stick
made of oak. A present from an Englishman.

He calculated that the journey would take him
three hours. Give yourself time, he muttered. Take
trouble, take care, follow the old rules. He was back
on autopilot.

He caught the metro, traveling against the flow. A
man followed him into the carriage, two doors down.
It took Anatol a full thirty seconds to come out of his
reverie. Look at the man's shoes and hat. What had
they said? Just the shoes and hat, the rest of him looks
the same as everyone else in winter.

The man was reading the sports paper. Anatol
scrutinized him but he didn't look up. They both got
out at Mayakovsky Square. On the platform Anatol
hesitated. Let him go first! He fumbled awkwardly in

his coat pocket. When he had finished the man had
gone.

On the street Anatol allowed the crowds to push
him along. He stopped at a taxi stand and waited
twenty minutes in line. By the time his turn came he
was frozen. He fell painfully onto the backseat and
barked *"Ostankino"* at the driver. The man didn't
turn his head.

"I want to arrive today," Anatol told him.

He saw the nod but there was no sound in reply.
They headed north. Occasionally Anatol turned and
looked out of the back window but there was nothing
to frighten him.

◆

Nikolayeva and her daughter were late for the
party. They reached the tall block on Leninsky Prospekt barely on speaking terms. Nikolayeva couldn't
remember feeling less like a party.

"What's the code to this door?" she demanded,
gesturing at the electric lock.

"How should I know, Mama? I come here once a
year and you're around almost every week."

"I thought you had a brain. Obviously I was mistaken," replied Nikolayeva tartly.

A young man pushed his way between them. "Let
me do it." He grinned at them. They glared back.

Marina brushed aside their apologies.

"What nonsense, you're not late," she declared.
"Everyone else was early."

The apartment was high above street level but the
noise of traffic penetrated the thin walls. Nikolayeva

could hear someone playing with a radio, switching from station to station. There were voices from the kitchen. Marina followed her eyes. "This is communal living for you. Lenin doesn't know what it's like. Ever since they moved Stalin out of the mausoleum he's had the place to himself." They all laughed.

Nikolayeva looked lovingly at Marina. Her oldest friend. Nothing to do with the network. A confidante, a woman of indeterminate age and politics. Marina was commonsense Russia, direct, devoted, leaned on. A doctor caught up in the bureaucracy of shortages, the machinations of minor officials. As time passed she saw more paper than patients.

Marina was stocky and wide, with short, straight black hair and the size bust that confers automatic authority. She was indomitable. Nikolayeva once told her, "If there's a nuclear war and the streets of Moscow are rubble and bodies, only you will be walking through the debris, stamping your feet, shouting for action and efficiency." Marina had blushed, but there was a kernel of truth.

"How do you feel?" she asked Nikolayeva.

"You know how I feel."

"I know how you are. Tell me, is the pain great?"

"I do not think of it now. I think only of enjoying myself."

Nikolayeva's eyes circled the room, taking in the other guests. Lena, she noticed, was deep in conversation with Sasha. She frowned.

Marina took her arm. "You don't like the boy?"

"I know him, I knew his parents too. It seems as if he's hung around for years."

"He is a great musician," said Marina.

"I know, I know. Maybe I just worry about everything at the moment. After all, Lena's old enough to look after herself."

They looked at each other thoughtfully.

Marina had pulled the table into the center of the room and stacked it with food. It looked magnificent. Nikolayeva knew the time and effort that would have gone into the shopping. Marina read her thoughts for the second time in a minute.

"In the West there is everything in the shops and nothing on the table. Here we have nothing in the shops and we put it all on the table." She smiled a smile of resignation.

They sat down, stiffly at first, but the uneasiness passed quickly. There were eight of them—friends and close friends. As they talked, each memory brought a toast, each toast a tear. In the end they drank to the drink and toasted the toasters. Marina beamed with goodwill. She loved them all, she told herself.

By eight-thirty Nikolayeva had tired visibly. She rose shakily.

"You must forgive me, all of you, but I have much to do tomorrow. It's been wonderful and I thank you most warmly."

Marina led her to the door. "I'll send Lena home in an hour or so. Sasha can take her. I don't want you to be alone."

"Don't be silly, Marina. I'm a big girl now. Besides, the devil looks after his own."

"Good night, my dear friend." Marina embraced her and continued waving long after the elevator had gone.

An hour later they turned off the main light in the room and lit candles. Sasha stood in front of the piano. "I'll tell you a story and then I'll play for you," he said. He told of his days as a music student, how a group of them had discovered some music notes from the composer Tamarsky, how he had written them just before committing suicide. Tamarsky, said Sasha, had striven to overcome mortal boundaries, he had set himself to compose the music of creation itself. And in the moment when he had stared at failure, he had jumped from an eight-story window.

Together with his fellow students, Sasha had deciphered the music and sent it out in secret to Paris. There it was performed by a well-known conductor at a one-night concert in Versailles. The next day the man had walked straight out of his apartment and been killed by a truck. The music was dubbed "The Devil's Concerto." "I'll play it for you tonight," said Sasha, "and I am the third to do so."

◆

Anatol arrived in Chertanovo just as Nikolayeva left the apartment on Leninsky Prospekt. Three blocks from her building he had telephoned to make sure she was out. The only risk now was the daughter.

The night was bitterly cold and there were few people on the streets. The buses had come to a stand-

still. Only a stray dog crouched by the curb under a
shelter. He passed a drunken man being beaten up
and dragged home by his wife. At one point she
seemed to give up, flinging the senseless tiny figure
onto the mound of snow and ice, piled high like a
railway escarpment along the street.

Most of the windows were lit. Only a few had curtains hiding the makeshift joys of Soviet flatland. Sex,
television, and vodka, Anatol reflected. The people
rotated through all three of them, the one bringing
relief from the others.

He knew he was conspicuous. He had to get off the
streets. Any militia patrol might stop and question
him. Any diligent comrade might pick up the telephone and report his presence.

He found the block next to Nikolayeva's. It almost
overlooked the metro. But there was no camouflage,
no hiding place. Cautiously, he stepped inside. The
light in the stairwell had been broken, but the streetlamp shone through clearly. Anatol remembered an
old trick. He lay down on the floor in the hall and
played drunk. Occasionally a resident passed him.
One woman even stepped over him. But no one
found anything suspicious about an old man suc-
cumbing to vodka. Anatol had entered the natural
landscape.

Nikolayeva was glad of the night air. The party had
exhausted her. All the way home she worried about
Lena. Why was she seeing so much of Sasha? Him of
all people.

And yet was it so surprising? The boy had been a

network baby. That's what they had called them—
the children of the courier network, the small secret
circle that had hunted, fetched, and carried for the
British for well over twenty years.

Its members had tried to lead separate lives, tried
not to meet. But inevitably husbands met husbands,
children met children. Their lives intertwined,
joined as they were by things secret and unmention-
able.

Sleeping partners, she reflected. Never knowing
the cause or the struggle but sitting at home. Awaiting the fallout. Like it or not, Sasha had been part of
the group.

And yet the group had been smashed and gone its
separate ways. He should not have returned. Tomorrow she would question him and find out why he was
in Moscow.

It took more than an hour for her to return to the
suburbs. By then the pain had returned, merging
with the fear. Despite the low temperature Nikolayeva emerged from the metro sweating. Her footsteps fell into the same path taken by Anatol two
hours before, but she was slower. From time to time
her left leg gave out on the ice and she stumbled.
How she longed to sit on the side of the road and let
the cold eat up what the cancer had left behind.

Anatol shivered as he saw her. He lifted his head off
the stone floor, his neck already stiff. Two apartment
dwellers had come out to berate him. One had
threatened to call the militia. But that was fine. He
remembered the old watchword—those who

threaten never do, those who do don't waste time threatening.

As he came out of the building he saw Nikolayeva some twenty-five yards out in front. He started a half-run across the ice, using the walking stick to steady himself. Jesus God, there was a man in the doorway of her building. He's saying good night, thought Anatol. I have no time. But Nikolayeva had stopped. Fifteen yards behind her Anatol could hear the labored breathing, the sharp cough. He started to turn away but the man was coming out of the building and walking briskly around the side toward the parking lot. Anatol didn't hesitate. Nikolayeva was about to move forward again when the stick caught her with full force on the back of the skull. It barely made a sound, cushioned against her woolen hat. She crumpled almost gratefully onto the ice. She didn't feel the second blow for she lay quietly, facedown in the ice, her eyes closed, no expression of pain or anguish.

Ira Nikolayeva released her spirit at the exact moment Sasha finished playing "The Devil's Concerto." In the apartment high above Leninsky Prospekt the guests sat back in their chairs as the music died away.

It had been loud, striking, and discordant. No one applauded. They were left with the feeling that something momentous and frightening had taken place. But no one knew what it was.

Chapter 7

DECEMBER 10

In August 1981 a South African businessman whose talents outnumbered his scruples many times over paid a short visit to the Romanian capital, Bucharest. Since the Eastern Bloc maintains no official contacts with Pretoria, the trip received no publicity.

The man spent forty-eight hours in the city, most of them inside the Soviet Embassy. Before leaving he sent two coded telexes, one to London, the other to Stockholm.

Three weeks later a Swedish entrepreneur drove his truck onto the ferry at Gothenburg, carrying the usual food supply for the foreign community based in Poland. The Swedish customs had no wish to plow their way through crates of fish fingers and avocados.

In any case, they felt sorry for the foreigners in Warsaw. So they waved it through without examination.

Soon after the ferry docked in the Polish port of Stettin, a dozen sealed fruit boxes were taken off the truck and loaded onto a Sovtransavto juggernaut bound for Moscow. Inside them were the disassembled parts of two IBM computers, both banned from export to the Eastern Bloc. The KGB couldn't have been more delighted. Even the truck driver received a bonus.

A month later the reassembled computers were fed the elaborate software that had been waiting for them and began to suck in the daily criminal digest from around fifty militia headquarters all over the Soviet Union. They were located thirty miles outside Moscow in the small village of Gorky, which suddenly acquired its own independent electric generator.

The forty or so residents of this hamlet believe the computers belonged to a weather station—one of the most efficient of its kind. What is more, they are inordinately proud of it.

In the early hours of that Friday morning the computers were treated to a transcript of Ira Nikolayeva's last telephone call. They duly filed it to await further action.

There it might have remained for some days had it not been for a small programming error at the Gorky station that same night. The duty record officer noted Nikolayeva's death as a routine homicide from Moscow CID but mistakenly routed it into the KGB's

Internal Security file. It was automatically cross-checked against the record of her phone call and registered an alarm within fifty seconds.

◆

"Where the hell is it?"

"Where it always is."

Lapkin hated bodies. Each time they found one it was like setting out on a long journey. All they could see ahead were forms and formalities, questions and more questions, shadows that darkened when probed.

He brushed his assistant, Sturua, out of the way, marched out of the office, and headed down the corridor to the mortuary. People's Militia Station Six on the Vernadsky Prospekt was waking up after lunch.

"Give me the facts. . . . No, wait." Lapkin eyed the three men curiously. They stood in a semicircle beside the single slab, a neon strip above them. In the corner a small electric fire fizzled dangerously. Two of them were from District Headquarters, standing awkwardly in their greatcoats, muttering their greetings. The third was unknown.

"I'm Lapkin, Sergei Ivanovich. Who are you?"

The man looked up but didn't move. He was small, balding, a thin mustache and a nose that pulled to the left. Cold, thought Lapkin. Like the old woman.

"Kovalyov." The man cleared his throat. "The prosecutor's office sent me."

"The prosecutor was awake early this morning." Rapidly, Lapkin computed the time. Just over sixteen hours since the body had been found. And the prosecutor's office was here now? Even before the last of the forms had been pulled out of supplies.

"Perhaps you'd tell me the nature of your interest?" Lapkin knew it was a forlorn request.

"Our office will be in contact later. For the moment, I have completed the preliminary investigation. I would ask that the body not be moved or tampered with in any way." The man from the prosecutor's office looked up. Lapkin returned the stare. But Kovalyov was already fastening his coat and heading for the door.

Lapkin watched it close and raised his eyes to the two militiamen from headquarters. He shivered. The dark cold room, the gray stone walls, and former citizen Nikolayeva half covered on a slab. None of them were going to make his day easier.

He never heard his door open, for he spent the next fifteen minutes on the phone trying to raise his own contact at the prosecutor's office. His eyes were closed tight in frustration, his boots wedged against the wall, his body slouched in the chair. A lanky figure, late thirties, blond. Such thin, pointed features.

Perminev stood in the doorway surveying the man's back, a half-smile on his lips. He knew he would enjoy this.

◆

Sasha had fallen asleep in the early hours, soon after they had returned from the militia. Lena had cried a little, but less than she had expected. Perhaps, she told herself, she had been prepared for it.

The doctors made it a rule never to tell patients

they were dying, and mostly they didn't tell the relatives. Telling was not the Soviet way. But Lena had known it, just as her mother had felt it.

Two militiamen had been waiting outside the flat when they had returned from the party—tired, drunk, and unaware of the violence of the night.

The officers had led them out to their car and swept them into the routine and the procedures that concentrate the mind and divert the emotions. Lena had even felt grateful to them. They were back at the apartment within two hours, while the dawn light was still in Asia.

She opened her eyes to see Sasha looking down at her, his hand on her forehead.

"I had hoped that it wouldn't be true this morning." She tried to sit up and he slipped a cushion behind her. "With time it will be easier," he said, "but the pain will last."

"But to die in that way . . . like a beaten animal. . . ." She rubbed her eyes. "They had no right. . . . My mother should not have died out there in the snow." She looked up and seemed to read something in his expression. For suddenly she became calmer and Sasha saw Nikolayeva's determination in the young face, puffy and tired, the black hair scraped back behind her ears. "We will find out," she said. "We will."

Sasha dropped her later at a friend's home and took the metro back into the city. For a while he lost himself in the crowds. He needed time to think before he made his calls.

◆

The orderlies backed out of the long room and shut the double doors soundlessly. Around the table twenty men fell silent abruptly. They felt the general secretary look up. You didn't need a cue. The meeting had begun.

Kalyagin sensed the power. It hung on the softly spoken consonants, the man's instant recall, his authority. Thursday afternoon. Kalyagin's first session of the Politburo. The innermost secrets of a superpower laid out on green baize in front of him.

For a moment he lost concentration, staring in turn at the taut, solid faces, cloned by communism, all deficiencies detected and corrected before they hit Moscow. They were the state's chief troubleshooters, the guardians and designers of its policy. The tacticians of the Communist movement worldwide, they were dangerous men—absurdly powerful. They made the rules. They changed the rules. Only *their* rules counted.

Kalyagin's mind was jerked back to the discussion.

"Your assessment please, Comrade General!" The leader was glaring at the deputy defense minister.

"What you ask, Comrade, does not seem possible at this time." The man moved slightly in his chair and reached for a glass of water.

"Then how long would it take?"

"I cannot say. Three months, maybe longer."

The general secretary took off his glasses and stared at the man across the six feet that separated them. "I would remind you that the Defense Ministry is on record as promising the completion of this project by the end of December. Or am I mistaken?" The irony was heavy.

"I am aware of the Comrade Marshal's optimistic assurances."

A few heads turned to look at the deputy minister. They hadn't missed it—the jab of betrayal, the merest hint of a colleague's inadequacy, the sleight of foot that marked out a fighter from a victim. Viktor Afanasyev, Deputy Defense Minister, was trying to save himself.

Kalyagin could feel the tension. It hung heavy in the airless room. What if the roles had been reversed? What if he had been deputy minister? Here more than anywhere else, you stood alone. You left your friendships at the door, never knowing if they'd wait for you.

"We will return to the matter in a week's time. By then I expect to have your submission in writing." The Soviet leader's mouth turned down in the familiar expression of distaste.

The deputy minister put his glass back on the table.

"As you wish, Comrade General Secretary."

"Indeed." The man looked around the room. "We shall all be looking forward to your forecasts."

So that was it. Kalyagin released his breath. There'd be no blood today, just a public warning. Little wonder that the apparatus called these meetings "crucifixions."

But what had he expected? Talk of the grandchil-

dren, the wives, the weather in the Crimea? Not at
this gathering. For here the subject was power—the
open or covert uses of it, the pressure points at home
and abroad.

America dominated the meeting: the ceaseless
competition with it, the push for superiority. And
how the push would turn to shove.

Kalyagin knew little of the Defense Ministry's new
project and the briefing papers gave few details. But
they were enough. Leafing through the file, it was
clear that Soviet technicians were interfering regu-
larly with U.S. reconnaissance satellites, "fogging"
their film, disrupting the spying, forcing the Americans to change their orbit. Both sides played the
game. But now there were new orders. And if the
Defense Ministry could manage to carry them out,
the enemy satellites would face a far more substantial
threat.

The general secretary released them an hour later.
Upstairs, in the private apartment, he stood by the
window watching the squat, black shapes climb into
their cars. His wife looked at him quizzically.

He took her arm. "It's just the way Andropov said
it would be," he told her. "They sit like lambs but
they have eyes like wolves. It's been too easy. Soon I
shall have to strike just to prove I can do it."

He stopped for a moment in the corridor and
looked down into the square. Dmitry Kalyagin was
getting into the last of the black cars. The set of the
shoulders, the confident movements—it all seemed
to indicate a man of purpose.

◆

Lapkin knew Perminev by instinct. Not his name
or even his rank. But his function and pedigree. They
all stand like that, he reflected.

He was suddenly aware that Citizen Nikolayeva
must have possessed special qualities. For she had
joined the select few who become more important
by dying than by living.

"Sit down please, Comrade. . . ." Lapkin waved
Perminev toward the metal chair in front of his desk.

"Thank you but I won't." Perminev still had his
coat on. "I don't want to hold you up. In fact, in a
moment I want you to forget that I was ever here.
The old woman's body is ours and will be collected
within twenty minutes. You never had this body, and
no one died last night within your area of competence. Whatever paperwork there was is now being
destroyed."

He looked over his shoulder, back into the outer
office. Two men in plainclothes were rifling the desk
of Lapkin's assistant. Papers were already strewn
across the floor.

"You have no right . . ." Lapkin was on his feet.

"I have every right, Comrade." Perminev had advanced on him, holding out the red card with the
gold letters and the unmistakable shield. The Committee for State Security, KGB.

"Please hand me the file on your desk."

"I don't believe this. I'll have to speak to the station
chief."

"I have done so already. The file, please."

Lapkin tossed the folder across the desk. It fell into Perminev's outstretched hand.

"I hope what I have said is clear. If you have questions, please ask them now. The opportunity won't present itself again."

Lapkin sank back into his chair. He knew that this was the end of it. The big feet from Dzherzhinsky Square had marched all over his office once before. Big feet that left no trace.

For a split second the noise of a truck jamming on its brakes made him look out the window. When he turned back Perminev had gone.

◆

"Hallo, James."

"Stuart." Dawling nodded at the man and shuffled cautiously into the room. The prison guard shut the door behind him.

Dawling looked around him, at the flowery wallpaper, the bright curtains, the soft gray carpet.

"What's this all about?"

"I thought we'd talk in a little more comfort, that's all." Stuart gestured him to the sofa. "The governor's away for the day and offered his flat, so here we are. Tea?"

He leaned forward to the pot and began pouring. "Milk and sugar? I'm sorry I've forgotten."

"Both," said Dawling greedily.

The man handed him the cup. "How's it been lately, James? Everything all right? No bother, no hassles?"

"Cut out the crap, will you? Remember, I used to be in the business."

The man took a package from his pocket and placed it on the coffee table. It was one of the few ways to reach Dawling, the child in him, the one that had emerged during his interrogation. The mental breakdown had delayed his trial and left lasting damage. And now they were left with Dawling the traitor and Dawling the child and they were obliged to deal with both.

"Oh, it's a box of sweets. That is nice." Dawling had torn the wrapping off the box and was smiling broadly. "Want one?"

"Thanks, but no. They're for you." Stuart paused. "I was a little worried about you after last time. You seemed to have Moscow on your mind. Anything we can help with?" The tone was measured, soothing. Take it slow, they had said. Really slow.

"It's funny." Dawling put his head in his hands. "I've been thinking it all over and the pieces don't seem to fit. I mean there always seemed to be so many couriers, so much information, but where did it all come from? I never got to the center, never knew who was behind it."

"Why should you think that? Look how many poor souls you succeeded in betraying. You want their names. I can remind you if you want. Andrei, Alex, Mikhail—"

"Stop it." Dawling spoke quietly. "It's not that," he said vacantly, and looked out the window over the prison courtyard. "It's just . . . it doesn't make sense." He turned back and the vacant look had gone. "But it will do. I'm sure of it. I'll get it in the end."

Again Stuart telephoned his report to London from a pay phone three miles from the prison. But this time no signal was sent to Moscow.

Chapter 8

DECEMBER 11

George Parker sat in Her Majesty's embassy and wrote his Christmas cards. The last diplomatic pouch before the holiday was leaving that afternoon.

There was a special one for the office back home. An old black-and-white picture of Dzherzhinsky Square and the Lubyanka with the words "Happy New Year." Such a tasteful little card, he reflected. Just the kind of thing they'd like.

It was six months since London had briefed him. The final briefing. He recalled the last-minute phone call as they were packing the suitcases. His parents had arrived to take them to the airport and they were standing awkwardly in the apartment in St. John's Wood, a little nervous, a little excited.

The voice hadn't said much. "Won't take more

than a few minutes, but we'd like you to come in on
your way to the airport." There had been a short
pause. "If it's no trouble, of course."

It had been of course. His parents were upset.
Steven threw a tantrum in the car. They had all
waited around the corner from the office while he
had gone inside.

"I don't know whether we made this clear or not"
—the deputy chief had hung his head like an expec-
tant Labrador—"but amongst all the mess that you'll
be picking up from . . . er, Dawling, there's a little
something that survived it all. A little someone in
fact."

"Oh?"

"He's a rather valuable fellow in fact. Well on the
way up the ladder. Actually we haven't heard from
him for a while. He's hibernating. Been out of sight
for about three years. We recommended it. Didn't
want him overheated. Anyway, we're sure he's still
with us, if you know what I mean."

Parker did.

"Oh, just one more thing. Your ambassador. You
can tell the old boy what you're doing in vague
terms. After all, when the Russians lay a crate of shit
at his door, he has to have a shovel." The head hung
again. "But if I were you, I wouldn't mention our
little someone. Understand?"

Parker smiled at the recollection. He was still smiling when the ambassador's secretary summoned him
to the cage.

"London is worried." Sir David glared at him across the table.

"I beg your pardon. I think I'm the one who communicates with my office, thank you, sir."

"There's no point getting testy with me. I go out to Helsinki with Harriet to do some shopping and find I'm turned into a bloody messenger boy. Anyway, I tell you they're worried. I'm hauled into the embassy there at a moment's notice—an appalling building by the way—and wheeled into head of chancery's office. Harriet by this time is having to kick her heels in Stockmanns. Well, who should be there but Hargreaves from your lot who says they're very concerned. They're not at all sure the ends have been tied up, since the Dawling business."

Parker was angry. "Dawling is over. They know that. And anyway, isn't it a bit bloody late to be getting cold feet? They handled his interrogation."

"Dawling was your predecessor and I don't think I need to labor that point." Sir David looked up sharply. "Mmm . . . ?"

"Look, I'm not sure why this has come up again now. I've been through this a thousand times in London. Dawling is sewing mail bags on the Isle of Wight. It's history. The network closed with him. The KGB got most of them and we managed to retrieve Sylvia. And that's it—period." He moved to get up from the table but changed his mind. After all, there was nowhere to go. The cage was aptly named.

"They wanted assurances that Dawling never handled anyone else—anyone major."

"Who?"

"How should I know? I don't control your operations."

"We went through Dawling's records, tore them apart. No reference to anything that didn't get shut down. I've told them that till I'm blue in the face."

"You don't have to tell me, George. But I had an odd feeling in Helsinki. They seemed to think someone had slipped through the net." Sir David took off his glasses and laid them gently on the table. The blue eyes faced Parker unrestricted.

◆

Upstairs, Lady Harriet White screwed up her eyes and bared her teeth. It was the most practiced of diplomatic greetings.

"Everything all right, dear?"

Sir David grunted and eased himself into an ugly old armchair patterned with vine leaves.

Lady White moved in closer to examine him.

"Sure you're all right?"

"Yes, fine. You?"

It was their daily routine. Sometimes the mutual interrogation would last an hour, until one of them gave up and admitted a headache.

"You're worried about something, David. I can tell."

To deflect her he reached for his copy of *Pravda* but she knelt beside the chair, eyeing him over the top of it. He laid the paper down.

"I assure you, my dear. It's all going jolly well."

"Hmm." She bared the teeth again. "I'm sure it's nothing that a hot toddy won't put right."

She padded off to the kitchen. Into a glass went lemon juice, brown sugar, brandy, and hot water. The recipe had traveled the world in her suitcase. Sir David could hear her stirring the mixture with a teaspoon. Poor soul! She tried so hard to be interested and involved, but the old scatterbrain didn't know a thing about diplomacy, probably thought arms control was something to do with aerobics. There were times when he missed the intellectual match, a foil, someone to spar with.

There'd been so many crossroads where he'd have valued a second opinion, a judgment, something more that the inevitable "It'll be all right, dear, I know it will" or "Never mind, better luck next time."

And yet there was safety, comfort in platitudes, in habit and predictability. And a little peace of mind to be found there.

She passed him a saucer with the glass on it and he sipped the toddy slowly, gratefully. She noticed his hand was shaking but said nothing.

◆

There were days when it snowed and fewer days when it didn't, but it seemed to make no difference in the roads. At any hour they were cleaned with clinical efficiency.

The traffic was light and Parker drove home easily in the early afternoon, the weak sun disappearing behind the Kremlin cupolas. Moscow had been blessed that day with more than the nine minutes of sunshine it averaged in winter. Perhaps there wouldn't be any at all tomorrow.

There was a lousy evening in prospect. Buffet dinner with the Harrisons, casual of course. They'd be wearing T-shirts, with the Slazenger logos on the sleeves, white sneakers.

They'd ooze health and happiness. There'd be talk of jogging. Perhaps Harrison's wife would ladle out potatoes with a tennis racket.

Parker skidded a few feet at the traffic lights. The militiaman on curb duty looked up expectantly.

Of course they were nice enough. She had been something awfully successful in a London bank and he was trying, yes, *trying* in the Foreign office. God!

As he put his key in the door he could hear Suzy shouting at Steven. And he swept the boy up in his arms, carrying him into his room, ignoring her, implicitly taking the child's part. Around him were the posters of Frog and Toad and the volumes of *Sam Pig.* There was a haven in children's Moscow.

Parker took off his coat. It was typical of Suzy, venting her frustrations on the boy. She did it too often. In London, of course, things had been different. No pressure. She had done the housework and doted on her son. Oh, and cooked the dinner. Not a worry in the world.

But the little clockwork life had ended in Moscow. Each setback, each delay, seemed enough to blow her off course. If one thing fell through, everything fell through.

Parker recalled a row they'd had the week before

when the embassy driver had forgotten to take her to the market. She had burst into tears on the telephone —how she would have to walk, how she would miss skating, miss a tea party, miss a Russian lesson. The list of tragedies had been endless. And Suzy had sulked for days. Moscow did that to you.

◆

They changed in silence, opening the door to the baby-sitter—Sharon, once from Blackpool and now from downstairs—closing it behind them, deciding not to wait for the elevator.

They heard the bonhomie blaring out across the courtyard as they tripped gingerly over the black ice. Cracked Beatles records, wholesome stuff, from the days when pop stars still wore ties. Good clean fun. Parker wished he'd taken them a porno movie instead of the 1982 Bordeaux.

Harrison beamed at the bottle.

"Good to see you, George, Suzy—my dear, how splendid you look. May I?" He did. Kissed her, pushing the great suntanned face right up against the pale English rose. Skinny, elegant Suzy. She blushed. Parker angled her through into the corridor. People were everywhere with their plastic plates and cups. Over on a table he caught sight of a mound of French crumbs, left over from the French bread. Beside it, a half-hacked Stilton.

"Hallo, George." He knew he'd heard it somewhere.

A foot below him the tanned features of Harrison's wife were winking at him, the small twitching nose,

quick-blinking eyes, the mouse-colored hair tied
back with a rubber band.

"Oh, hi! How are you?"

But she had already reached out to Suzy, pulling
her toward a plastic drink. And Parker turned to
watch the awkward, nervous dancing; embassy protocol exploded; first secretaries with second secretaries; the minister with a typist. And, alone on the
periphery, one of the Russian switchboard operators,
just to prove they all knew they were abroad.

Parker didn't like it. They were all touching each
other, touching him. It was something he had never
come to terms with. Every time someone passed
they'd stroke his shoulder, or his arm, or his back.
"Excuse me, old chap" . . . " 'Scuse please" . . .
"Budge up a mo." It was like riding the London un-
derground. Your body belonged to the crowd.

He shook himself like a wet animal and moved
back into the kitchen, noticing too late that Harrison
was crouching in the corner.

"Oh hello, George. Just sweeping up a glass.
Bloody fool Jenkins knocked it off. Actually it's one of
the Waterfords. Quite valuable, I think." Suddenly he
looked depressed.

"Shame," said Parker without much conviction.
"Still you can probably claim. I think there's a form
for that sort of thing."

Harrison stood up and emptied the dustpan into
the garbage.

"While you're here, George, any chance I might be

able to do a bit of chancery work sometime? You know the consulate isn't exactly intellectual."

"I wouldn't call chancery intellectual either. Depends what you want really. Anyway, I don't see why not in principle—maybe in the summer."

Parker turned around as he heard footsteps. Harrison's wife was standing awkwardly behind him. They both stared at her.

"Whoops, so-rry," she said in an embarrassed, singsong voice, and walked out again.

"I say, George, that would be great if you could fix it." Harrison had cheered up. "Let's go and get another drink." He ushered Parker toward the living room.

"I haven't had a first one yet," Parker protested.

But Harrison had stopped listening.

◆

They had reached a truce on the way home. The pressure of her hand on his arm told Parker that peace had been restored.

"I'm a pain in the arse, aren't I?" She looked up at him, wide-eyed, uncertain. He suddenly recalled their first date.

"Of course you are." He smiled. "You always have been."

For a moment she said nothing. The car crossed Gorky Street.

"George."

"Mmm?"

"I've been very silly about Moscow. I'm sorry. I let it all get me down a bit. I'll be better, I promise."

Parker put her hand in his. She giggled.

"D'you know," she whispered, "I heard today that the wife of a French diplomat hasn't got dressed and gone out for nearly a year. She's too scared. She just sits around the flat all day in her bathrobe, feeding the cat and eating chocolates. Now I'm not that bad, am I? . . . Who knows?" she added. "I might just get to like it."

Like it? thought Parker. If you do, you'll be a lot better off than me.

In the apartment they found Sharon asleep and Steven wide awake, as if he had baby-sat her. But then, as Parker reflected, things in Moscow were seldom the way they seemed.

Unable to sleep, he got up an hour later and tiptoed into Steven's room. He put out his hand to the boy's forehead as he did every night and then felt it a second time just to make sure. This time there was no doubt. Steven was running a high fever.

Chapter 9

DECEMBER 12

No waiting this time. The questions began even before Perminev could sit down. The anxiety hung there unspoken, the heartbeat of intelligence.

"You have the body?" The voice came from the back of the room. Which one was it?

"Yes, and all the paperwork. The instructions were quite explicit."

"Good. It was lucky the old lady's tape came to us as it did. An original idea—a telephone confession." The voice rose but it wasn't a question.

"Unfortunately it wasn't enough. A dissident turns a Party man twenty years ago and the man reaches high office as a traitor. But who is it?"

"With time, Comrade, I feel sure—"

The voice cut him off. "Time is in short supply. The

chairman is worried sick about leaks. Now we know his paranoia is justified."

For a moment no one said anything. Perminev could hear the elderly breathing across the table.

"What about the old woman's daughter?" The question lashed out at him.

"I am approaching her quietly to try to avoid anyone panicking."

"Indeed. Don't forget that so far we have nothing. Maybe the old woman was mad. Maybe she made it all up. We don't know yet. And nor, it appears, do you. Now leave us."

When the door had closed the old general leaned back in his chair and yawned. His younger colleague faced him.

"You look tired, Melor. Does the chase begin to wear you out?"

The general swallowed hard and coughed. It was seven o'clock and already there was thick gray stubble on his face. He undid the bottom of his tunic and sighed with relief. In the light from the single desk lamp he cut a bleak figure. A large, squashed nose leaned out from the flat Slavic cheeks. The small eyes were almost closed. It was a moment before he spoke.

"You know, it was simpler in the fifties. And maybe it was more interesting. Now it's all a question of degree. Does a man betray us in his thoughts or in his deeds? Is he loyal enough? Is he efficient? Maybe he's not efficient enough. Does that make him a threat? Who can answer such questions?"

The younger officer raised a single eyebrow. He knew the mood, knew the philosophy. Melor Inozemtsev, one of the most ruthless heads of department, was airing his soul, searching for a conscience he didn't possess.

"How do I know about you, even you, my friend?" Melor went on. "How do I know that you don't have secret designs on a fur coat from Leningrad or a silk rug from Kazakhstan? And what if you did? I could judge you a criminal today. Tomorrow you might be a hero. This week a fool, next week a genius." He looked up and the monologue was over. Almost.

"As for our present problem, we must shake the tree a little harder—that is, if we wish to enjoy our retirement. The chairman wants results, we must get them." He looked down at his desk and toyed with a pencil. "Of course we could try making the British an offer . . ."

There was an audible gasp from the other side of the room. The general walked across and patted his colleague on the shoulder.

"Don't worry, my friend, we have seen all this before."

◆

"Hullo, James. Good to see you."

The visits were more frequent, Dawling reflected, and the tone friendlier. The message under his door had prepared him for that. The game was back on again, and they hadn't forgotten him. They really hadn't.

He returned the man's smile. "I do believe we're

going to get some snow soon," he said. "How're things in London?"

"Oh, you know. We stumble from one departmental cock-up to another. Nothing changes."

"You're so right, Stuart, so right," Dawling replied. They were back in the prisoners' visiting room. London had advised against reusing the warden's flat. Give him a few conflicting signals, they'd said. Be nice, but make him feel he's in a real prison. No more gifts. We can't let him play baby all the bloody time.

But it was Dawling the traitor who sat at the table this time. A more confident Dawling, thought the man. More dangerous somehow. And yet he was in jail. How could he be dangerous?

"Ever play chess, Stuart?" The question came out of the blue.

The man looked surprised. "Can't say I have." He thought for a moment. "Played with my dad once on a wet afternoon, but that's nothing to write home about, is it?"

"But you know the pieces, don't you? You know how they work?"

"I think so. Why?"

Dawling felt the nerves suddenly. After all this time, he thought. Nerves!

"Well, you know how it is sometimes, you get to the point where you decide to lose a queen to get one. I've heard of it happening that way."

Dawling tried to keep his voice steady. "D'you know if it happens very often? Do people still play that way, you know, queen for a queen?"

The man looked at him curiously. "I expect they do," he said slowly, "but only after very careful consideration."

Dawling smiled for the first time that day.

"That's what I thought you'd say."

◆

It was hard watching Sasha. For he passed lightly and easily through the evening crowds. Sometimes, though, he would stop dead in the street, turn and gaze into a shop window or duck down an alley. But he never looked back and they assumed he hadn't noticed them.

There were two on foot and three in a car acting as backup and radio control. The walkers had the new CIA-style wrist microphones and the transparent plastic earpieces. They didn't believe they could lose him. The technology was too good.

But they reckoned without Natasha Keramova, a pretty, scatty twenty-year-old from Kiev who wasn't really watching her niece for she was too busy watching the shops and dreaming of bargains. She didn't see the child step out into the road and neither did the hundreds of other passers-by on Kalinin Prospekt. But she heard the screech and the scream and for years afterward feared she had heard the thump as well. Although they told her she couldn't have. But the watchers couldn't ignore it because they had families as well, and few Russians can turn their back on a child. And so they lost him.

Within eight minutes another car had been called

in to patrol and search the area, but they didn't find
him either.

In fact, it took a man who was much more experi-
enced. And as Sasha headed quickly toward Tver-
skoy Boulevard the figure stepped out from the
courtyard and forced him up against the wall, his
chin touching the brickwork. The delicate fingers of
Sasha's left hand were twisted back with excruciating
force while the man whispered carefully into his ear.
He had known his target. There would be no piano
playing that night.

Sasha found the pain so great that he couldn't even
shout. And when Perminev released him he sank
quietly onto his knees in the snow, whimpering
softly, like a stray dog.

◆

In the hours that followed Sasha traveled the
metro from Rechnoy Vokzal in the north to Kakhov-
skaya in the southeast, losing himself in motion, nausea, and pain.

It seemed that his entire life had been spent on the
move. He recalled a frightening kaleidoscope of
travel as a child. Summer in Moscow, his father's
hurried arrival, his face flushed and fearful, his
mother pulling a suitcase from the top of a wardrobe,
so little to pack, so little they owned. Money came
from the hollow insides of a book, tickets, documents
from behind a wooden panel. And the little eight-
year-old was dragged out by his parents for the start
of an odyssey—destination unknown.

Only later did he understand what had happened.

How the little family was handed from town to town, apartment to apartment, by people who said little, kept their faces covered, and moved only by dark. Anxious, frightened people, but held together by a secret link.

They had traveled more miles, more days than the little boy had thought possible. Surely, he had reasoned, they would fall off the edge of the earth and that would be the end of them.

He knew nothing of the more tangible risks. And on the journey his father had said little.

Sometimes they didn't see their route, hidden as they were in the backs of food trucks or bakery vans, once a government Volga, even a military truck. The arm of the secret network guided them smoothly to the south, skirting the cities, crisscrossing the sleepy hamlets of rural Russia, into Central Asia and Kazakhstan.

Seven months later they were carried on the back of a horse-drawn cart into the ancient city of Tashkent, their clothes changed, their faces red, their hair swept by the wind. The escape line was at an end.

The new life brought with it a new name. Sasha Treshkov became Sasha Levin. His father began working in an asbestos factory. It brought the old man his illness and hastened his death.

But Sasha never heard him complain. Instead his father would rejoice in the musical talent of his son and praise God that life had been good to him.

Later, as the sickness intensified, his thoughts had returned to Moscow. Hesitantly, painfully, he had

come to speak of his courier work for the British in a
thin high voice that barely carried across a room. It
became almost a confession as the soul looked to its
future and sought forgiveness for the past.

At times the old man would recite names, even
addresses. The discipline left him. The illness unlocked his memory.

There was Potapov and his daughter Zina, Anatol,
Nikolayeva, and Lena. His father had spoken of their
warmth, their passion, their humanity. None were
more selfless, he had said, more courageous. And
Sasha had promised himself he would find them and
join them.

It had not been hard. For his music took him to
Moscow at the age of twenty. Zina lived where her
father had lived. Nikolayeva had never moved. And
the path they showed him led, by care and cunning,
by deduction and subterfuge, to a meeting with
George Parker. Just as he had planned it.

But tonight's encounter? That was not in the plan.
And yet Sasha had long expected it. For different
reasons, certainly. But he had known it would come.
He was to get Lena out of Moscow, persuade her to
leave, sweet-talk her, cajole her if necessary. Perhaps, Perminev had suggested, she was in danger.
Whatever the case, they wanted to talk to her in
peace, well away from the crime, away from the
police. Understand, little boy?

Sasha had known it was a lie, known it without a
doubt in his head. But he knew he'd deliver her.

There was no choice. His own operation depended on it.

◆

The snow and the silence seemed to stretch unbroken for thousands of miles. Russia was locked into its winter.

The car had dropped Kalyagin at the country home of the deputy defense minister. It was getting dark. There were to be drinks, then dinner. But before allowing himself to be ushered inside Kalyagin turned, feeling the snow crisp under his feet, watching his breath swirl up into the birch trees. He tried to picture the miles of impenetrable countryside unaffected by history, older than politics. He shook the snow from his shoes, wondering why the old stoat Afanasyev had invited him, but knowing the answer already.

"Stoat" was a good description. Kalyagin smiled to himself as the minister shuffled toward him, nodding his head at the ground. Amiable, but desperate, he thought.

"How good that you came, my friend." The minister held out a large sweaty hand. "Welcome to the club—no dancing girls, I'm afraid, no roulette, but a club just the same." He winked at Kalyagin. "And such special members."

Nothing had prepared Kalyagin for the wife who got up as he entered the living room. She must have been twenty years younger than Afanasyev, not slim, not perfect, but with the high Slavic cheekbones and the full mouth that engaged the eyes when it smiled. She tilted the blond head when she spoke.

"I can see we should have invited you much sooner." She looked him up and down appreciatively.

"It was kind of you to invite me at all."

"Nonsense. I know we shall get on well together and you will come to see us frequently."

They sat him uncomfortably between them, and it wasn't until he was on his fourth vodka that the warning tugged at his brain. What had they told him in Tallinn all those years ago? "The game never stops. Don't believe you can end it when you're tired. Close your eyes and you're dead."

Kalyagin shook his head clear. He was relieved to be told that dinner was ready.

The dining room had been furnished by Scandinavians. The table and chairs were made of light wood. Kalyagin noted the creaseless white tablecloth, the dark blue napkins. Above him the stained mahogany beams, across the room a wide low fireplace and a circular Italian rug in front of it. The taste was faultless.

◆

"You should try a little more sauce with the salmon." The minister's wife leaned toward Kalyagin with a bowl. As she did so her dress detached itself from her upper arm. He caught sight of a suntan that seemed to stretch forever.

"Thank you, a most exquisite meal."

"You should not have expected anything else." The

mouth tightened. "My husband is, after all, in charge
of the armed forces of the world's greatest nation."
She threw back her blond head and looked Kalyagin
straight in the eye. "At least," she added, "in all but
name."

The minister put down his fork noisily on the plate.
"I'm certain Dmitry Ivanovich doesn't require political reeducation or indeed any special pleading."
He cleared his throat and chuckled. "Tonight we
promised ourselves we would not speak of politics.
And we won't. My dear Dmitry, a toast of welcome
for your first visit to our little . . . home." His right
hand indicated the paneled walls. They all raised
their glasses.

"To your health and success, Dmitry Ivanovich,"
echoed his wife. "If there should be anything we can
do for you at any time"—she paused—"you have only
to say."

She licked away her smile, dabbing her mouth
with a napkin. A single serving lady cleared the
dishes. The minister bore down on Kalyagin with a
wine bottle.

"Perhaps we should go to my study, finish the
wine, and try some cognac," he said. "And then you
can tell me about your family. I hear your father saw
service at Stalingrad. Perhaps you know I was there
myself."

Kalyagin rose as directed but Madame Afanasyev
remained seated. "Viktor, it is rude of you to lead our
guest away so suddenly. Besides, I have not finished

my meal." She picked up her wineglass, holding it to the light, toying with it.

"I'm sorry my dear but—" And suddenly she was standing in front of him, blocking his path.

Kalyagin smiled but knew in that instant that she was not joking.

"I think we should all talk some more in the living room—*vmyestye*—together."

"That is not appropriate." Afanasyev wasn't smiling. "If I were you, I should go to bed. We shall be talking about battles and wars and I'm sure you would be bored . . ." He jerked his head suddenly, motioning her to get out of his way. It was an ugly gesture and she didn't move.

Kalyagin had only a vague inkling of what was coming. He saw the beginning of the movement and gasped in disbelief, for Afanasyev's hand whipped out from his side, catching his wife flat on her right cheek. The smack reverberated through the room and for a moment there was silence. Then Madame Afanasyev screamed like a child and ran out into the hall. Kalyagin could hear her high heels clattering on the wooden staircase.

The deputy minister turned to face his guest. There was a single bead of sweat on his forehead. "Forgive me for this little scene." He sounded out of breath. "You are not married but you know what women are like. Occasionally they have to see that a Russian is master in his own house. It does no one any harm."

◆

There was little traffic on the roads as the Zil sped back into Moscow. It was 1:30 in the morning and the city dwellers were reveling in private. Kalyagin had been sickened by the minister's behavior. And yet, he reflected, it might not have been a spontaneous performance. Afanasyev had been offering an alliance with benefits, making an incentive out of a threat.

And yet the man had rambled wildly, making little sense. The wine and the vodka had taken their toll. The cognac had finished it.

Afanasyev had tried to talk about satellite weapons but forgotten what he wanted to say. Instead he had droned on about the old defense minister hurrying off to his deathbed, promising the world to everyone and leaving his deputy to cope with the mess.

Kalyagin sat back in the seat and tried to doze. He didn't want to get involved, but it would be difficult to stay out. He knew well enough who had helped him into power, who had become his silent patron so many years ago.

One man had watched his progress through Estonia, accelerated it, and marked him out for a slice of power in the Kremlin. One man, who had come first in the uniform of a lieutenant, then in an old Zhiguli and finally in a staff car with the hammer and sickle on the hood. That same man over all those years. He had known him simply as Viktor. Viktor was shrewd, Viktor was generous, Viktor talked much and expected little in return. Only loyalty, he had said. He had talked quite a bit about loyalty.

And it hadn't been a surprise to meet Viktor again in Moscow. Of course he hadn't wanted to talk about their earlier contacts. That's our little secret, he would say. We'll keep that to ourselves, won't we? And they had.

And now he had eaten dinner with him for the first time ever, and Viktor was about to call in his marker.

Kalyagin didn't remember falling asleep.

◆

Madame Afanasyev could see her husband in the reflection of her mirror as he stood awkwardly in the doorway. She was sitting at the dressing table brushing her hair, long deft strokes, exposing the neck. Afanasyev felt his hands go clammy.

She tossed her head, acknowledging his presence.

"Don't just stand there. What are you looking so stupid for?"

Afanasyev advanced a few paces. She saw that he had unfastened his trousers.

"Viktor, you forget yourself." She pointed to his crotch. "Of course you forgot yourself a long time ago where that's concerned."

She turned back to the mirror and Afanasyev stood behind her. Why did she make him nervous? I control an entire fucking army, he thought, and my own wife makes a clown of me.

"I thought it went well," he muttered, trying to smile.

"Of course it did. D'you think I can't handle boys like that? If I can handle a fool like you, Kalyagin is no problem at all." She continued brushing her hair. "In fact, I quite enjoyed it."

"What will you do next?"

"Wait a day or so, then telephone him. I shall tell him what a bastard you are. He will feel desperately sorry for me and say so. And then"—she smiled—"then we shall meet and I will ensure his cooperation."

"Brilliant, my dear." Afanasyev put a hand on her shoulder and beamed drunkenly into the mirror. "Don't wait too long, though. He must feel sorry for you."

"He will. It's just as well one of us can manage your career." She reached up and pushed his hand off her shoulder.

Chapter 10

DECEMBER 13

Dmitry Kalyagin awoke at 6:30 with a start. In the kitchen he found Zina Potapova making his breakfast. She had been reassigned from his old quarters but there had been no explanation, no warning or consultation. She had arrived because someone had signed the form. You didn't ask why because you didn't know where to ask.

She stood at the stove—a stocky figure in her flowery apron, stirring kasha. Kalyagin smiled at her back. She was Russia.

He left the flat at 8:30. The car had been warmed up and the smoke from the twin exhausts drifted out over the icy courtyard.

Zina Potapova watched from the window. She had exchanged a brief smile with her employer as they met in the corridor and both had gone about their morning ritual.

"How is the weather this morning?" he had asked, as he had done for more than a year.

"It is cold," she replied. "And they say it will be colder by the evening."

I am glad to see you again, he told her. But it was only his eyes that spoke.

It was enough for the microphones embedded deep in the walls—a legacy from the Stalin era when the old man was said to have derived his evening's entertainment from reading the wiretap reports on his closest colleagues. No one had ever dared authorize the removal of the devices, so they had remained there through the decades, giving faithful, if erratic, service.

Each leader had publicly abhorred the practice but none had discontinued it. The evening reading sessions had become something of a Kremlin tradition.

Zina Potapova wandered from room to room with her carpet sweeper, reflecting on the good fortune that had smoothed her transfer from the minister's old quarters to the block on Kutuzovsky. It was the sort of luck you couldn't buy, let alone wish for. Perhaps God's smile had truly fallen on the inner ring road. She began humming to herself, a long-forgotten tune that meant nothing to the man six stories above who heard it.

When her work was finished she descended in the elevator to the caretaker's office to ask for instructions about the laundry. But as she approached the door she found it ajar, the noise of voices and laughter coming from the inside. She pushed it open and tiptoed inside. It wasn't what she'd expected.

In the darkened hallway, balanced on an ancient deck chair, a plump strawberry blonde was sitting on the caretaker's lap, tears of laughter pouring down her cheeks. The old man's face was bright red and he was singing. A girl rushed out of the kitchen, caught sight of Potapova, screamed, and ran back. Loud music screeched out from a tiny transistor. It reminded her of a theatrical comedy.

The caretaker had a glass in his hand and beckoned her over. "C'mon, Zina Dimitrievna, join the party. It's my birthday, have a swig, we're a happy little group. Let's have some fun."

Potapova looked back toward the door. "Don't worry," he told her. "All the bosses have gone to work. There's only security downstairs and they'll be up for a drink in a minute. So, come in. Come in." He tickled the blonde under her armpit and she slid giggling onto the floor.

This wasn't what Potapova wanted but she stayed half an hour, propped against the wall in the kitchen as the cleaning ladies clinked the tiny vodka glasses and swayed to the music. They were real Muscovites —sharp and cheeky.

"Got a man, dear?" A spiky-haired blonde peered skeptically at Potapova. They all roared with laughter as Potapova turned red.

"Got plenty of men here if you want them," the

blonde's friend added. The two had their arms around each other. "At least they look like men, but we've never checked. It'd frighten some of the old donkeys to death."

"Don't you believe it." It was the oldest of the women speaking. A thin, gaunt creature, once blond, once pretty, leaning on the kitchen table. "A few of them still know that it's not just for making holes in the snow. No, my little doves, drop your guard and they'll leap on you like a fox in a sheep pen."

They fell about at that, cackling raucously.

"What would you know about it, old cow? The last time you lost your knickers was in the revolution." Spiky shrieked with laughter, wiping the tears from her cheeks.

"Ha, think you know it all, don't you? What if I told you some old stick had set me up—a little bolt-hole, a love nest, eh? What would you say to that, fathead?"

Spiky was still guffawing. "I'd say you were dreaming, old girl. Your mind gone the way of your body, down the fucking drain."

At that Spiky crawled drunkenly onto the table, stood up, and began swaying grotesquely to the music. But suddenly there was silence and Spiky was swaying to nothing.

"Hard work, ladies?" A short man in a gray suit stood in the doorway. He raised an eyebrow, then caught sight of the caretaker sprawled out under the table. "Ladies and gentlemen," he added sarcastically. "Party's over, don't you think? Time to go back and look after our leaders. Deserve a bit better, don't they? *Nu shto?"*

As they drifted into the corridor Potapova felt a tug at her arm. "I did have a little place, you know." The old woman was whispering. "Gruzinsky four, apartment three, can't forget it somehow. The shit's probably got someone else there by now, but"—she winked and put a finger to her lips—"enough of all that nonsense."

◆

They buried the body of Ira Nikolayeva on a stretch of open ground in the southwest of the city, where the wind blew the snow in their faces and froze the tears.

It was a corner of the district cemetery to which the KGB had delivered the coffin, pulling it from the back of an unmarked Volga station wagon and entrusting it to the unsteady grasp of the two gravediggers. The men had demanded extra money because of the cold.

Lena and Sasha walked behind them. Marina Alexandrovna followed, and with her a Jewish friend who had come to recite the kaddish.

It was barely audible, for the man had to speak through his scarf and the wind carried away his words. Lena felt numbed by the cold. At one point she thought she heard a plane taking off from the nearby military airfield. For a moment she felt a long way from Russia, standing out in the urban flatlands, unwatched and unhindered as the earth covered Citizen Nikolayeva, removing her from Soviet life.

She wondered what her mother would have wanted said; there was always something appropriate for every occasion. Russian was full of little phrases or couplets to trot off the tongue and explain away life's mysteries. Lena thought hard but no words came.

Sasha took her left arm, Marina her right, and between them they steered her inert figure over the rough ground, through the rows of gravestones, emblems, and inscriptions to where the yellow taxi waited—its engine running, its grille coated up with a blanket. None of them spoke as they drove back into the city.

Chapter 11

DECEMBER 14

The nights had dissolved into one another as Anatol crouched under his blanket in the tiny apartment, fearing the daylight, dreaming his way through history and memories, no longer knowing where one ended and the other began.

At times he rose shaking from the bed, shivering and barely able to stand. He would make tea, drink a mouthful and return to shroud himself, semiconscious from the day outside. Frequently he wept. Once he laughed and the fever turned him alternately hot and cold until he no longer knew his name and began calling out those he had long forgotten.

His mind raged at the killing, raged, too, at the collapse of its shelter. It had taken so many years to build the barrier that separated him from terror, from the treachery that had hacked his life apart.

On the fourth day he awoke lying exhausted on his back, hearing the stillness, the bang of a door in the distance, a woman's voice many floors below. Niko-layeva had been right about one thing. There were only fighters and cowards and he had fallen from the one to the other. Twenty years ago he had run the most efficient network in Moscow. Dozens of agents and a model system of cutouts and fallbacks that left the center secure even if the lifelines were cut.

Secure. Anatol laughed. So secure that he hadn't seen the traitor—the long line of traitors that London had allowed to infiltrate and track them. Silent treachery, the systematic penetration of the dissident movement that even the KGB had been unable to mount. In the end the British had done it for them.

He coughed painfully, easing himself up on his forearms. His hand reached under the curtain, feeling the ice on the inside of the windowpane. With a nail he scraped at it a little and tried to put it on his forehead but fell back exhausted.

Anatol recalled the years spent running after the operation had been blown. He and Nikolayeva had gotten out, so had two or three others. But a dozen or so had been caught and still more had died resisting.

This was a story the world had never heard. The survivors had gone to ground, he to Kiev, where there were relatives, the others God knew where. They had known the rules. All contacts severed. No returns or reunions.

But seventeen years after his escape Anatol had gone back to his father's apartment and Nikolayeva had remembered the address and found him there.

Of course the old man had died, but the place was between tenants. A friend had bribed a blowsy fifty-year-old blonde on the housing committee, given her flowers and chocolates and one or two afternoon kindnesses she had been lacking. And the flat was his, the records falsified.

Anatol's mind searched back over the details, putting the facts into boxes, cross-checking them, seeking out the gaps and inconsistencies.

He wanted to lie down again but a shadow seemed to pass in front of him and he sat upright, throwing the blanket on the floor, dressed only in a long, coarse nightshirt. What had Nikolayeva boasted? . . . "I still have my contacts." That's what she'd said. But there should have been no contacts. Nothing at all. What had she meant?

It could have been nothing more than the bravado of a vain old woman, but it was possible there was more. He staggered to the kitchen and prized the top off a bottle of mineral water. What if Nikolayeva had done her damage before dying? Would the British ever realize the danger? A twenty-year-old operation could have been blown apart. The biggest ever. Questions and more questions. They banged inside his head in time with his heart.

For more than an hour Anatol sat on the bed, oblivious to the draft that tore through the crack in the window frame. He had a goal, a purpose. Pulling back the heavy curtain, he saw it was evening, the last traces of the sun streaking the horizon. As he peered down into the dark street he knew exactly where his logic would lead him.

It was vintage adrenaline, old, bottled, and lost, he had thought, forever. Wrong! Wrong once again.

Seventeen summers and winters had dented his memory but there were things he could never forget. Anatol dressed clumsily under the single light bulb. Long strands of his hair hung lank from the balding scalp.

He met no one in the corridor or on the stairs but he couldn't chance the yard. Quickly he prized open the windows and slid into the side street.

Serebryany Bor lay four miles across town. It took Anatol almost as many hours to make it. Moscow had been hit by a blizzard. A driving wind snatched at his coat, blowing him from side to side, covering each footstep with snow as he walked. A bus took him a mile and a half, crawling along the deserted streets, the driver blinded by the snow. Anatol could recognize only the outlines of buildings.

"Go home," the driver turned and shouted at him. "This is a night for dogs. Get out here. I'm not going any farther."

The hydraulic door had frozen and Anatol had to fight his way out. For a moment he stood still and looked around, a dark giant, powerless before the storm.

He had no strength, no warmth, and his numbed feet sank deep into the snowdrifts. But an ancient

prayer fixed itself in his head, a childhood supplica-
tion that God deliver him that night from evil and
confound his enemies. Anatol knew that he had for-
feited the right to pray to his God but it made no
difference. He knew no other.

And then he saw it—the long, straight road that led
to the river beach. He didn't hesitate. Not now. This
was known territory. Five hundred yards away was
the small turning to the left, through the woods. He
stumbled toward it, a walking snowman. The animals
saw him and kept clear, but the moon was hidden
that night and no human eye caught sight of him. In
his mind he held on to the image of the boathouse.
Pray God it was still there.

Anatol never heard them but the bells of the
Kremlin tower struck midnight across the city as he
climbed the steps of the old shack, half conscious, his
chest in agony.

With a single movement he pulled the lock from
the door and lurched inside. Behind him the wind
died away as he tripped on the uneven boards and
crashed painfully, his head catching the edge of a
table. In the moment he fell it seemed to him that
God had not, after all, decided to hear his prayer.

◆

He regained consciousness with pain thudding in
his temples. Even after so many years he knew the
place. He had seen it last in summer in the days when
all memories were touched by sunshine, when he
lived on a high of intrigue, an intensity that had
taken a decade to settle.

The last visit had been so different. It had been a hot evening early in September and Anatol had been in a hurry. He recalled the desperation. He had run home from the Leningradsky station after waiting an hour for Sylvia. The instructions were to try the next day, same time, and every day for four days. He didn't know what would happen after that.

But as he ran through the courtyard, past the old gossiping grandmothers, he had glimpsed the two chalk crosses on the upper left side of the door. Such a simple message. And so confident had he been, had they all been, that he might have missed it. But something had drawn his eyes upward and he had stared in disbelief while the grandmothers stopped talking and looked around to see if he had been struck by a devil.

Perhaps it had been a mistake. Maybe some children had been scribbling idly on the wood. But as he looked again he noticed the telltale circle that linked the crosses and knew there was no mistake.

It was an emergency signal. Only one meaning. Get out. Save yourself. A once-only contact. No follow-up. The plug was being pulled.

Anatol remembered it all and the sickness of fear returned to him. Outside in the distance an animal barked. A stray dog, a wolf perhaps. He peered into the darkness but saw nothing.

He hadn't waited that day, taking the stairs three at a time, rummaging for the battered suitcase and the plastic bundle, running as never before, knowing that life depended on it.

He had found his way to the boathouse, half hoping that Sylvia or Andrei might meet him there. But it had been deserted then as now. So Anatol had taken his time with the package, memorizing the location, repeating the lesson they had taught him so carefully.

Never lose equipment, bury it. Nothing is forever —not even failure. Remember everything for the years when you may need it again.

They would have been proud of Anatol, he thought. An emaciated shell, his skin gray from sickness and fatigue, sitting on the floor of a freezing boathouse, reciting his lessons word-perfect into the night. He began laughing until the tears came soundless and bitter.

He never doubted that he'd find the bundle and he thanked God for the care with which he'd packed it. A metal paint can, with its special plastic lining, sealed with rubber, airless and watertight. Two pressure screws on the lid. He had made it himself.

Chapter 12

DECEMBER 15

The militia patrol noticed the old man hobbling along the frozen bank. Dawn had broken half an hour earlier. The man carried a bundle on his shoulder, wrapped in plastic, and the officers assumed he had been fishing in a hole in the ice. Plenty of people did that with no more than a length of twine and some bait. Just the same, they followed him with their eyes until he was out of sight.

◆

It was a tribute to the technology of the sixties and the customizing skills of the British.

The Motorola had begun life as little more than a walkie-talkie. But the engineers had converted it to Morse with a miniature key molded to the bottom. It transmitted less than four watts on the six-meter am-

ateur band, the range just over three miles. It had
been enough. The set wasn't designed for lengthy
operation—fifteen to twenty seconds at most using a
shorthand code.

In fact, the experts had considered it a dangerous
form of communication, virtually assured of inter-
ception. There were only two uses: occasional dis-
information and an emergency signal to arrange a
crash contact in a predetermined site.

The virtue had been simplicity. A set frequency on
54 megahertz using a length of wire as an antenna
and flashlight batteries. It had been a problem finding the right ones. Moscow was always short of batteries. But once found the set could then be carried
in a shopping bag and even operated surreptitiously
in a moving bus or car.

That night Anatol sent the simple ZA code from
the back of a taxi as it rounded Revolution Square
heading for Kalinin Prospekt. Across the river in the
British Embassy the digital detectors locked on to it
within a millisecond and printed out the frequency,
recording the transmission automatically.

The VHF carrier wave was scanned continuously,
twenty-four hours a day, year in, year out. It was just
a precaution. No one took it seriously, but since the
equipment was there, they thought it best to use it.

◆

Sasha dropped her at the domestic terminal at
Sheremyetyevo One, sitting like a distant outpost
among the white fields and forests around Moscow.

Lena had sat in the taxi not wanting to go.

"Sasha, why? Maybe I can help you. There is so much to do."

"It's better this way. It won't be for long." He didn't wait to see her off. She watched him from the warmth of the terminal, hoping he might turn and wave, but he didn't. He had arranged everything so quickly—the call to her cousin in Murmansk to say she was coming, the ticket, for which he had stood in line for nearly two hours at Aeroflot—and now he had left her and that was that.

"Forget about Moscow for a while," he had said. "Things will be easier when you return and then we can continue the way we were."

She couldn't find the energy to argue.

Ninety minutes later, with the smell of sheepskin and leather coats around her, the TU 134 banked sharply through the evening clouds over the city. Soon Lena could see nothing but the deep, clear blue sky. She knew she was doing the right thing.

The feeling lasted through the flight, through the landing at the single bleak terminal, right up until the airport police saluted her politely, introduced themselves, and drew her, unprotesting, into the patrol car. It was the Arctic night, she reflected, peering through the dirty windows. There would be little if any daylight for months to come.

They took her to an apartment block, one of six that looked down from the hill onto the football stadium, where the children romped noisily in the snow, shrieking and laughing at each other. She cursed herself for not looking at the number on the door and then remembered there hadn't been one.

"I am to ask you to wait here." The uniformed militiaman gestured to a chair in the tiny living room with the livid orange wallpaper.

"Wait for what?" she asked.

"Everything will be made clear shortly." And with that the officer had wiped his mustache with the back of his hand and left the room.

Lena could hear his footsteps on the stone landing outside, the whine of the elevator, the clunk of a door, and then there was silence. She wasn't frightened, she told herself. They had been polite and civilized. Perhaps it was something to do with Mother. Maybe they had some news for her. Could they have found the murderer so quickly? She caught sight of the telephone on the sideboard and rummaged in her handbag for her cousin's number.

She was genuinely surprised that the line had been cut.

◆

Two miles across the city on the road that winds over the hills to the naval base at Sevyeromorsk, her cousin picked up the telegram and threw it angrily in the wastepaper basket. It was typical of people from Moscow. First they said they were coming, then they found something better to do. Never mind that she had gone to the Arktika fish shop, bought enough to feed a regiment. Shrimps too. Just to show the girl how well they live in the north—and how much better the food was. And what was she to do with it now? Feed it to the dogs?

She picked up the local edition of *Polyarnaya Pravda* and scanned it for the personal ads. "Student, thirty, seeks lady for companionship. Interested in the theater." Whoever heard of a student aged thirty? But she put a big red cross beside it. By the time she had finished there were four crosses on the page. And she felt a little better. Maybe this time she'd find a friend, someone with whom she could pass the godforsaken Arctic days and nights.

She went into the kitchen, spooned a dozen of the shrimps into a saucer, and poured some mayonnaise over them. Damn the waistline and damn the god-damn relatives.

◆

The two cousins heard the storm begin and both shivered at the same moment.

Chapter 13

DECEMBER 16

"What do we have on code name Unicorn?" General Inozemtsev looked across his desk. On it was scattered the debris of the night. Files, computer printouts, stained coffee cups with the cold dregs at the bottom. Seven hours since the radio intercept.

The lieutenant pulled himself awake. "Unicorn was used several times in the late sixties and then terminated. Department Four suspected internal subversion, possibly a courier network operated by the British. Transmissions ceased abruptly soon after one group was arrested. You will recall we had a certain amount of success at that time."

The general glared at his assistant. "I not only re-call it, my friend. I was largely responsible for it. We took over what began as a military intelligence operation. True to form, the GRU were about to bungle it completely. It is fortunate that we had a friend who was able to bring the matter to our attention."

The general got up and walked over to the window. Far below, a trolley bus had become disconnected from the overhead wires. The driver, rope in hand, was trying to reattach the long arm.

It was a painful process. Not the only one, he reflected. He sighed audibly. "What are the British saying?"

"We expect to hear soon. They appear to be considering." The junior officer sat back in his chair. It was good to have some cards to play, especially with this old bastard.

The general scratched his forehead. "Get Perminev here and let me know when you hear something." The general rested his head on the back of the chair and yawned. His body wanted to sleep, but his mind wanted to play on.

◆

Parker shut the cage door. Inside it seemed to him a grotesque little gathering, like crows perched on a wall. Dark faces, dark clothes, and nervous, pointed little features. The light was far from flattering and the air had become unwholesome. The room was meant for only two and there were four of them, sweating and arguing.

He regretted calling the meeting. Too many people in the know. Strictly speaking, not even the ambassador should have been there. But Parker needed to talk it through, the way they used to in London.

Mary Cross was there to inject some sanity; Jim Farrar, the signals clerk, to lead them into the boring world of codes and diodes. Parker wondered how much use they were going to be.

Farrar nodded his head pedantically and pointed at each of them with his pencil.

"It's unbelievably childish, you know. I mean this sort of thing went out with the ark. When you look at all the technology that's available, even here. Even the amateur radio stations, the sort of worker's club thingamajigs, what are they called . . . ?"

"They're called trade unions," Parker interjected. "Just like we have in Britain."

"Yes, well, that's the one. Anyway, you know what I mean. This little transistor johnny isn't much more than a walkie-talkie. If you ask me, it was a bloody miracle we picked it up at all."

"So you think it's an amateur job?" asked Sir David. "Is there any way it could simply be made to look like that? I suppose what I'm asking is, were there any professional hallmarks at all—any known signatures?

Farrar scratched his ear. "Just can't tell, sir. I mean look at it this way. . . . The man knew enough to send the message and do it from something that was moving. I can't say fairer than that, now can I?"

"No, indeed you can't, and thank you so much for joining us." Parker noted how the ambassador had suddenly seized control of the meeting. Farrar caught it as well and flushed. He hadn't imagined he would be asked to leave. "Oh yes, fine," he muttered, and disengaged his legs from the table. "Er, see you all later, perhaps?"

The air locks shut behind him. "Now then." The ambassador grimaced. "Your thoughts."

They all shifted in their chairs, as if Farrar had taken an unpleasant smell with him. Parker fumbled in a manila file.

"You know what that code is?" He turned from one to the other. "It's twenty-odd years old. That's what it is. Last used in 1968 by a local unit under embassy supervision. We lost them in the summer of that year. KGB terminated the group, although some were thought to have got away. We never heard and, of course, we never asked. The rules were quite specific even then. They were good people—courier work mostly but there were one or two long-range attempts at penetration. Something of a new project at the time, I believe."

Parker delved deeper in the file. Suddenly he felt elated. The page was shouting up at him.

"Mary, what about you?" asked the ambassador.

"It has all the signs of a decoy operation. Standard ploy to get some sort of reaction from us, force our hand, get us to reveal whoever it is that works for MI6."

Parker continued leafing through the file.

"So you'd advise us to drop the whole thing, forget we'd heard it. . . ." Sir David seemed anxious to make a decision.

But Parker wasn't listening. Near the bottom of the file one paragraph had caught his eye. The ZA

code that signaled an agent in place—a code that not
even boring Farrar, with his head full of cryptology,
had known. As he read to the end of the page, he
could feel his mouth go dry.

"Anything more, George?" Sir David seemed
happy with what Mary had told him.

"Nothing." Parker slapped the file shut. "Junk. All
sorts of nonsense about miniature cameras. That sort
of thing."

Sir David looked at his watch and stood up. It was
ten to six and the first of the diplomatic circuit's cocktail parties was about to begin.

"Let's talk again in the morning," he said. "Doesn't
seem to be anything urgent about this one."

◆

It was pitch dark outside. Moscow was encased in a
wall of cold. Parker waited until the embassy was
virtually deserted. It took him forty minutes to get
the files from the basement safe to his room on the
ground floor. Quickly he drew the thick velvet curtains and turned on the desk light.

For a moment Parker stood still, listening. Then he
locked the door and blew the dust from the top
cover.

The investigators had decimated the records.
When the Dawling business had broken three of
them had appeared from London in the guise of a
Foreign Office inspection team and gone through the
intelligence data line by line. By day they had
checked budgets, looked at the living quarters, chatted to the wives. But at night they had torn open the

top-secret files with the vengeance and thoroughness that always follows a major betrayal. Dawling's contacts, his notes, doodles, his assessments, phone numbers, jottings—everything before and after him had been put under the spotlight.

Some of it had gone back home in the diplomatic pouch, but those were bad days in London. And trust was in short supply. The new policy was to avoid centralizing information as much as possible. Keep it where it is, they had said, distribute on a need-to-know basis, cut out the sorters and the couriers. Ironically, Moscow records seemed safer left in Moscow. At least the enemy there had been visible. Mostly.

From the missing pages Parker could follow the route the investigators had taken. The casualties had been immediate. They had ripped the old network apart. Not that they needed to. In the aftermath of Dawling's arrest, the Russians had done it for them. Within forty-eight hours there had been swoops in Moscow, Leningrad, and three other cities. Further raids had come a day later, following a series of brutally successful interrogations.

But the London investigators had kept to established principles and insisted on sending the emergency signals as soon as they arrived in Moscow. The breakup codes. The warning of betrayal and treachery. Just in case there was anyone who had survived long enough to hear it. British intelligence considered that a final act of faith.

Parker yawned and rubbed his eyes. He could only imagine the mess.

For everyone there are moments of premonition, split-second warnings, most of them harmless and without consequence. And so it was that Parker knew the black telephone was going to ring. The direct line, the one that mattered.

You don't ignore this call, because when there's only one light in the building and only one room occupied, they know you're there and you have nowhere to hide.

"Steven's much worse," she told him. "Come *now.*" In that instant he recalled, she had never before spoken so forcefully.

◆

In the back of the Rolls-Royce, Sir David cuddled his "sweetie" as they sped down the fast lane on Kalinin Prospekt. One Spanish party over, one Australian still to come.

He permitted himself a wet kiss on her neck, but Harriet was not to be distracted.

"You know we don't seem to talk at all these days, dear," she murmured. "There's so much I want to tell you."

"Tell me now," he whispered, and kissed her again. She looked out the window.

"I have *tried* to like it here." She turned back to him. "But it's all so gray and ghastly. Couldn't we just take an early retirement or something?"

He took her arm. "I thought you loved it. That's what you always tell everyone."

She laughed. "Well, what am I supposed to say? Go

into a great moaning session every time someone
asks 'How are you?' "

"But what's wrong? You seem to keep pretty active."

"Yes, but it's always the same thing. Bloody flower
arranging, bloody walks, bloody keep fit—"

"I say, keep your voice down, old girl." Sir David
gestured toward the Soviet chauffeur.

"That's the trouble. We can *never* talk. And you
don't seem to want to. Don't you remember, before
we came here? We were always chatting about . . .
you know, a little cottage in Wiltshire or somewhere
like that. And you did promise, David. You did say
we'd do that."

He took his arm away but she tugged it back.
"We're still going to do that, aren't we, David? I don't
think I could bear it if we didn't have something to
look forward to."

But the car had stopped and someone had opened
the door, and there was a crowd of people standing
by the embassy gate and Harriet wasn't at all sure
she'd heard what David had said.

◆

It's the most secretive building in the world but
there are no moments of privacy. The thought struck
Kalyagin as he examined the bank of colored telephones beside his desk.

Each one spoke status and power. He had only to
ask and the calls went out or came in within seconds.
Towns, villages, coal mines, post offices, guard posts
along the border with Mongolia—the operators

found them and dialed them in an instant. Distant
nervous voices. Kalyagin could visualize the sweating faces to which they belonged. A call from the
Kremlin, from the Politburo no less. Enough to make
the tundra tremble. Careers and lives made or shattered along a shaky connection thousands of miles
long.

In the first few days Kalyagin had sat nervously
between the high stucco walls. He had chosen from
six portraits of Lenin that had respectfully been offered him. He had sensed the power he held but was
unsure how to use it.

He recalled the time when his old mentor,
Afanasyev, had put him right. "You want something,
you get it. You read a report, you don't like it, you call
the man who wrote it. You don't like *Pravda* today,
you ring the editor and tell him why. It's a family
business, only you're the troubleshooter. Anywhere,
anytime. Pick up the phone"—he giggled a little—
"pick it up and you'll be fulfilling your norms. It's the
way we work."

Kalyagin had shrugged.

"No, I mean it. Only remember one thing. You
have a dozen senior members above you. Each of
them with their networks and friends, in Moscow, in
Leningrad, you name it, in Kamchatka. Learn who
their friends are and don't cross them. Get it wrong
and you could wake up to find fifteen people standing over you with a hammer." He had giggled again,
coughing phlegm noisily into his mouth and then

swallowing it. "You see, Comrade, these are high stakes."

And Kalyagin had known it. In the early days he had stifled the desire to send London reports hour by hour. The sudden access to information was breathtaking.

Each document represented a jigsaw piece to a puzzle most Russians could only guess at. Raw intelligence came to him in every file, on every page. From all over the Soviet Union, from its missions abroad, from the intelligence directorates, their agents and controllers, he saw a picture of Soviet activities that defied his imagination.

It would take years to absorb, years to trace the patterns—but the daily record was sufficient by itself. Only now did he realize the sophistication of the state's machine. Half the world took them for bumbling, backward peasants, incapable of keeping a tractor on the road—they should read some of this, he thought—the political analyses, the leaks from the White House and from London, yes, London. Kalyagin would draw in his breath in amazement. If only they knew!

From the pile of riches he stole just a few gems. Long-term assessments rather than bald facts. They were too risky, they could be traced, he would save the best for the end—whenever that would come.

Kalyagin never knew what was done with his material. He received no feedback. The traffic was one way. No cards, no thank-yous, no bonuses for productivity. And yet nothing was asked of him, nothing required or demanded. Whatever he handed out they swallowed. As far as he knew, he had never been wrong. To Kalyagin it meant there were two jobs, and he took pride in both.

In the Kremlin office he would often work from dawn till midnight. Afanasyev's advice had been useful. He would pick up the phone, not once, but twenty times a day and well into the evening, when the Far Eastern republics were just awake, when the local officials were sleepy and disoriented.

He had questioned, ordered, even threatened on occasion. And the results had begun appearing. A drug ring had been broken up in Georgia, two senior Party figures dismissed, and he alone, through diligent research and long hours, had uncovered one of those age-old criminal mirages that the Russians so love to create—the Potyemkin factory, the one that takes funds, hires and fires, makes profits, loses profits, and never, ever exists.

Kalyagin enjoyed himself.

The only dark spot had been Perminev, constantly beside him, newly promoted and appointed, charged with feeding him the reports and digests, the conduit between country and Kremlin. There was no bypass.

"They say Perminev has a friend," Afanasyev had warned him, "and it isn't you."

◆

It was two minutes to eight when she telephoned, using the direct line unlisted even in the Kremlin switchboard, the green phone, made by Siemens of West Germany, the phone that never rang because no one knew the number. No one except the general secretary.

"This is Irena Afanasyev." The voice was flat, unexciting.

"I know." Kalyagin sat very still.

"You could say 'Good evening.'"

"Forgive me, my mind was far away."

"I could call back if . . ."

"No, please . . ." He couldn't help it. In his mind he saw the full mouth, the suntan glimpsed beneath her dress. He didn't want to let her go.

Her tone softened. "I do not wish to disturb you, but I must apologize for what happened last night."

"My dear Madame Afanasyev, there is nothing to say. What happened was—"

"Between me and my husband?" she interjected suddenly. "Is that what you were going to say?"

"I . . . I . . ."

"I wish it had been otherwise. Unfortunately, these scenes are becoming a little too frequent. I'm sorry, again. I did not wish to bore you with family problems—"

It was his turn to interject. "But you haven't, not at all. Please don't apologize. I had a splendid evening."

"Well, I did not. Anyway, that is of no consequence to anyone but myself. I hope that despite the unpleasantness, we can meet again."

"I hope so too." For a moment there was no response and Kalyagin was on the point of asking if she was still there. The line crackled suddenly.

"Tomorrow, five o'clock," she said.

"Forgive me. I did not hear you correctly." He could feel the flush on his cheeks.

"I said five o'clock tomorrow. Don't be late."

Kalyagin listened for the click, but she had already hung up. Quickly he picked up his coat and made for the outer office, nervous suddenly, furtive, aware that she had left him with the guilt that was still to come.

◆

By prior arrangement he met her husband that night in the courtyard of the Kutuzovsky block, but it was staged to appear a coincidence—two of the country's leaders just meeting by chance for a breath of the icy air after a large dinner.

They didn't stay out long. Afanasyev took Kalyagin's arm, steering him into the darkness of the archway. For a moment they were lost from the television monitors.

It was the second approach, and Kalyagin was shocked at the depth of the man's resentment of the general secretary. It seemed to be growing daily, fueled by hatred and ambition. He shook his head in amazement as the deputy minister talked in rapid bursts.

"Not much time left," Afanasyev told him.

"For what?"

But the older man put a hand to his lips.

By now the infrared cameras had found them again but all they could see were the short puffs of breath from the two figures, like smoke signals across a valley.

They moved inside the main hall, nodding at the security detail, taking in the scrubbed marble cleanliness, the aura of sanctity that surrounded high office.

The elevator door slammed shut and the ancient box began climbing.

"What about the space weapons?" whispered Kalyagin.

For a moment Afanasyev said nothing, then turned slowly and looked at him. His nose was dark red from the cold.

"He wants to destroy an American satellite."

"I know . . . but when?"

"End of the year."

"And you don't want that?" Kalyagin had tried to slow down but the question came too quickly.

"Of course I do." Afanasyev grimaced. "If I thought the weapon would work."

The door grated open and Kalyagin found himself dragged by the forearm around the corner, as if to climb the steps to the next floor. Afanasyev was panting.

"Look, the general secretary wants to test Washington. He thinks the old President is soft, lot of piss and wind about the evil empire but no backbone. You see? Understand?"

Kalyagin nodded.

"Anyway, he wants an incident, a big one, wants to know what he's up against. They all do it when they come to power. It sets the guidelines, establishes the pattern. A bit like a policy statement. Anyway, if it backfires, he'll just say it was an accident, play dumb, apologize, promise greater international cooperation to prevent such things happening in the future. The Western media love that sort of crap."

He stopped for a moment and scratched his ear. "The point is that the Americans are so easygoing, always have been. They're not going to launch an attack because of one satellite. Just look at them! Take the farmers. They're now so greedy they won't even let the President cut off grain to us. Idiots!"

"What's the problem then?"

"The problem, my friend, is that our much-hailed kinetic-energy weapon couldn't shoot a partridge out of the sky, let alone a satellite. It's failed every test we've given it."

"But the reports? I mean . . ." Kalyagin looked astonished.

"We rewrote the reports. D'you think we're mad? What were we going to do—type out our own transfers to Siberia? Anyway, that's the past, we've done it now, and there's no turning back."

For a moment Afanasyev stopped. There were voices in the distance, footsteps coming toward them.

"You have to help," he whispered to Kalyagin, "there's no other way."

As Kalyagin watched, speechless, the minister opened the door to his apartment and stepped quickly inside.

◆

For a long time Lena had sat by the window as the gale whipped at the building. Now, in the stillness, she eased open the catches, shaking and battering the ice with her fists, watching the top layer of snow cascade down into the street. The cold jabbed straight at her eyes and mouth and she gasped in surprise, wrenching the two frames back together.

During the first hours no one had come to see Lena. She had lain down. Then a woman was shaking her awake, telling her that it was morning, there was food for breakfast, and that she—plump earth mother with the chattering mouth, the long black hair fastened with a rubber band, and the kopeck-sized mole on the chin—she had come to look after her.

"You see? Not so bad here, is it? Eh? It's the Arctic up here. We know how to treat visitors, huh?"

Peasant talk, peasant logic, thought Lena, but she smiled gratefully and warmed to the old lady's words. So she didn't see the eyes begin to narrow, didn't notice the chatter had changed direction, and failed to wonder at all why the woman had placed a cassette recorder on the table between them.

In fact, all she did was drink her coffee gratefully, put her legs on the sofa and wrap her free arm around them. And the woman chatted about her past, ever more deeply, ever more precisely while the drug coursed headlong into Lena's bloodstream, compelling her to talk and talk. In the end, though, she wasn't talking. Lena was singing everything she knew.

◆

Parker could feel that the boy's fever had risen. He didn't need to be told. Steven's cheeks were bright red and he was breathing with some difficulty.

He switched off the bedside light and tiptoed into the corridor. Suzy was busy in the kitchen.

"What did the doctor say?" he asked her.

"You know what Steeles is like . . . 'Give him some aspirin, lots to drink, and bring him in if he gets any worse.' " She was angry. "Bring him in. It's minus twenty out there tonight and he expects me to bring over a child with a temperature over a hundred and two. For God's sake, who hired him as the embassy doctor? I was at the playgroup this morning and no one's satisfied with him. He just doesn't bother. And besides, some people heard from the Swedes that there's been meningitis in the city. What do we do then?"

Parker wasn't used to this Suzy—determined, demanding—but she must have been gearing up to it for hours. Surrounded by listeners, she had no one to talk to.

"We can't fly him out if he gets it. . . ."

Parker put out a hand, steering her gently into the sitting room.

"I'll see Steeles in the morning and stick some dynamite under him. It'll be okay. Don't worry."

◆

Later, after Suzy had gone to bed, Parker sat in the armchair and listened to the traffic along the ring road, the trucks and snow clearers, the stalwarts of

Soviet life. It seemed as if they just cruised the circles, never deviating, like the foreign residents when they first arrived in Moscow.

He recalled how difficult it had been to navigate in the city. So hard to find landmarks. In summer it was a city of yellow ocher, of plane trees, of cracked, dusty back roads, of courtyards and alleys where the old had sat out the revolution and the young went to hide from it. Some buildings had numbers, others had lost them, and if you asked a passer-by, no one seemed to know . . . or wanted to know. You could lose your way in a city of nine million people—this city.

In winter there were icicles and slush, sharp, angular buildings with their towers and turrets enveloped in snow. Gray snow, never white for long in this industrial powerhouse. But in the small country roads outside Moscow it hung heavy in fir trees, pulling the branches down low over the ground. Thick forests, crisscrossed with hunters' tracks and the paw prints of the animals they stalked. Bears and foxes, wolves and stoats. The Russian forest. A quiet, daily battle for survival.

To Parker there was magnetism in the Soviet Union. Man against climate. Thousands of square miles where nothing lived. Deserted steppe and tundra where you could lose whole countries. All this unified behind the fir trees and the Kremlin wall. Silence and intrigue. And if you stopped and listened hard—the whisperings of the few who ruled the many.

Somewhere out there a lost soul was trying to reach him. For Parker had read enough to believe the message. It was too shabby, too amateur to be a fake. There was something childish about it. The signature for instance. Unicorn was straight out of nursery rhymes. What was it . . . the lion and the unicorn?

Parker got up, took a flashlight from the desk drawer, and went into Steven's room. On the bookshelf beside the bed he found what he was looking for and returned to the living room.

The lion and the unicorn were fighting for the
    crown,
The lion beat the unicorn all around the town,
Some gave them white bread and some gave them
    brown,
And some gave them plum cake and drummed
    them out of town.

So that was it. Parker looked out over the rooftops, covered in snow, smoke coming from a few chimneys. They all looked the same, but Unicorn was out there somewhere. Unicorn was back in Moscow.

Chapter 14

DECEMBER 17

In the gray light it took nearly ten minutes to dig out the car, two minutes to spray the deicer on the windows, and Parker was driving through the embassy gate by 6:15.

Steven had been hot and restless, Suzy was dozing. He had wanted to stay with them, should have stayed with them, but he had to find out.

In the courtyard the embassy drivers were clearing the snow with shovels. They nodded to him as he clambered up the ramp to the main door. Through the glass he could see Jenkins pulling off his cardigan, reaching for his jacket, lurching toward the security door, sleep in his eyes, the stubble on his chin.

"Hell of a morning, Mr. Parker, sir. Brass-monkey weather, this is."

Parker nodded a greeting and hurried down the left-hand corridor into the chancery section. The papers were in the filing cabinet where he had left them. Nothing had been touched. His eyes checked the desk, the window locks.

Two hours later Mary Cross brought him coffee in his own mug, with the big G on the side. Embassy protocol, morning routine.

"The meeting's at nine, you haven't forgotten, have you, George? You look pretty much stuck into it, whatever it is." She nodded to the pile of envelopes and files. Parker looked up, taking in the fresh perfume, the long brown hair waving over the shoulders.

"Got to sit this one out, Mary. Cover for me, will you? Bit bogged down here."

It must have been ten o'clock when he next looked up because he felt sure he had heard the Kremlin bell in the distance. But it could have been imagination, or elation, or the adrenaline that came from knowing he had gotten it. Page and paragraph. Got you, Unicorn, you bugger! Got you, God love you. You're there and I know how to find you. George Parker has found you and is going to bring you in.

The coffee had gotten cold but it didn't matter. He raised the mug in a gesture of triumph, a salute to Unicorn. That was all that mattered.

It was true what they'd told him. Intelligence was nothing more than reading the right things. Finding and interpreting, straining and squeezing till you have it all in the pot. Then sifting piece by piece, picking the truth from the lies, the clean from the dirty. After twenty years you could hold it up fresh as the day they'd devised it.

He checked his calculations—the time of the transmission, the day of the week, the final digit in the message. It was all there. The key was in the files. No room for misunderstanding. There were two hours to go.

◆

Friday. Anatol's Friday. The fourth day of the cycle, the last day in the code book. You go to the rendezvous four days running, same time, same place, and then you crash out. That's the rule.

Make another contact, set another date. Repeat the process after ten days. And maybe it's too late. A lifetime too late.

Only that was something they never told you. Believe you can do it and you will. "But what if the odds are too much? What if there is no chance of success?" he had remembered asking.

"Things like that have never stood in the way of intelligent men." The answer had come pat.

In the end, he told himself, you do it because you have to. You're too deep in to get out, too scared to go back or to stand still. They, too, had seen the realization on his face. It was the day Anatol had looked in the mirror and told himself he was a spy.

Already he had his hat on, the coat draped over his arm. But wait. Take a minute of silence, sit by yourself on the unmade bed, the way the family used to do at the start of a long journey. A moment of quiet for the souls to converse, a moment to unite the past with the present, to pray for the future. It was tradition.

Suddenly he looked up at the ceiling and smiled at an old vision. A young Anatol embracing his father, their arms tight around each other in an unspoken declaration of love. A minute later he was out on the street, carried forward by the lunchtime crowd.

◆

Entrance two, staircase four, second level. Maybe it had all been changed. Maybe the whole place had been rebuilt. For all he knew, the staircases could have fallen down. George Parker was counting the risks, but he didn't believe them. The venue for the contact was quite precise. The Moscow Hippodrome, the racetrack, the only place in the Soviet Union where you can gamble legally. Very appropriate.

Take the car to the Mezh, Trade Center. A taxi from there. The drivers are all security men who watch the foreign business people. Nothing strange about going to the races. They did that all the time. Russians and foreigners. Like a football match. Totally innocuous.

He had his coat on and was walking down the corridor.

"George, hang on a minute." It was Eileen running after him, one of the juniors from chancery. "George, thank God you're still here. It's your wife on the phone. It sounds urgent."

Parker looked at his watch. Plenty of time. An hour and a quarter to go. It was his only thought as he picked up the receiver. Steven had got worse, she had called Steeles and he'd been around within twenty minutes. There was no doubt. The boy had meningitis. Severe headache, stiff neck, his temperature now hovering around 105. He'd have to go to the hospital. They'd called the ambulance and were waiting. They didn't know how long it would take. Could he come now? Please.

Parker sat down, unable to think straight.

"George, are you there? You have to come now. Steeles doesn't speak any Russian. You're the only one who does. We need you."

His mind was running in circles. Steven going to the hospital, the little face on the stretcher, Suzy crying, the orderlies babbling away in a strange language, lifting the boy from her arms, barring the door in her face, carrying the screaming child away down a darkened corridor. His child. And out there was Unicorn taking his first mortal risk in eighteen years, desperate for a contact, his life depending on it, and God knows how many others.

George Parker, you have to make a decision, and in years to come, when you are old, incapable, and infirm, you will have to live with it.

He pressed the intercom. "Get Mary Cross in here, quickly."

◆

She had never been used for field operations and Parker knew why. Blue-suited, demure, with a flush that came all too easily to those rounded English cheeks. London must have assumed she'd be an instant giveaway. A Christmas gift to the KGB.

Mary Cross swallowed hard and sat down on the sofa.

"I'm not sure I can handle this, George," she said.

"Don't piss about, Mary. I wouldn't ask you if there was any other way. Fact is, I have no choice, and neither does the poor bugger out there."

"What's the code again?"

Christ, thought Parker. Talk about giving a blind man a map. "Look, get it straight now, okay?" he told her. "You'll have one shot at it, and then he's gone, probably for good. Now listen to me. It's betting talk, right? You ask him how he did today. 'Nu kak vygraly?' And he says, 'No, it was better yesterday— Nyet, vchera bylo luchay.' And you take it from there."

"And what if he doesn't show?"

"You don't hang about. Get back to the Mezh. And before you go, lose those high heels and get some other clothes on. Try the ambassador's secretary, make some excuse, and do it now, hurry."

"Where are you going?"

"I'm going to the hospital to make sure my son doesn't bloody die."

◆

They sat in the corridor because there was nowhere else to sit. The lighting was poor—cheap neon strips that lit the center but left the edges in shadow. A row of chairs stretched away down each side. On the opposite wall hung a sign saying "A healthy child is the future of our nation." At intervals Parker could make out the faces of some of the other couples. Beside him a young woman wept softly while her baby sat on her lap playing with a rattle, unconcerned by his mother's distress.

The nurses had taken Steven as soon as the ambulance had arrived, confirming his worst fears, wheeling him away into the emergency room, the boy too ill to shout. He had looked up from the stretcher but Parker wasn't sure if he could make them out. The little face was expressionless, as if the spirit were half here, half there. How many parents, he wondered, had taken a last look at their child in this room?

He turned to look at Suzy, her fingers clutching Steven's coat, his boots tucked under her arm, eyes somewhere in the middle distance. She didn't want to talk to him. Not now, maybe later. Maybe.

Parker could feel only hatred and anger. What had made him take this posting, risk his wife and child, play with their lives the way he and the department played with others? Whatever happened, this was the end.

London had been wrong, he reflected. You couldn't mix this business with a personal life. Good for cover, they had assured him. An ideal couple with a child, the Parkers. No one suspects a happily married man. Spies are loners, misfits, human wreckage. They don't have families. You'll do great. Parker could still hear the voice.

"Please come with me."

She must have said it twice, for Parker caught only

the last two words. He looked up to see the face
leaning over him, a kindly face, a woman in her thirties, hair swept back in a bun. He took in the white
coat and the bulging pockets.

"Please, Mr. Parker, just for a moment."

Suddenly he realized what had surprised him. The
doctor was speaking perfect English.

◆

It was just as Parker had described it, except for
one detail. The entire Hippodrome was swarming
with militia.

From her vantage point in the stands Mary Cross
could see the patrols picking their way through the
crowds, stopping at random, checking documents.
There must have been five teams. Mostly two-man
units. But as she looked more closely she could see
several senior officers positioned by the staircases. In
front of her an elderly man was peering through his
binoculars but they weren't on the racetrack.

God, it was cold. No climate for her. No climate for
Unicorn either. She turned to the track as the troika
race began. The wind was whipping the snow into
the horses' blinkered eyes. It was bearable in the
relative comfort of the stands. Down by the track the
conditions were brutal.

The horses were pulling the sleds into the straight.
All around her men were shouting, but for a moment
her eyes fell on the enclosure. From high up she
could see the pattern. The uniformed officers were
fanning out rapidly, like beaters on a grouse shoot.

As she watched, a handful of people carefully detached themselves from the main crowd, split up, and lost themselves in the throng. The racecourse mafia, she decided—petty thieves or tricksters. But something was wrong. Surely the police wouldn't advertise a raid on such a grand scale and then let everyone slip out.

She turned by the staircase and looked down. You could see right through to ground level. And then she understood. Lined up in full winter gear, cap flaps tied down, a detachment of Internal Security police had ringed the outer barrier of the racecourse. A few of them even wore the sweet smile of expectation.

The elderly man had seen it too. And as he moved behind her a question seemed to come out of the crowd, from no particular direction. It could have been for her . . . or someone else. Mistake or intention. She turned around to see the figure encased in the shapeless black coat, the beard speckled with flakes of ice. The eyes held a smile.

"Were you not wanting to ask me a question, young lady?"

She flushed, despite the cold. "I . . . I had been thinking about placing a bet." She recovered quickly. Russian was her strength. She knew how to lose herself in clichés or proverbs—wonderful language.

But the old man was turning away. "How have you done?" she asked quickly. "Have you won?"

The smile left the eyes. The movement was barely perceptible but she caught it.

"Perhaps you will permit me to buy you a glass of tea?"

"I should like that," Mary Cross told him. He took her arm, guiding her gently upward through the crowd.

In the clammy warmth of the cafe Anatol looked at her as they stood in the line for tea. She had done a good job on her outfit. Faded blue jeans that could have been bought on the black market and an almost-shabby three-quarter length camel coat. It wasn't quite racetrack Moscow, but he had to admit not bad. After all these years they had sent him a woman, fresh out of school, clearly, but at least she was a contact. God almighty, it was all happening again.

His hands shook as he reached for the glasses, passing the change across the counter. Of course there was nowhere to sit. And why should there be? This wasn't get-to-know-you time at the Ritz. This was a crash contact. Pass the message and get out. The thought struck both of them at the same time.

"Why all the militia?" she whispered as they leaned against the wall in an alcove.

"Russian police don't like crowds, they don't trust them," he told her. "There are always militia here. That's why the venue was chosen."

"I don't understand," she said.

"It's the last place anyone would expect people like us to meet." He grinned at her. "Let me give you some advice, my little one. Worry about the police only when you can't see them. But listen to me carefully." He was speaking rapidly now. "I am assuming you are not the boss—please don't be insulted by this. It is merely an observation, and I have been trained to make them. I have to talk to your senior officer. Give me a name, any name, by which I can know him."

"Call him George, but . . ." Over his shoulders she caught sight of two uniformed militia entering the cafe.

He must have seen the look in her eyes, for in a fraction of a second he had scooped her hand into his, held it, and bolted across the room. As the two officers turned to examine a document, he darted past them and through the door. Mary Cross was amazed at his speed.

It was only when she looked down that she noticed the tiny scrap of paper stuck to her palm. Like a communion wafer.

◆

"Please sit down, Mr. Parker." The doctor gestured to a low wooden chair in front of her desk. "I thought you might prefer to talk in private."

"That's kind of you, Doctor. Your English is first-class."

"I was fortunate enough to participate in a medical exchange program, so I spent a year in Leeds. But I did not bring you here to discuss language." She raised her eyes from the table and looked straight at him.

"I cannot hide from you that your son is seriously

ill, and we do not, in this hospital, have the drugs to treat him. I have sent a message to the emergency center at the Ministry of Health asking where these drugs are to be found and I have asked for an answer now. So far, I do not have it." She shook her head. Parker had the impression that she had been down this road before. She looked terribly tired.

"Until we have news, I cannot tell you more. Your son's condition appears stable but that could change rapidly without medication. We will try to keep his temperature down, but it will rise by night unless we have the medicine we require. Anything that you could do . . . perhaps you have possibilities from another source. This might help. Please know that for our part we are doing everything we can."

"How serious is it?" Parker returned the stare.

"He could die. You should know this. I do not believe in hiding reality from parents."

She looked so white, thought Parker. Pale right through to the roots of her black hair. Probably spent most days in the hospital. Never saw the sun in the middle of the sky. Sunrises and sunsets only. Daytime for the dedicated. He knew how hard the doctors worked, were working. There would be pride there too—wanting to do the best for a foreigner, wanting to be thought capable and, yes, equal.

She handed him a slip of paper. "This is what we need. If you can get it, somehow, today, it would greatly improve his chances."

◆

It was one-thirty. Embassy lunch hour. Please God let them answer the phone. Of all the days to be on duty, let it be this one.

"The embassy is closed for the moment. Please try at two-thirty." It was Irena, one of the Soviet switchboard operators.

"Hallo, hallo, Irena, don't hang up, it's me, George Parker. Please put me through to chancery, quickly now."

"Oh yairs, Meester Parrkerr," the voice purred its way back onto the line. "One second."

"Harrison, thank God. It's Parker here."

"Oh, hello, George. Couple of people been asking for you. When you coming in, old chap?"

"I don't know yet. I'm at the hospital. Now listen very carefully and write this down."

◆

An embassy courier brought the package to the hospital just after five. It had been dark for an hour. George Parker and his wife had been sitting in silence listening to the traffic building up on the street outside. The trucks were having a hard time on the hill, grinding away in the slush, overloaded and underpowered. In the distance a train snorted once loudly, clattering out into the snowy suburbs. Where did they all go to? Parker realized suddenly how little they all knew about the country. All the analysts, all the departments, all the satellite pictures—but what were these people really like? People like Unicorn.

The courier shook himself and sat down. He was new. Parker had seen him only once before.

"We got it from the French Embassy in the end, sir," he said, gesturing to the packet. "Thing was, they had it all the time and there we were, trying to get planes from I don't know where and all that sort of thing. I don't mind telling you, it's been quite an afternoon." He looked accusingly at Parker.

"Thank you for all your trouble," said Parker hastily. "I won't forget it." He turned and ran to find the doctor.

She took the package from him and headed down the corridor. He couldn't help noticing the thin, spindly legs below the white coat.

◆

The soldiers hadn't been looking for him and the knowledge comforted Anatol as he cleared the stadium, his breath coming in short bursts, his chest heaving. It must have been a blitz on deserters. There'd been rumors about a batch of recruits escaping from the Kantemir Division, the crack troops that secure the capital for the general secretary. No wonder the search parties were out in strength.

Once through the turnstile, he didn't look back but strode rapidly to the main boulevard, Byegovaya Street, and tried to hail a cab. Not much chance. Friday afternoon and more snow on the way.

He was thirsty now. Passing a Pepsi kiosk, Anatol bought a bottle, lifting the ice-cold liquid to his mouth, draining it in gulps. Sugar-sweet syrup. It made him think of the girl.

Strange that they had sent her. Young, inexperienced, and yet she had shown no fear, no apprehension. Almost as if part of her hadn't been there. She had spoken no more than a few words of Russian but it had been fluent and idiomatic.

The British had a good language school—the new one in Beaconsfield. Anatol had seen a picture of the town once in a foreign magazine. Pretty streets, pretty name. He stumbled on toward the metro— three thousand miles from Beaconsfield.

The rush hour had begun early and Anatol rode the metro with the crowds, crossing the city once, then a second time, taking elevators to the surface and then back down again to the platforms, then onto the buses, squeezing in at the last moment, standing close up against the people, daring them to smell betrayal.

It was around seven when he arrived home. Instead of putting on the light, he got a chair and sat down in darkness beside the window.

His eyes were far from perfect. For years they had strained to see in poor light. But the eyes knew. If he had turned away for a second, they might have missed the movement of the tree, its branches white, its trunk shades of dark, for there was something else as well.

You believe your eyes, Anatol told himself, because they alone give you the facts.

And the facts started to appear. Fifty yards down the street, same side, there was a car, a foreign model, he couldn't place it, windshield covered with snow, inches deep. But seen from a distance, some of it had melted from the inside. Wasn't there a face against the glass?

It was enough to ask the question—and the question became the answer. Anatol stayed motionless for a full five minutes. No traffic entered or left the street. Had everyone moved out?

I could stay here, he told himself, and maybe they won't come at all. They don't know I'm here. They missed me on the street, missed me on the staircase. I'm safe here for a few minutes and the door is locked, and if I stay quiet, they'll go away.

But he knew they wouldn't.

And yet they had taught him well a generation ago, because somewhere in his memory he recalled there could be no surrender. It couldn't be done. Ever. No exceptions. For a moment he stood still, looking around the room, remembering, calculating. Imagine it empty. How would it look after a search? Where could you hide a sign, a signal? What would be left?

It didn't take him long to work it out. From the shelf beside his bed he took a pencil and made a few jottings in the darkness. Satisfied, he turned on the light and moved back to the window.

As if drawn by a beacon, he saw three of them emerge from the street and walk unhurriedly toward the building entrance. One from the plane tree, two more who had been idling farther down the street.

Carefully and without the slightest trembling, Anatol pulled on his gloves and climbed out onto the windowsill. It was hard because he was tired, not just

physically, but deep down in his mind. Hard to concentrate. He raised himself to full height and looked
down into the courtyard. He hadn't wanted to die in
a room, boxed in and screaming. Not that way.

◆

Mary Cross never got out of her car. She simply
turned on the windshield wiper, letting it brush away
the thick, flaky snow. The city was quiet as she pulled
out of the side street and headed east along the Embankment.

◆

They came and went—the hospital people. Shifts
changed, the tired headed home, the night workers
took their places. Shrill greetings echoed down the
corridor, someone wished them a prim "Good evening," but Suzy and George Parker sat alone.

"We must find the doctor!" Her hand felt wet on
his.

"What good would it do? They'll give us news
when they have it." But even as he said the words the
sickness rose in Parker's stomach. It was hours since
the drugs had been delivered. They should have
done something. Why wouldn't they let them see the
boy? For God's sake, I'm a British diplomat! Doesn't
that count for something?

He got to his feet, his face hot, body cold. The twin
symptoms of fear.

"I'll go and look for the woman. She's got to be
somewhere."

Parker strode quickly down the corridor, through
the swing doors. Ahead of him a row of wards

stretched away into the distance. The light wasn't bad, but the scores of faces seemed blurred—the sick, the bedridden, the half-well, the nurses. He wandered among them, searching, scanning, and the panic edged closer. "I'm looking for my son—his name is Parker," he shouted to a nurse.

"You shouldn't be here. It's not permitted."

"I must find my son—please."

"Supervisor," she told him. "Ground floor."

"I . . . I . . ." But she had lost herself in the bustle. For a moment he stood still in bewilderment. A seeker of information, the loneliest species in Russia. In desperation he began retracing his steps, but a hand caught at his shoulder, and he turned to see the woman doctor, smaller than he'd remembered, wearier.

"I was coming to find you," she said. "Please, this way."

She took him into an office, closing out the noise and the suffering.

"I'm about to do the evening figures," she told him, and the voice was matter-of-fact. "Four people have died today, one was born, and a foreign child is much better tonight and can go home in two days." She looked up and smiled.

"You were in time, Mr. Parker."

"Thank you, Doctor. I . . . I can't thank you enough for doing this."

"No need to thank me. I tried hard for your son, just as I would have done for a Soviet boy. Only the Soviet boy wouldn't have had the drugs, and it might have been different." She paused, looked down at her papers and up again.

"When you go home to England, Mr. Parker, don't think badly of us. Remember there was just one night in Moscow when we fought for you."

◆

It was 8:30 when he reached the embassy. Suzy had refused to leave the hospital. She had a cause. She would not leave the hospital till she was certain her son would survive. She wanted to see for herself.

Through the hall, Parker could see the light in the ambassador's study. The old man appeared in the doorway, dressed in dinner jacket.

"George, you better come upstairs a moment. Something we should talk about."

Sir David put his elbows on the little trestle table and leaned forward into the light. Parker noticed a yellow stain on the velvet bow tie.

"Where's Cross?" he asked.

"Look, this is what happened." The ambassador breathed deeply. "As you know, young Cross went out to make contact with some chappy—I didn't know anything about it and of course it's up to you the way you run your section—"

"Look, hang on a minute. . . ." Parker felt the anger rising in his throat. "You're damned right it's up to me how I run the section. We keep you informed as a matter of courtesy from time to time and at my discretion, but it doesn't give you the right to cut in on operations in the middle of them."

"Listen to me, Parker. You were out, for whatever

reasons—and I'm sure they were the best—but things were moving quickly and Cross needed guidance."

"What happened, for Chrissake?"

"Well, she made contact with this fellow. No name, no code. He was in a terrible hurry, didn't identify himself. But he did give her an address, some little rendezvous where he wanted you to go. Said he had to talk to the boss of the section. It was urgent. Anyway, she came back here, of course, and time was marching on. No word from you. We had no idea how long you'd be, so I sent her out again."

"You did what?" The words came out in a croak. Parker could scarcely believe what he was hearing. "You ordered one of my operatives out on a mission, about which you had no knowledge, no background, and no control? I can't believe you did something that stupid." He was shouting now, the self-control gone, anger pouring out. But his heart wasn't in it. He shook his head. Laughable really. The head of the MI6 station in Moscow screaming away at his ambassador in the middle of a padded soundproof room a hundred yards from the Kremlin. Suddenly he felt cold.

"You don't know what you've done, Sir David. And the worst thing of all is that I don't know either. Not yet. I expect we'll find out pretty soon and then you'll go into the damage-containment business, cook up a story, tell London there was a fuck-up, but never mind. Just another agent, plenty more where he came from. Occupational hazard, that sort of thing."

He banged his fist on the table. "I won't let it end there. Not this time."

The ambassador stood up. "I don't have to take this nonsense from you, Parker, and I suggest you get yourself under control. Never heard anything like it. But let me tell you one thing." The old man stepped forward until his face was about three inches from Parker's. "Be very sure of yourself before you take me on. Understand?"

It was an ugly look. As Parker reflected later, quite the ugliest he had seen since crossing the Urals.

◆

Mary Cross was waiting for him in his office. And the anger gripped Parker and twisted his stomach. He turned away from her with disdain. "God, you look terrible."

"I'm sorry, George, I couldn't—"

"Don't whine, Mary. Didn't they ever teach you that in London? Don't bloody whine. Just give me the facts, good or bad, any order! Okay?"

The facts stunned Parker. He had never talked to Unicorn, never known his true identity, never seen his face, but something had passed between them across that cold, alien city.

Mary Cross put her head in her hands. "Look, George, there was nothing I could have done. They just got there ahead of me. . . ."

"How many?"

"Three. They'd been waiting. Me too. We must have all missed him going into the building. And when the light went on they moved. None of us could get to him in time."

Parker looked at the floor. Unicorn wasn't his agent, wasn't his loss. But he represented a debt that should have been paid. Parker had failed to pay it in time. And, worst of all, in his final moments, Unicorn would have realized the futility of ever approaching him.

"We let him down. You *know* that, don't you? Men don't cry for help, but this one did. You can see it, can't you? Make yourself *see* the death of a British agent."

He picked up his briefcase. Mary could see the hurt and tiredness in his eyes.

He opened the door. "Let's go. Nothing here for us." The security guard let them out into the courtyard. Parker was struck, as so many times before, by the beauty of the Kremlin across the river—the contrast between appearance and reality. It wasn't so much that he had made the wrong decision. He'd do the same again. And yet he couldn't leave it there. Even from his unmarked grave, Unicorn demanded better than that.

◆

"Sit down," she said softly. And in that instant Kalyagin knew.

All the way out to the dacha he had pretended it would be different. They would have drinks, discuss the weather, some politics, a new joke. He would kiss her on the cheek and go back into Moscow. Now all he wanted was to kiss her and stay.

You can't match that moment, he thought. You don't have to say anything, don't have to ask. The path is in front of you, the weather clear, you have only to walk.

They had sat for less than a minute before she stood up and reached for his hand. She was in the same gown she had worn when they had last met. Everything was the same, the blond hair, the smile that wouldn't go away, the lips that took so long to open and close, the suntan that spoke of a world a thousand miles from winter Moscow.

It didn't matter that the shutters were drawn, that they had to feel their way to the bed, that the gown tore, that he lost sight of the face and the figure. For there were fur rugs, and silk-covered pillows, and the warmth of a woman who wanted him. And an hour later, when he felt himself falling asleep, there was no one to tell him why, no one to explain.

◆

Minutes were wasted hunting for the light switch. Kalyagin could feel the cold in the house. The central heating had been turned off. He looked around the bedroom, fearful suddenly, retracking the hours that were lost, fighting disorientation. His clothes lay in a heap where he had left them, one shoe by the window, the other beneath the bed. Memories.

Hurriedly he opened the shutters, but the darkness was impenetrable. He called her name but the house spoke only his echo and he knew he was alone. Alone and burned by a woman. Again. Dmitry Kalyagin, betrayed by a skirt, after nearly a generation.

He turned on the lights as he went, angry now, moving swiftly along the landing and onto the stairs. A small desk light shone in the sitting room, but there were no signs of life. Kalyagin pulled on his coat and hat, fearful of what he would find outside.

It took him a moment to adjust his eyes. The snow and the black sky created a half-light, with hues and contrasts that were difficult to penetrate. He heard and saw the driver at the same time, saw the man climbing from the Zil, heard the "Good evening, Comrade Secretary" as he crunched toward the car. What did it mean? Where was the woman?

But he felt no fear as he got in. Russia was not about fear. The word, he reflected, was foreboding, the sense of being directed by unseen and hostile forces, the way it had happened so many years before.

The driver switched on the engine . . . or did he? Perhaps it had been running all the time. Kalyagin glanced back toward the house, saw the lighted sitting-room window, and gasped involuntarily at the face he glimpsed there.

His mind pieced together the features one by one. There was no doubt about the identity they created.

As the car headed for the city he recalled the way the KGB used to delight in frightening its victims. It had played a game to disorient them, to make them run, to render the chase and the capture more absorbing.

It would send the victim a face from his past, no one instantly recognizable but a face that would stick in his mind and worry him, that would force him from his sleep at night, that would ride with him on the streets till he could bear it no longer. A face that would speak of past sins, real or concocted, of corpses, maybe, or traitors, a face from the past that would bring it all back. And the victim would know. Just before they came and got him, he would know. The way Kalyagin now knew that Afanasyev had been out there in the dacha, in the middle of the forest.

◆

"He's yours if you want him." Madame Afanasyev was in bed. The minister couldn't help recalling that it was for the second time that night.

As he stood beside her the light seemed to catch the wrinkles around her eyes.

"What happened?" he asked quietly.

"Don't be stupid, Viktor. What happened is not important. What it *means* is important. He is now your ally, your tool." She looked hard at him. "You can use or discard him as you please."

And then, to his disgust, he saw she was smiling.

"If you want me to help again," she purred, "you have only to ask."

Bitch, thought Afanasyev. My own little bitch, cold as the wind outside and twice as dangerous.

Chapter 15

DECEMBER 18

For the first time Dawling received his message by word of mouth.

It was lunchtime Friday. Fish day. Even in British prisons they observe the traditions, just in case there's a convict who cares.

Dawling took his usual place at the end of the table. It was a bit like school, he recalled. There he had been on better terms with the teachers than the students. Somehow he had found little to say to his peers. And now it was the same. Long talks with the chaplain and the guards, barely a word to the other inmates.

So he was surprised to find himself engaged in conversation by an amiable young West Indian with teeth that were both black and gold. "Hi, I'm Tony."

Tony announced he was serving a six-year term for embezzlement ("Second time round, you see") and what was Dawling in for?

"Same thing," he replied. "Well, sort of."

"Know what you mean," said Tony.

The buzzer sounded, and they all stood up, 270 blue-coated convicts, guests of Her Majesty.

"If you're in the carpentry shop, I'll see you later," said Tony.

Dawling smiled. "By the way, I'm Dawling."

"I know."

Of course they weren't supposed to talk during carpentry, but the duty guard on Friday never seemed to mind. He spent much time on the phone in the outer office, giggling into the receiver and watching the room through the observation window.

" 'Spect he's got some bit of fluff on the side," Tony remarked as they glanced toward the door.

"Wouldn't be surprised," Dawling replied.

"Lucky bastard. What I wouldn't give now for a bit of the other. Worst thing about this place, and that's the truth."

They labored on for about an hour before either spoke again. Dawling liked to concentrate. The work wasn't difficult but he wanted to get it right. The prison had arranged a contract with a toy manufacturer to assemble dollhouses. He liked to think he was helping children; made it all worthwhile, he told himself. Well, some of it.

"You do that well," said Tony, glancing over the workbench.

"I've always worked and I enjoy it. Nice to be doing something useful."

"You happy?"

Dawling looked up, a smile making its way across his face. "What an extraordinary question."

Tony came across to the other side of the bench.

"It's just that some friends of mine were asking after you recently." He picked up one of the little houses Dawling had assembled. "You know this is very good," he said.

Dawling's smile had disappeared. "I don't like being fucked about," he said suddenly, quietly. "If you've got something to say, say it. There's too much time spent on pleasantries in this place."

"Don't get excited." Tony sat down on the bench. "My friends were saying it's been awhile since you had any visitors. You know, like that nice man from London who came once or twice. When's he coming back, d'you know?"

"He didn't say." Dawling scowled at the dollhouse. After a lifetime of subterfuge, he hated to be the object of it.

"Why not ask for him?"

"I have. They say he's busy."

"Ask again. My friends want to keep the ball rolling. See that it does."

◆

Dawling didn't see Tony that night. So he approached one of the guards with whom he chatted from time to time.

The man shook his head. "Don't know any Tony," he said.

"You must. The young West Indian. Tall fellow."

"Oh, Rasta. Oh, I know him. But he wasn't Tony. No, it was Cedric, or something like that. Cecil, that was it."

"Well, where is he?" Dawling was irritated.

"Oh, he's out. He wasn't one of the regulars, put here by mistake, I think. He was on remand for something or other, an accident, I think, just a few miles from here. Anyway, he's gone now. Hearing was today."

Chapter 16

DECEMBER 19

Stuart arrived after lunch. He was visibly annoyed.

"You wanted to see me?"

"Of course I did," said Dawling. "I thought we had discussed a rather important topic last time we met. Something about a queen for a queen, I seem to remember."

"Oh yes." Stuart spread his hands. "Was I supposed to act on that?"

Dawling gripped the table. "I see you want to be stupid about this, so let me help you out." He removed his hands and relaxed. "Certain friends of mine are prepared to do a deal. A sort of slate-clearing exercise. Of mutual benefit, I feel sure."

Stuart said nothing.

"The deal is this. You have an agent in Moscow and

we have an agent in Moscow. Both valuable, both highly placed. My friends want to trade the identity of theirs for the identity of yours." He looked up. "I trust you can follow all this."

"Perfectly."

"Good. There's only one other thing. We—I mean they—need your answer rather quickly."

Stuart got up to leave but changed his mind. He went over to Dawling, grabbed his double chin, and yanked his face up so it was staring into his own. Dawling yelled with the pain.

"James," he said. "Why don't you piss off."

◆

"There's some shepherd's pie in the oven." Suzy put her head around the sitting-room door. Parker took off his coat, threw the hat and gloves in a basket on the floor. Moscow custom.

"Thanks."

"Well, you don't have to eat it."

"I said thanks."

Her head disappeared back into the sitting room. Parker stood in the doorway.

"How's Steven?"

"We can get him about five tomorrow. You'll have to sign a form, I think. I wasn't quite sure what they were saying. That doctor—the one who speaks English—wasn't there today."

"That's great." Silence. "I'll go and eat something. I've got to go out again in a little while. Back to the shop."

She was flicking through a magazine, feet curled

up on the sofa. "So what's new?" She didn't look up.
Parker clenched his fists. He felt drained, the way
only Russia can do it. His day at the embassy, hers at
the hospital, and they had nothing to say. Moscow
was a graveyard for marriages. The city took away
your intimacy, your trust, the little things that keep
the big things in place. Finally, it took the love as
well.

He sat in the kitchen and chewed the shepherd's
pie. Maybe it was just Moscow blues, either that or
they'd end up in the divorce court. Hard to tell.

◆

An hour later he drove out of the compound heading for the river. By 9 P.M. he had entered the street
where Anatol had lived and walked the length of it
twice.

He had acquired the aimless, unhurried step of
suburban Russia. Occasionally he nodded to passers-
by who didn't know him. The glasses had gone; so,
too, had the forelock of brown hair. On his head he
wore a blue beret, an old light mackintosh, a scarf,
and thick black lace-up boots. Not peasant Moscow,
but faded intellectual, in keeping with the area.
Faded and poor. On his arm hung a basket of apples.

In the darkness he could see little groups of
homecomers standing gossiping in the courtyards,
their shadows long against the snow. You don't keep
secrets in a place like this, he thought. The caretaker
would probably have been notified first about the
body. After that the clean-up unit would have operated through her. Then the secretary of the housing

committee and so on down to the odd-job man who kept the central heating going. They'd have been chatting about it all day. All comrades together.

A little girl gave him the excuse he needed to loiter. A pretty thing, in a blue woolen coat, no more than five years old, he thought, she threw her ball to him because no one else wanted to play. He caught it and threw it back, following it with light questions about her family and kindergarten, her grandmother, and where they had gone for their holidays.

It gave him time to look around, searching the odd man out. There's always one, he told himself. They always leave one behind. And if it's important enough, more than one.

He was dressed in a shiny red parka and a jaunty fur cap, and Parker could place him instantly. He was KGB from the district, a minion, not an officer. But flashy all the same, pleased with himself, a big shot in the neighborhood, where he would let it be known that he was someone without ever saying who. Maybe special friends would get a glimpse of the little red card or maybe he'd just show it to the girls. Tall and athletic, Parker reckoned he was the good, knockabout sort of fellow they looked for.

The girl's mother was approaching now and Parker was thinking fast. He grabbed her hand, introducing himself, as if it came automatically to him.

"Nekrasov, Georgy Petrovich," he told her, beaming broadly.

She withdrew her hand awkwardly.

"Velikhanova, Tatyana Ivanovna."

It was good enough. "Lovely child," he muttered, and looked around. The KGB man had moved away from the main door and was now in a group about ten yards away. But the caretaker was still blocking the entrance. Anyway, he thought, it was now or not at all.

"Very pleasant to meet you," he told the child's mother, "but please excuse me. I have to deliver these apples."

The caretaker accosted him ten yards from the main door. "What are you wanting, young man?" she asked.

"I'm with Tatyana Ivanovna." He pointed over his shoulder, hoping she wasn't near enough to hear. "I'm just dropping off her basket of apples. Just visiting for the day."

The old lady looked at him suspiciously and then broke into a smile. Parker caught sight of a row of gold front teeth. "I'm sorry," she told him, and then put her head close to his ear. "Spies everywhere today. It's like a film. Never seen anything like it." He squeezed her hand reassuringly. "I know," he told her. "I know just what you mean."

He had calculated that the apartment was on the third floor, but was surprised to find no special lock or seal. He opened it, second try, with a skeleton key and moved soundlessly inside.

But there was no reason for it to have been locked. For the little room was empty, and as he looked around in the half-light he could see that nearly half the floorboards had been ripped up and stacked in a corner. His spirits sank. They'd done the full number.

He took a small flashlight from his pocket and shone it at the little kitchen. The place was filthy, dust everywhere, marks on the walls, all sorts of graffiti. Hot and smelly. A lousy place for Unicorn to end his days.

As Parker turned to leave, a light was switched on across the courtyard, illuminating a portion of wall beside the door. He sank instinctively into the shadows, but as he did so he caught sight of an outline sketched on the plaster. It was something he had not seen for years, since the first of his briefings, two crosses linked by a circle, and he knew that Unicorn was in the room with him.

Minutes, perhaps just seconds, before his death the man would have scrawled the network's emergency symbol and below it a series of tiny figures. Parker copied them hurriedly into a notebook and crept out into the corridor. No one questioned him as he limped across the courtyard, thanking God for a man he had never met.

◆

The general didn't believe in luck. Life, he told himself, was a matter of odds. You could add to them or subtract, play them or ignore them. And at the end of the day they alone would determine success or failure.

It was no surprise that the British had rejected his offer. For the moment the odds were with them. Their information mattered more than his. In their shoes he would have played the same way. In the end they could seal off the embassy and dissect the personnel. It wouldn't be long before the traitor came under the knife. They had the time. He didn't.

The general yawned and switched off the desk light. Only then did he realize it was night. The days were getting shorter, it seemed, the hours of darkness overrunning the hours of daylight. One day he'd wake up, look at the clock, and there'd only be minutes left. It was always later than you thought.

◆

George Parker began decoding the figures as soon as he arrived at the embassy. He was struck at once by the detailed accuracy of Unicorn's work. Normally, agents made errors, they became nervous, omitted words, misspelled them, confused dates—but not this one. The coding was perfect, the writing unhurried. To Parker it was the signature of a man who knew his fate and accepted it.

He completed the first section and sat back in his chair. It was as if Unicorn was talking to him by name, warning him to be careful, priming him to face an imminent danger. Across the city, in the inner suburbs, the old Russian had been visited by a sick, frail woman who still had the power to wreck a major intelligence coup. Unicorn had worried, agonized, sought guidance. And then he had made his own decision.

As he broke the last line Parker froze. It was a moment that he knew would live with him, the moment he had trained for so long ago in that dismal classroom with its twisted, cynical teachers, scrawling on blackboards, playing with all the flawed human beings who woke up scared and went to sleep terrified.

"One day you'll do this for real," they'd told him, "so pay attention." This day, he thought. This is the day.

He picked up the decoded text and tore it into shreds, then tore the shreds again. No one else would read it—the confession of an executioner and the question that he had taken to his own death unanswered. Had he killed too late and in vain?

Parker rose and made for the door. If that was Unicorn's final testament, it contained no comfort for the world he'd left behind.

Chapter 17

DECEMBER 20

Through the steam and the faded splendor Parker could see Moscow at rest. It was a chamber the size of a tennis court, filled with the pink and brown bodies of the world's first Marxist state. Scrubbing, lathering, and baking each other in an orgy of communal cleansing. He decided it was where East and West finally divided.

Long ago the swimming pool had been magnificent. There were ornate arches, stone figureheads, and Italian tiling that spoke of a culture and artistry that had not survived in the Soviet Union. It was shabby now.

Wandering out of the changing room, Parker was lost in the corral of bodies. The sauna room was so hot, he could barely stand. He left after less than a minute, fearing that his skin was on fire.

"Want yer back beaten?" an old man asked him, brandishing some birch twigs.

"Beat your own," Parker told him, but his throat was so dry that the sound was lost in the noise of water and the slapping of skin.

Naked and unarmed, he felt strangely ill at ease. For once on equal terms with the great Russian masses . : . and not enjoying it.

The only thing he wore was his wristwatch, and it showed Sasha was already fifteen minutes late. The boy broke the rules so often, they had all but lost their meaning. But what do you do? Parker wondered. You can't fire him, can't take him to the trade union committee and accuse him of skiving or absenteeism. The boy risked his neck, while Parker risked nothing more than his posting. If he wanted to be late, it was his affair. But when all was said and done, they didn't have time to play with.

He retreated to the changing room, which gave him back his modesty but not his patience. With the full-length sheet around him, he settled back to watch the comings and goings. On each side of the hall were little cubicles, no larger than four feet square but curtained off from public view. Inside them private parties or picnics were in progress. Attendants were delivering crates of mineral water and beer, and in the swaying of the curtains Parker glimpsed raw fish being unpacked from newspaper and jars of pickled cucumbers.

The hall held the essence of Soviet life, as much in the sights as the sounds, the raucous, spontaneous laughter, the poignant stiletto jokes about shopping or waiting lists for housing. It struck him that they laughed not because life was funny but because they felt they could make it so, that if they ridiculed their problems, they might somehow be easier to handle.

He didn't see the curtain move beside him, and he should have, because his glasses were on, and they'd told him so many times to keep his eyes roaming. He caught it the second time but it didn't register. Once is just an event, twice is danger. And Parker had missed it.

"Excuse me, please." The voice sounded familiar but Parker wasn't prepared for the naked body. The Sasha he knew had always been dressed. He looked up and was about to greet the boy when he caught the whisper.

"Don't acknowledge me, don't say anything, and look the other way. I think I may have been followed."

Parker rummaged nonchalantly in his bag. He found a crumpled copy of *Soviet Sport* and began checking the weekend listings. Sasha was drying himself, putting on his clothes, getting ready to leave. But Parker could sense the fear just inches away from him. There was nothing he could do to help. On the contrary.

"What is it you want?" Again the whisper. Parker turned the page, holding the paper up to the light as if having trouble with his eyes. He waited a full minute before answering. Sasha had a foot on the bench beside him, tying his laces.

"I think our man is in danger. Warn him. Not a final emergency, but tell him to be careful."

He wasn't sure the boy had heard him. He was putting his towel in his bag, gathering it up, heading for the door. At the last minute he turned and Parker saw that he had left a glove on the bench beside him.

Good man, he thought, well done!

"I'll do my best." That was all he heard and the boy was gone.

This time Parker had no difficulty catching the movement of the curtain or the fully clothed body that emerged right after it. The man had been alone inside the cubicle. But that was no comfort. Sasha was being followed and knew it.

◆

The North Koreans bowed their way out of the reception hall. To Kalyagin it seemed that they had spent the whole day bowing. They were the third fraternal delegation in as many days, the third fraternal cocktail party, with not a vodka bottle in sight and only a sprinkling of Georgian white wine to stave off complete sobriety.

The members of the Politburo looked around them and gave a collective sigh of relief. Next week, at least, it would be the French, and with them you could be as rude as you liked. No one would feel the need to pretend they were on the same side. They could have a proper row, hurl a few insults and recriminations, go through the ritual bash on human rights, and enjoy themselves. Kalyagin was starting to indulge the cynicism that went with the power.

He had tried to avoid Afanasyev but the man took his arm and led him down a corridor. He waited until they were alone. Kalyagin felt no guilt about the minister's wife—no remorse. He knew Afanasyev was about to seek payment.

"Perhaps you have thought a little more about our last conversation?" The older man leaned forward.

"I'm not sure that I fully understood it, Comrade."

"What is this 'comrade'?" demanded Afanasyev sharply. "Yesterday we were sipping wine together. And now it is 'comrade.' Why so formal, my friend? Something troubling you, something upsetting you?"

They fell silent for a moment as an orderly passed them, a tray of files in his hands.

"You would do well to listen to me my 'comrade,'" whispered Afanasyev mockingly. "My office in half an hour. Be there." He shambled off. Kalyagin stayed where he was, watching till he was out of sight.

The outer office was empty. It was after six. Kalyagin felt sure the staff had been dismissed well in advance. For as he pushed open the door to the inner sanctum, he caught the unmistakable smell of alcohol. Afanasyev held a glass, three quarters full of colorless liquid. It wasn't water.

"Come in, Comrade. Shut the door. Over here, over here." Afanasyev beckoned him to a small sofa in the corner. He pulled another chair from the opposite wall and sat down beside him.

"You will forgive me, Dmitry Ivanovich. I was perhaps a little sharp with you back there." He smiled affably. "Have a chocolate." He groped for a box on the cocktail table beside them. "Go on, take one, take one. They're Belgian. That's better." He paused. "By the way, my wife sends greetings."

Kalyagin took a chocolate but said nothing. At least it was all out in the open.

"I asked you here, my friend, because we can speak frankly. No one is listening. No one can over-hear us. I made sure that the relevant experts took precautions. We in the Army have our resources, as I'm sure you know."

Nearly there, thought Kalyagin. He can't take for-ever.

"And so," Afanasyev continued, "I am in a position to render you certain favors, that is if you will render me some in advance." The deputy minister cleared his throat. "You are aware of the satellite problems. We have spoken of them before. But there's more. Just recently the Soviet Army has had very little rec-ognition. All we've had were the dirty jobs, like baby-sitting the East Germans, revving up our engines on the Polish border, and then, of course, getting our balls cut off in Afghanistan. All part of a soldier's trade, we're told. Well, I'm telling you that not all the soldiers are so happy about that." He jabbed a finger in Kalyagin's direction and fumbled for a chocolate.

"We intend to do something about it. Of course we *would* have done something already if there had been enough of us when Chernenko died. But there weren't and we've been wasting time. Now, with the weapon problems—we have no choice." He leaned over to Kalyagin. "Can I count on your support?"

"I don't think you've spelled out what you want me to support."

"Haven't I just? Well, let me make it clearer and see if you're subtle enough to understand. Our new general secretary has been in power for just six months. He's sharp, speaks well, and that goes down big in Moscow. But in the provinces he's weak. The congress'll show that. Oh, he'll get his way most of the time but they'll block him where they can. Irkutsk is still a long way from Moscow. And that's the point of it."

Kalyagin looked up. Afanasyev was warming to his theme. Traces of froth were visible at the sides of his mouth.

"You see all this talk of reform is upsetting people. This anticorruption drive has to be stopped. Some of the best men in the Party have been led to the wall. He's got to stop it." He waved his hand to encompass the country. "The Army, the police, everyone's worried sick."

"So what do you do about it?" Kalyagin was prompting.

"You raise it at the Thursday meeting and put it to the vote. As things stand now, he'd lose."

"And what then?"

"What then?" Afanasyev snorted. "He's out— that's what." And his laughter filled the room, echoing up to the high ceiling and into the outer office. Far farther, in fact, than Afanasyev had intended.

◆

Mary Cross finished her work and drove straight to the International Trade Center. Gudrun was to meet her there at four. They'd have a swim and a sauna, and then indulge the other favorite pastime in Moscow—spending money in the hard-currency stores. It was always fun, picking out the nineteenth-century classical works in the bookshop, hunting for jewelry or fur hats, being a "have" when the "have-nots" were all around you.

The swim was wonderful. They'd even played ball in the water with a good-looking man, enjoying the pool at the same time. Twenty minutes in the sauna, then out for a beer and chicken in the German-style bar on the next level. The man had even joined them and offered to pay.

And it wasn't until he showed up again in the hard-currency clothing store that Mary and Gudrun became at all suspicious, cutting short their browsing, hurrying instead down the corridor and out into the parking lot, turning just in time to see him come out of the main gate and stand for a moment gazing after them.

It shouldn't have surprised her, thought Mary. This was Moscow after all. City of the odd and the sinister. But why follow her now? Was it a warning? A sign of mild day-to-day interest or a threat?

She looked out at the grim, gray streets. No answers there.

◆

The dim street lighting in Moscow has always favored those who hide and not those who seek. But Sasha had been carefully marked.

A dark green Volvo—special to the city's KGB detail—had been outside the baths for twenty minutes, engine on, windshield wipers slow-wiping the snow. There were three of them inside, chain-smoking but otherwise fresh. They'd been on shift for only an hour and were looking for action.

Even so, the boy didn't make it easy for them. He sprinted for a bus, catching it at the last moment as it slithered away from the curb like a giant caterpillar and headed north toward Ostankino.

Sasha was pleased with himself and so were the men in the Volvo. The bus was almost pitifully slow, stopping every quarter mile, and once stopping altogether. Swearing and muttering to herself, the driver climbed down onto the road, opened the hood, and appeared to dive inside. The watchers could see nothing more of her than her legs, booted to the knee, her coat flapping in the wind over an ample bottom. They began joking and then lapsed into sullen silence. It wasn't even fun anymore.

At the television tower the bus turned right and headed for Prospekt Mira, and it was there that Sasha made his move. If anyone was following, he'd lose them in the crowd around the permanent exhibition halls—the tributes to national achievement.

He cleared the subway, half running toward the ceremonial arch. His right leg hit something soft and a child screamed but he kept his head down, kept moving. And yet at six in the evening you stick out running through a Soviet crowd, and the people don't like it. One or two tried accosting him. "Why the hurry, young fellow?" cried a pensioner, raising his walking stick at him. "Perhaps he's a thief or a hooligan," someone suggested. Sasha could feel the antipathy around him, rising like a wall.

And then, suddenly, the people no longer parted for him. And he looked up into the faces of the followers, recognizing them for what they were. His body told him that it was, after all, a relief to stop running.

Sasha was taken, not to KGB headquarters, but to the police station on Petrovka Street, a building that had acquired its reputation at the height of the Stalinist purges and kept it in the years that followed.

The three officers led him to a cell on the first floor, elbowed him in, and handed the key to a uniformed sergeant at the end of the corridor. None of them exchanged greetings, for the men had come off the streets, still sullen, knowing their role was over. There would be no chance to question their catch. The instructions had been quite specific.

For an hour Sasha sat on the bed, trying to collect his thoughts. A guard had been in to take away his coat and boots, but nothing had been said. And now his mind was full of the sayings of George Parker: "Don't believe the old myths. . . . They don't always have the evidence. Mostly they're just fishing. . . . Don't give up, don't assume you're finished simply because you're there."

Sasha had stored the words. It had been spring a year ago when he'd first heard them. They had met at one of the cafes in Gorky Park, beside the boating lake. A hot, dusty day and the two of them had been in shirt-sleeves. Everyone had looked happy. It was the first really warm day since winter. Cause enough to celebrate. He had listened to Parker's warnings as if they were coming from one distant planet destined for another. He hadn't believed he'd ever need them.

And yet, he told himself, it might not be so serious. After all, he was a pianist of some repute. One of the better-known students at the Conservatoire. The state respected such people. Sasha had even begun to feel moderately confident when the door slid open and Perminev appeared.

He looked unhappier than ever, his hair was uncombed, and Sasha could see his shirttail had gotten caught in the belt buckle.

They had tracked him down at the Trade Center. And why not? He had to have some pleasures, although the tone of the general's voice over the telephone had suggested that the pleasures were somewhat premature.

"He's over at Petrovka. Get there as soon as you can." And the receiver had been replaced. But Perminev had understood all the same. They didn't want the boy at the Lubyanka until the evidence was solid. Someone might talk, might question, might ask to see documents. And when a case went as high as this one, it was better to be careful.

Much wiser to use Petrovka. Petrovka could lose him or throw him back. It was ideal. The militia there didn't ask questions. Questions weren't part of their heritage. And no one had ever won medals in that place for keeping records.

He looked down at Sasha for a moment without saying anything. Better to get this one over with as quickly as possible. Then he could go back to the Trade Center and continue where he'd left off.

"You remember me, don't you?" It was a quiet question.

Sasha did not reply. Perminev edged closer.

"Speak to me, boy. Silence is a luxury they don't sell here. I could have broken you last time, when we met in the street, but I didn't. You carried out my instructions then, the girl, Lena, was delivered to Murmansk and has not been harmed. If you cooperate again, you could be out of here tonight. Not many who come here get a deal like that."

Sasha looked up, wanting to believe.

"I need information on a matter that is far more important than you can imagine." He sat down at the foot of the bed and unbuttoned his coat.

"How well did you know Nikolayeva?"

Sasha's spirits leapt. Was this what he wanted? Did the man have no idea of his involvement with Parker?

"I did not know her well. She was there sometimes when I went to see Lena. I don't think she liked me."

"Why not?"

"She never said."

"What did you know of her background?"

"Nothing much. She never talked about it."

"And Lena's father?"

"I think he died when she was a child. Lena said she didn't remember him."

Perminev relaxed visibly and leaned against the wall beside the bed. Sasha began to feel more confident. So he had no warning at all of the punch that caught him on the side of the head, knocking him to the floor. He rolled onto his knees on the stone floor, clutching his right temple. The boy was probably telling the truth, thought Perminev, but it didn't help much. He stood up and pulled Sasha off the floor, letting him sink down onto the bed. In the light from the single bulb his face looked ashen, the tall, thin body lay lifeless like a puppet. Perminev drew back his fist to hit him again but thought better of it.

"Think, Sasha, think carefully. Who did the old woman know, who did she see?"

The boy sat up painfully. He held the side of his face. It felt as though a car had run over it.

"I . . . I can't think of anyone. Only her doctor visited. Marina Alexandrovna lives on Leninsky Prospekt. She once went to supper there. No one else."

Perminev stood up. He'd had enough. The boy had been a waste of time. The general was jittery. Soon he'd be picking up half of Moscow just for the hell of it.

"Try some more thinking," he told him. "It would not be clever to lie. Not clever at all."

He locked the door behind him and made his way to the sergeant.

"Keep him for an hour and then throw him out," he told the man.

The sergeant raised his eyebrows, Eastern eyebrows.

"What, let him go?" he asked in poor Russian.

Perminev smiled bitterly. "Listen, peasant, I can see it's a new experience for you. But that's what I'm telling you. Let him go. Lead him down to the door and open it. Understood?"

He brushed past the sergeant and headed for the stairs. The man was clearly an animal. You expected them in the countryside. But in the cities? In the capital? Bloody animals.

◆

Afanasyev sat back in his armchair and breathed a sigh of relief. He could hear the car move off down the track. And then there was nothing. Just the peace of Russia.

It had been the third visit of the evening. Pyotr Pelkhin, Politburo member and overseer for agriculture, had been the last to leave.

He had taken his drooping clothes and his melancholy face with him, pausing only to give a little wave before he got into the car. A small affectation for a man with such power.

Afanasyev had been drawn to him as a natural ally. No one in charge of agriculture had much of a future in the Politburo. And Pelkhin had used up most of his. Every year the harvest was a disaster, every year brought fresh criticism from the Central Committee.

Only the general secretary had risen above the post, shelving the problems onto Pelkhin in a way no one had managed before. But Pelkhin was tired of being leaned on, tired of being the scapegoat, tired of having every faulty tractor and rained-out wheat field laid at his door. Every time *Pravda* found an absentee peasant or a beetle in the potatoes, he'd get a call. So Pelkhin had been more than ready to listen, more than ready to pledge his support.

On his fingers Afanasyev counted the members of the Politburo who were with him. Pelkhin made six, Kalyagin the seventh. Eight of them in all. Nearly half the supreme policy-making body of the Soviet Union, half the kings and king-makers, half the rulers of the fifteen republics. Not quite enough. But there was still time.

The minister climbed the stairs wearily to his bedroom. It was an old house full of creaks and strange noises, but there was nothing to worry about. The grounds were patrolled twenty-four hours a day by a KGB protection unit armed with rifles carrying infrared night sights. No one had ever attacked so he assumed the deterrent was effective.

He slid into bed beside his wife. She had retired an hour earlier. Afanasyev didn't really know if she was asleep or just feigning. He would have liked his conjugal rights, but he hated having to beg, and in the end it was easier for his assistant to arrange it in the usual way and then no one owed anyone anything.

He was halfway into a dream about just such an arrangement when there was a loud knocking at the main door downstairs. It was well after midnight.

◆

The pain had not eased in his head and Sasha felt dazed and disoriented as they pushed him out into the night. Since childhood his health had been poor, and a succession of specialists had failed to recommend effective treatment. They concluded that his heart was weak and urged him to lead a quiet life.

The thought crossed his mind as he swayed along the street. Petrovka was almost deserted. He turned right and made it to the ring road, but the going was hard. A hammer beat his head in time with his footsteps and he knew he should see a doctor.

Marina Alexandrovna. The name floated into his consciousness. He'd known her for years, played for her in the flat on Leninsky Prospekt. More than a doctor, she was a friend.

A bus took him across the Krimsky Bridge. He got off before the underpass and walked the rest of the way. The pain made it hard to see, hard to concentrate. But his feet knew the way.

She came to the door in her dressing gown.

"My God, Sasha, what are you doing here, what's going on? It's past midnight." She brought him into the light and fell silent, pulling him across the communal hall and into her room.

"Sit down, boy, let me look at you. Here, sit here." She patted the bed.

"Don't ask questions, Marina Alexandrovna. I

came because I need to stop the pain. I hit my head. Badly, I think."

"You don't need to tell me that." She laid a hand on the swelling. "This bump . . . I must know how it happened."

"It was a fight, nothing serious, a punch . . . that's all."

"That's not all. I think you should go to the hospital. There's a severe swelling. Some fluid might be trapped inside." She took her hand away and grimaced. "We'll go now. I will admit you to the clinic, and then there'll be no more problems."

Sasha took her hand. "I can't do it, Marina. Sit down for a moment, here, beside me. Look, there is someone I have to see. It's very urgent. More than that even. It's vital."

"As a doctor I must insist. There could be serious consequences. . . . What are you doing?"

Sasha stood up and pulled away from her. "Marina, I have to go. I'm sorry, but it is more important than anything else."

She saw then that there was no point in arguing. There was only one thing she could do. "You can go, but I will drive you where you want and *then* to the clinic. And that is final." She reached for her coat.

The car was an old Zhiguli, stronger and more reliable than the newer models. On the private market they fetched a fortune. As a doctor Marina had easy access to snow tires, but that night the streets had been well cleared.

At least three militiamen noted the car's number

plate, which identified it as belonging to a doctor.
There were no stops or document checks. Doctors
who travel fast at midnight are doctors with errands.
You leave them in peace and hope they'll come your
way when you call.

Two streets from Potapova's building Sasha called
a halt. "I'll walk from here. It's just around the corner. You shouldn't be seen close by." He opened the
door. "Thank you so much, Marina. . . ."

"Thank you nothing," she retorted. "I'll wait for
you."

"No," he breathed.

"Yes!"

◆

They had given him little time for pleasure. Two
hours after returning to the Trade Center, Perminev
was summoned again by the general.

It was 1 A.M. when he reached the Lubyanka. The
building was awake and active—like a troubled conscience.

Inozemtsev's face was flushed. Perminev took in
the open shirt, the sweat marks under the arms, an
eye that twitched uncontrollably. Signs of pressure.
A man in trouble.

"You're an idiot, Perminev." The general got up
and walked around the desk. "The finger is pointing
at Kalyagin. D'you know what that means? My God!
D'you have any idea . . . ?" He wiped spit from his
mouth. "Who got to him first? I'll tell you, shall I?
Kremlin security. How d'you think that will look?
Huh?"

Perminev didn't answer. He took a step back, his mind computing the damage, assessing his chances. Maybe it was a mistake, still worse a setup. But Kalyagin? The newest, the brightest. His man! It was bad no matter how it had happened.

The general turned, slammed his fist on the table. He could read Perminev's mind, the calculating, the damage assessment. "Don't even think it, my friend." The voice had turned cold. "Have no doubts, no questions. You want to know why? I had a phone call an hour ago. A tip from an old friend. A drunk old friend . . . who wanted to talk . . . wanted to return a favor. . . ." The general coughed noisily and spat on the floor. He turned away, reaching for a glass of water. "It's fortunate that I made my own arrangements."

Without knocking a messenger opened the door and handed the general a slip of paper.

"When did this come in?" he demanded.

"Thirty seconds ago, sir. I've come straight from the control room."

The general pulled himself to his feet. "Tell them to pull him in. Now. And run!"

He stood in front of Perminev, brandishing the message.

"Did you interrogate the boy, Sasha Levin?"

"Of course. He knew nothing."

"What did you do with him?"

"Let him go. You wanted it quick and quiet. There was no reason to hold him."

"No reason?" The general waved the piece of paper in Perminev's face, slapping his nose with it. "No reason? The boy has just been reported outside the building where Kalyagin's maid lives. Kachalov Street. Don't you see the link, idiot?" He went back to his desk. "This time the boy will be brought here and I'll do the questioning."

◆

Sasha never saw the watch on the building. The door of the caretaker's apartment was ajar and he tiptoed past it without looking in.

Potapova lived on the ninth floor, reached by an elevator that banged and jarred its way up the shaft. Enough noise to wake the whole building.

She wasn't in but he knew what to do. Taking a piece of chalk from his pocket, he began to draw on the doorframe beside the lock. And then he stopped. Parker had said to give them a warning—not a final emergency but a warning. Should he change it after his stay at Petrovka?

For once he decided to follow instructions. One cross and one circle.

Downstairs the message came back from the Lubyanka as Sasha was leaving the building. Two of them grabbed him from behind. One held him around the neck, the other punched him in the stomach. A black Volga arrived at the front steps within seconds and Sasha was bundled inside. He was trying to say something so the larger man hit him on the side of the head to keep him quiet. Sasha moaned once and then lolled back in silence.

An easy one, thought the two officers, who had no

idea who he was. Not like the usual dirt they picked up, most of them shouting and waving their fists. This one wasn't a problem at all.

On arrival at the Lubyanka they were surprised to find him unconscious. One of them slapped his face and informed the inert figure that if he didn't like that, there were 210 volts waiting for him, which would do even better.

In the end they flung him into a cell, and after chatting a few moments to the duty officer, decided to summon the medical orderly. The man was having supper in the canteen and insisted on finishing his meal first. Sasha Levin died long before he reached him.

◆

Marina Alexandrovna waited for twenty minutes without moving, then left the car and walked around the block. She could see no sign of Sasha, just a jumble of footprints on the fresh pavement snow. There were too many to be distinct. She got back in the car and turned on the engine to start the heater.

After an hour she drove around the side streets, but then returned to the same place and parked again.

At 4 A.M. Marina gave up and went back to her apartment. She couldn't sleep. Instead she sat in her dining room, next to the piano where Sasha had played for her and her guests. As the dawn light appeared over the city the sounds of "The Devil's Concerto" came back—and with them the warning that Sasha had given the night he had performed it.

She decided to sell the piano, now certain that her friend would not be playing it again.

◆

The snowstorm hit Murmansk that night with unusual ferocity, and despite her drug-induced sleep Lena woke up and heard it. She had come to accept the comfortable world of house arrest. A plainclothes officer had told her it was for her own safety, and the constant, daily supply of sedatives left her disinclined to question.

The company was gentle enough. The peasant woman cleaned in the morning and made breakfast. In the evening one of the housewives across the corridor came in to sit with her for a couple of hours. In between she would sleep and sleep while the dreams merged one into another.

Once Lena asked if her cousin could come and see her. They replied that her cousin had gone away on business and no one knew when she'd be back. What about returning to Moscow? "Soon," she was told.

And Sasha?

They said they'd find out about him.

Next day the reply came back.

Sasha was fine.

◆

Steven was fine. Parker signed the hospital release, handed chocolates to the nurse, and took him home.

He had cried a little in the car and fallen asleep in the child seat, his head slumped forward on his chest. So small, thought Parker, to have been out in Russia alone.

Suzy took the boy in her arms, carried him to his room, and waited till he slept again. Then she tiptoed into the sitting room.

"How d'you think he looks?" She sat opposite Parker on the footstool, distant again, anxiety around her eyes.

"I think he'll be okay. The hospital said he was." Parker could see her jaw tighten and knew she'd made a decision.

"Well, I'm sorry, but that's just not good enough. I'm taking him back to London and getting him properly checked over. God knows what they've done to him."

The tears came then, just as he'd known they would. He went over to put an arm around her but she stood up before he got there. She was shouting now.

"If we hadn't come to this stinking place, this would never have happened. D'you realize he could have died—the son that you profess to love so much? D'you realize that?"

Parker stood in the middle of the room. Hard to know what to say. The listeners would have fun with this little scene. And in his mind's eye he saw a man slouched over a tape recorder, headphones on, grubby shirt-sleeves rolled up, a smile on his unshaven face.

Suzy had gone, slamming the bedroom door, leaving Parker alone. Maybe the listener would take a break, have a beer, smoke a cigarette, and then transcribe the marital problems of a British first secretary. There would be no hurry. It had all been heard before.

◆

There are many ways of seeing Red Square. Most people pay twenty-two kopecks and trail wearily behind an official guide who summons her flock beside the giant shopping complex Gum and spends an hour bellowing at them through a megaphone.

At dusk she wanders home, leaving the visitors to tread the cobbles in ignorance—to gawk at the slick guard change outside the Lenin mausoleum, to chat with the locals who stroll around offering friendship to the unsuspicious.

Illuminated by night, the Kremlin is half dream, half myth. Moscow's fortress, a hundred times the size of the White House. You can't remain indifferent to it. All through history there have been attempts to build it up or pull it down. Few could bring themselves to leave it alone.

Hitler was perhaps the major exception. He just wanted Leningrad, arranged to install himself in the old Astoria Hotel beside the cathedral, even printed invitation cards to his celebration party there. But Moscow? He didn't seem to want Moscow at all.

At the end of the war the Red Army took as many of the Wehrmacht's banners as they could find and flung them down in the mud beside the Kremlin wall. Since then no one has really had a go at the city. It's too far for conventional armies and too well fortified. Nothing may enter or leave the city without close scrutiny. Thorough and practiced.

Everyone is an enemy until shown to be a friend.

It wasn't always like that, although many historians say it was. But the Kremlin's modern history has been one of such limitless violence—executions, suicides, and gratuitous barbarism—that it would have been a miracle if any other attitude had prevailed.

Life there is lived on quicksand, fast-moving, unpredictable. And Viktor Afanasyev would not have had it any other way.

After waking him they had sped through the deserted streets from the dacha, stopping for nothing. He had barely had time to adjust his tie, button his cuffs, run the razor over his chin.

But it was often like that. Crises blew up at a moment's notice and then blew away. Too many of the commanders in the outlying republics got nervous and referred matters back to Moscow. Any time of the day or night. Still, better that than some of the ghastly incidents of recent years.

Afanasyev well remembered the South Korean airliner, the failures in communications, the flagrant insubordination among junior officers, the total ignorance of basic military practices. They'd thrown the rule book at those bastards and kicked their asses all the way to Siberia. Since then they pissed themselves every time a sea gull crossed the border. Probably had done the same tonight.

The Zil entered Red Square, heading for the Savior's Gate. Afanasyev recalled the years when the Kremlin had been closed to the public. The worst years of Stalinism, the awful years that followed the end of that awful war. And then in 1955 they had opened up parts of it as a sign that things were getting better. But "better" wasn't what Russia needed. Russia needed control—and loved it. Always had. *And who better than me to give it to them?*

Inside the archway the traffic light turned from red to green and the car was lost from sight within the Kremlin wall.

◆

He noticed it as he got out. No sense of urgency, no lights, nobody rushing in and out of doors. And there was something about the hand on his arm as he was led through the corridor to the general secretary's apartment that made Afanasyev wonder.

This wasn't an invitation. It was an order.

The man was behind the desk in his study, only half his face visible in the light from the single lamp. He wrote quickly, his left hand jerking across the paper.

"Sit down, please." No eye contact. No greeting.

It was only then that Afanasyev felt the stirrings of fear. The first doubts. But what could he know? What could have gone wrong?

The general secretary stopped writing. "Did you know that this room was once occupied by Napoleon?" Afanasyev looked perplexed.

"I . . . I should have . . ."

"Yes, it was in 1812. He stayed a night in here after looting the palaces. The next day he ordered the entire place blown up. Fortunately, Russian soldiers arrived in time to prevent the order being carried out. Napoleon was, of course, the last pretender to stand here. Until tonight, that is." The eyebrows lifted, gauging reaction.

"I'm sorry, Comrade General Secretary, I don't quite see what you wish me to do."

"I wish you to accept a job, my friend. A job, nothing more, nothing less. It's just that I need your answer rather quickly."

Afanasyev had begun to sweat nervously. He took out a handkerchief and wiped his forehead.

"It's quite simple." The leader had sat back in his chair, relaxed, expansive. Dangerous, thought Afanasyev. "The job is President of the Union of Soviet Socialist Republics. It will fall vacant in a few days. You want it?"

The minister swallowed and wiped his wet hands on his trousers. What was going on?

"This is a great honor, but I am not sure I'm suited to it. I am after all—"

"Do it," the younger man cut in, "do it." He leaned forward on the desk and looked Afanasyev in the eye. "Because if you don't, I'll have you tried and shot as a traitor." For a moment there was silence.

"I must protest, Comrade General Secretary—"

"Don't bother. If I want comic acting, our theaters are full of it. So let's get on to business. You are, of course, not fit to clean the people's streets, still less to be their President. But for that there's a price. Before you leave here you'll write down the names of everyone involved in your pathetic treachery. Understand? All of them."

Afanasyev was breathing heavily. He could see defeat but he was too old, too long in Soviet politics to give a younger man a gift. Besides, he had a card.

"Assuming you're correct, Comrade, and I have indeed opposed you—in the best interests of the state, of course—what guarantees do I have that your offer is genuine?"

The leader slid open his desk drawer, removed a cassette, and placed it in a player beside him. The voices of Afanasyev and Dmitry Kalyagin blared out, echoing across the darkened room and up to the high ceiling.

"You see," he told him, "I needn't have bothered to talk to you at all. You could have been a pile of bones in the gutter."

Chapter 18

DECEMBER 21

Back in the sitting room, the general secretary's wife was waiting for him. The curtains were open and across the Moscow River the first red tints of sunrise were in the sky. A beautiful Russian day was approaching, the finest winter day in the world.

"Is it really necessary to make him President?" she asked.

The general secretary sat down. "There are too many with him, too many of the old guard that hung around with Brezhnev and Chernenko. If I don't give them something big, they'll try again in six months, or six years. Like dogs from the steppes they always return. Better to give them a sop now and be done with it. Anyway, I know who they are. And they'll know that too."

"Were you surprised about the young one, Kalyagin?"

"I'm surprised only that he got so far." He looked out the window. "You know it's not so strange to have all these plots and counterplots. Brezhnev told me once that Andropov used to ring him up almost every day about some coup attempt or other."

He wiped the sleep from his eyes and turned back to his wife.

"The old ones can stay. But Kalyagin must go—quickly. There has to be an example."

"What would you have done if he'd gotten away with it this time?" She raised one eyebrow. "If it hadn't been some old idiot like Afanasyev but someone who really stood a chance? Would you have stepped aside."

He returned her look calmly.

"Only with a bullet in me."

◆

All the way home in the car Afanasyev had prepared the little speech. If only she had been the empty-headed bitch he had once taken her for, like her mother. But no! She was sharp. She would see it for what it was. From Politburo to President—opening factories, waving at airports, offering the tray of drinks, chief government entertainer, and no say on anything ever again. She would know.

Perhaps if he left it until after breakfast. "My dear, I've some good news for you." That was it, that was the way. But she would wonder why he had kept it to himself. Subterfuge would be useless.

He looked out at the early traffic, the early shifts. The funny thing was, you could lie to all of them. No, not could. They expected it. They didn't want the truth, didn't want the details. Let the Party manage it all.

Afanasyev pulled his coat tighter around him.

"Turn up the heating."

The driver pulled a lever on the dashboard.

It was a pity about Kalyagin, but there were always casualties. There were plenty this time. Half the Politburo almost. He had written down their names without a second thought and handed them to the general secretary. Another funny thing. He had enjoyed doing it.

They were almost there now, turning off the main road, down the freshly cleared track, the militia just around the bend.

Perhaps, after all, it was time to slow down. Just turn up for the meetings, sign the papers. No need to argue or even think. Just sign. With more time at home, more evenings, perhaps the two of them would even . . . well, more frequently.

He told her over breakfast. In her anger she refused to speak to him for the rest of the day.

◆

Zina Potapova had spent the night with a childhood friend in the southeastern suburbs near the Zhdanovksy metro.

Nastya—born Anastasia—was a lady of such transparent kindness and good humor that the entire neighborhood sought her company.

And so it was that an evening that began with just the two women, a half bottle of vodka, and some boiled ham ended with a roomful of singing comrades, six bottles of Georgian wine, and enough food to satisfy the entire block.

Zina looked around at the plates of pickled cucumbers, the cold chicken, the sturgeon and salami, and marveled. They were the fruits of shopping expeditions that had lasted many hours. A tribute to Russian endurance and ingenuity.

Half the inhabitants of the staircase had trooped in, hearing the clink of plates and glasses. She recognized a young schoolteacher in his shirt-sleeves, a car mechanic, a nurse from the local hospital. They had left behind their troubles and brought their jokes instead. And Potapova laughed until the tears poured down her face and the clock hands twisted around well past midnight.

Nastya had thrown them all out, gracefully and with much charm, and the two women lay down on the sofa, nursing their heads, the room lit only by the heater's electric element. We Russians, thought Potapova, no one has fun the way we do.

She awoke at five but her dreams had brought a change of mood. In front of her was the vision of her father. She had been six when he had waked her that sunny morning in January 1950. He had made her breakfast and walked her the three kilometers to school.

She remembered turning to wave as he looked through the wire fence and began walking down the street to the factory, his *shapka* pulled down over his head, his collar up around his ears. It was the last time she saw him.

Since then her mind had carried the image of a labor camp a thousand miles north of Moscow. An image of snow, and suffering, but one that she had never seen. It was standard practice for the authorities to notify prisoners' families of their deaths, even when they were still alive. That stopped the annoying letters and parcels. Potapova and her mother had received notification of her father's death and they had tried to believe it. It was easier that way. Except in the early mornings when he seemed to stand before them, challenging their belief, pleading with them to acknowledge him.

He had disappeared on a morning much like this one, Potapova reflected. And the joy and jollity of the previous night had gone.

◆

By 6:30 she had arrived at the Kutuzovsky apartments, ready to make Kalyagin's breakfast. Today would be pancakes, because a man who worked as hard as he did needed something substantial.

"A busy day ahead," he informed her, sitting down at the long dining-room table. "Many problems to solve, much to do."

He looked up at her and grinned. "Good pancakes!"

Later, as the Zil flashed down the center lane and the traffic militia held back the hordes to let him pass,

Kalyagin recalled it was a day he had looked forward to for some time.

There was a meeting that afternoon with a group of British businessmen. Three of them. They wanted to sell high tech to the Soviet Union, although they would have to try a little harder. Kalyagin intended to turn them down.

He wondered idly if they were genuine, and if not, whether they'd have a message for him. He smiled at his reflection in the side window. Like a twenty-year-old, he thought, waiting for a letter from his sweetheart.

◆

It was morning in prison, but Dawling's thoughts were on the night. God knows how he'd done it, cajoled, threatened, shouted. But the governor had been unsure of his ground and Dawling had been allowed to use the phone after all. Just once. Special. Okay? And now he wished he hadn't.

If only the dreadful man had come to see him, he wouldn't have done it, wouldn't have called the long-remembered staff number at MI6, chatted up the overvetted operator, tried to worm his way to the deputy chief with an out-of-date password.

He'd almost made it. How typical that they hadn't changed the phone numbers! Arrogant slapdash bastards!

And yet he had really wanted to talk to them, find out why they'd cut him off, bypassed him, taken away his new role even before he'd perfected it. Dawling

the mediator. Dawling the go-between. A useful
man. A man other men came to see.

Back in the cell, Dawling lay still on his bunk and
shut his eyes. He tried to remember the scenes of
Moscow—the exhibition park, the zoo, the bookshop
where he had once met Arkady, standing just inside
the main door beside the poster section. Dawling had
lined up with all the other students who were engaged in bulk buying because posters were cheaper
than wallpaper, and maybe there wasn't any wallpaper in any case.

Arkady had been there. Good old Arkady. Bit fatter than the last time they'd met. God, it had to have
been at least four years.

But he still had the beard, still had the slogans, and,
deep in his inside pocket, still carried the envelopes
with the money. Sterling bank notes, with a special
export permit, just in case Customs asked questions.
Nice and legal.

They would take a few glasses of tea together.
Arkady would explain that the money was really just
a sign of goodwill. They liked him, thought he had a
good future.

Dawling had no illusions about all the sweet talk.
He had understood it from the beginning. It began
during his first year of Russian studies at Oxford. Father had died unexpectedly after a short illness, leaving behind him the boy, his mother, and all the debts.

Of course there was a state grant available to him
but it wasn't enough and the old lady had been far
too old to go out to work. It was decided that Dawling

would leave the university and get a job with his uncle. The man owned a cake shop in Covent Garden. He'd give him work.

It had all been settled, until just two weeks before the end of the Christmas term. The university Russian Club had thrown a party for some visiting Soviet lecturers, and Dawling had found himself pouring out his problems to a pleasant young man from the city of Kizhi.

He remembered little of it. Perhaps he'd had more vodka than he'd meant to. But the man had asked to see him again, met him in the Queen's Lane Coffee House at the corner of New College Lane, and three days later the money had begun arriving. The lecturer's name had been Arkady.

There were no more problems with the bills, no more nastiness—unless you counted the uncle. In a fit of rage he declared he was giving the job in the cake shop to a less ungrateful relative.

As for Arkady, Dawling hadn't seen him again until the language course in Moscow, his second summer at the university. Then again when he was posted to Moscow as second secretary, and seven years later, of course, when he returned as head of chancery. Arkady had been waiting at the Foreign Ministry, Second European Department, where he claimed to have worked for years.

Arkady, Arkady. Three and a half hours flying time from the prison, three hours ahead of him.

Dawling eased himself under the single blanket,

trying not to remember the promises he had kept
and the ones Arkady had broken.

◆

An English breakfast in an English home in Russia.
An odd mix, thought Parker. Cornflakes and communism.

Steven was loud and mischievous, banging his mug
on the kitchen table, spitting the cereal back into his
bowl. He'd be four after Christmas. By his fifth birthday he'd have forgotten he'd ever been to Russia.
Parker envied him.

There was Suzy on the other side of the table,
"Silent Suzy," he called her. Not to her face, but to
himself. After all, there was no one else to speak to.
Not here. In the family. Exiled to Russia.

He finished his bacon and toast, pushing the plate
to one side. Of course Suzy would get over it—the
fear for Steven, the problems of life in Russia. He
looked over at her, slumped in her nightdress across
the table, chiding the boy. Of course she would. They
had a great life to look forward to. There was the
house in Richmond, nice friends—Robin with his
boat, Jonathan with the cottage in Brittany, Chris
and Jane, Sue and Pete, Alfred and Natasha—interesting couple, that one. They'd all be there to welcome them home. And they'd all live happily ever
after in boats and cottages.

But not Unicorn. Dead three thousand miles from
Richmond. Not Unicorn.

He got to his feet.

"Bye, Dad."

"Bye, Steve." He came around the table, laying a hand on Suzy's hair. "Bye, luv."

"Bye."

◆

Two-kopeck pieces. That's what you need. Parker took off his glove, fumbling in his pocket for the tiny coins. The phone booth was freezing, the window-panes cracked, the receiver like a block of ice.

Busy. The number had been busy half the morning. That was the problem with this contact. You rang the Mir movie house on Tsvetnoy Boulevard to find out the film time. There was a recorded message. Only sometimes the time and the digits meant more to you than anyone else. Because Sasha had a friend.

Finally it rang through. Parker listened for about thirty seconds and then hung up. It wasn't right.

He trekked back to the car and climbed in. No signal from Sasha. There should have been three pairs of threes. Nothing. What did it mean?

The car shuddered through the snowdrifts and lurched onto Gorky Street. Drive carefully and think. But that didn't take long. And on arrival at the embassy it seemed clear enough.

He hurried through the hall, greeting no one, and sat at his desk. The worst-of-all-worlds scenario. That's what they called it, and that's what it was. He couldn't even send Kalyagin the breakup codes because he didn't have a courier. The man was sitting in the Kremlin, just a hundred yards away but totally out of contact. No threes, no signal, no Sasha.

"George, have you got a moment?" Mary Cross poked her head around the door.

"No I haven't, Mary. Get out, will you?"

The phone rang. He ignored it. *I need time to think. I have to think. Then I'll send the cable. And then it'll all be over because they'll bring me home. But first I must think.*

"George, you'll have to see them. I'm sorry there's no one else." She was back, standing her ground, refusing to leave the room.

"See who, for Chrissake?"

"The people from IBM, you know. They've got a meeting with Kalyagin this afternoon. Don't you remember? You promised you'd brief them on trade prospects."

My God, I forgot that. I forgot it as if it had never happened. But it could help, could even save him. Just a chance, George Parker. One chance.

◆

Two big men. One small. Parker noted the crumpled suits. They were travelers, northern accents, refined in a hard school. They would know how to push for what they wanted.

He gave them the embassy's commercial lecture: "Don't underestimate these chaps, they know us better than we know them."

But even as he spoke he was assessing them. Who had the brains, who was the calmest, who was streetwise?

After forty minutes he knew. The man had a pleasant, ruddy face, almost boyish, with short hair, army style. He hadn't asked many questions, but Parker knew he was taking it in. It all made sense to him. The eyes said so.

As they got up to leave he showed them to the door, led them through it, and then, as if suddenly remembering something, motioned the big man back into his office.

He looked him up and down and the voice was an urgent whisper:

"I haven't got long so I won't mess around. I need you to pass a message to Dmitry Kalyagin this afternoon when you go to the Kremlin. And I need it done discreetly."

The man said nothing and Parker was relieved. Here was a thinker.

"I'm sorry to have to ask you this. If there was another way, I'd take it."

"What's the message?" asked the man slowly.

"It's just this. 'Ira says it's time to go.'"

"And you don't want anyone else catching on to that?"

"No, it's got to be private. No one else must hear."

The man turned to go.

"Does that mean you won't do it?" asked Parker.

The salesman looked back over his shoulder. "Of course I'll do it. What d'you think? You want to pass a message. That's good enough for me. I assume it's important?" He raised an eyebrow.

"It could change his life."

◆

Ivan Kulakov, chairman of the KGB, looked whiter than ever. He stared up at the general and decided to leave him standing.

"Let's not waste time. You know it's Kalyagin. I know it's Kalyagin. And that's worse than any of us expected." He swung his chair to the side. "If it had been one of the old, senile idiots—Sazonov, Pelkhin —that would have been easy—almost natural." He waved his arm around the room. "But Kalyagin. An apple that went rotten even before it was ripe."

The general shifted his weight onto a different foot.

"What concerns me is that your department carried out the vetting of this man. This trusted figure, this perfect product of the revolution." He sneered.

The general read the signpost. He knew where it led. It wouldn't arrive today, maybe not tomorrow either. But the blame would be delivered to his office sooner or later and there it would stay.

"May I know more details, Comrade Chairman?"

"Some remain to be clarified. But I believe Kalyagin was the ringleader in an attempt to vote the general secretary out of office at the next meeting of the Politburo. At any rate, he's to be detained tonight and escorted out of Moscow immediately to Elektrostal. Your department can handle that, I take it?"

The general nodded. So that was the plan. Take him to a city just east of Moscow. One closed to foreigners. They had used it for some of the dissident trials. But this time there couldn't be any leaks. They didn't want to hear this one on the BBC.

The general shifted his weight uncomfortably from foot to foot. "May I sit down, Comrade Chairman?"

Kulakov nodded.

The chair creaked under the general's weight. "If you'll permit me, there are one or two other facts you should know."

As he talked Ivan Kulakov's face turned whiter and his small, bony hands clenched the papers on his desk as if he imagined he could do them physical harm.

◆

It was a short message. No details because there weren't any. No need to tell them about Sasha because they wouldn't care. And Parker didn't want him written off, not like that, not by the people in London, who had never met him.

And yet he should warn them of the dangers. A major operation was unraveling, potential casualties, prepare a net. They'd know what he meant.

At four o'clock Parker got tired of pacing his own office, tired of the Ministry of Works watercolors on the walls, and went out into the corridor. When he returned a few minutes later the ambassador was sitting in the armchair across from his desk.

"I hope you don't mind me looking in like this?" he asked amiably. "I just wanted to clear up that bit of unpleasantness a couple of days ago."

"Nothing to clear up," said Parker brusquely. "Ended rather finally, I thought."

"I was just wondering if there'd been any developments since then."

"Look, Sir David, the man's dead. What further developments do you expect? The Soviets are quite capable of looking after their own corpses without my assistance."

"I just thought there might have been something. I notice you sent a snap priority earlier this afternoon. Isn't that something I should know about?"

Ah-ha, thought Parker. The bastard's worrying about his own position. Well, he wasn't going to give him this one.

"Sorry, sir, operational matter. Nothing I can tell you at the moment. I'm sure Foreign Office liaison will be in touch in due course and brief your people at the FCO. We wouldn't want anyone to be out of step on this one, would we?"

"I see." Sir David got to his feet. "You're not being very helpful, George, least of all to yourself. Think about that, and try to take my meaning on board, mmm?"

As the door shut behind him Parker laughed inwardly. A fine time to be helpful, he thought. I'll be on a plane home before the week's out.

◆

The face-lift at the Lubyanka was almost complete. And yet the great yellow-ocher rectangle looked much as before. Cleaner, perhaps, but there were few enough who cared and even fewer to stand around and gawk at it.

Perminev watched them pour out of the giant toy-shop Children's World, which lies across the square, and hurry down the hill with their bags and parcels, past the ticket scalpers for the theaters, past the Berlin Hotel and the antique bookshops, back to the comfortable Russia of the picture postcards. The Bolshoi and Red Square.

He felt the excitement the moment he entered the general's office.

The general sat down at his desk. The room was full of shadows and Perminev could see only his profile. He yawned noisily and rubbed his eyes.

"Get it right," he told Perminev, "and we may still claim some of the credit. Pick him up tonight, just after two A.M. at the Kutuzovsky Avenue apartment. Don't tell Domestic Security, I'll get your authorization another way. We don't want them treading all over him. I'll call just before you leave."

"And then?"

"There's a home lined up for him in Elektrostal. Shouldn't think he'll be there long. But it's convenient. A number of people are going to want to talk to him before he's sent on."

"Who else knows about this?"

"Four people, that's all. And the general secretary is one of them. Take who you want but don't make any mistakes. There's no safety net."

Perminev left the building and drove to the Leningradsky station. The place was crowded. Everywhere he could hear the shouts of porters and tour guides as they hurried through the slush. He made for a public telephone and put in a call to a town about thirty miles outside Moscow. A man answered, so quietly that Perminev might have missed him had

he not known the voice and strained to catch it.
Perminev spoke for about thirty seconds, then hung
up. He'd have to fetch the man but it was always
better using a retired free-lance. Better than the staff
they employed these days. Just in case something
went wrong.

The drive out was slow and difficult. The police had
blocked one lane and were checking trucks.
Perminev guessed it was part of the crackdown on
petty theft.

In the town fresh snow had fallen. It lay thick on
the new apartment buildings and the low wooden
houses with the smoking chimneys. And from a long
way off he could see the dark figure standing stiff and
motionless against the white buildings, an army kit
bag on the road beside him.

He didn't wave, just opened the car door and sat
down. Perminev turned and said good evening. But
he knew then that, whether from the long wait in the
cold or the years of killing, the man's warmth had
died inside him.

◆

The protocol was exact. Three on each side of the
table. Two interpreters, both Soviet. Pencils and paper courtesy of the Central Committee, mineral water from Georgia. It was perfect in every detail.

Kalyagin was disappointed. The British seemed to
know their business and that was a bad sign. They
were probably genuine.

It was an exploratory discussion, for the Russians
wanted little more than to probe. How long would

the embargo on sensitive technology last, was there a
way around it, what was the political temperature?
Not questions you could ask aloud but issues to touch
on, reactions to assess. Useful and painless.

After an hour they shook hands for the Kremlin
photographer, a fussy little man with cameras hanging from his neck like Christmas decorations. Kalyagin suggested they drink some coffee before leaving. They sat awkwardly on two sofas in the
reception area.

Later he couldn't be sure how it had happened,
but the Englishman next to him contrived to spill his
coffee over both of them. The effect was immediate.
His two colleagues dashed to the side for cloths and
napkins, the interpreters followed, someone went for
a fresh cup of coffee.

In the midst of all the exaggerated gestures of assistance, he found himself quite alone with the English
businessman. They smiled for a moment and Kalyagin shrugged his shoulders as a sign of helplessness.
And then, quite casually, the man leaned over and
whispered something, and the Russian felt his stomach heave.

The words caught him badly off guard, like a
punch thrown by a drunk. Six words—six blows to
the head. The words he had hoped never to hear.

He looked around to see if anyone had heard. But
no one was close. An assistant approached and began
to sponge down his jacket and trousers. The Englishman was making effusive apologies, the interpreter

struggling to keep up, and Kalyagin had broken out
in sweat.

He dabbed at his forehead with a handkerchief,
faltering for a moment, his balance gone.

An arm was supporting him from the side. His
discomfiture must have been obvious. He couldn't
hide everything, couldn't hide that. No one could.
Something so clear and final. And after twenty years
they tell you over a spilled cup of coffee.

He felt them all shaking his hand. Good-bye, good-
bye—*do svidanya.* Till we meet again. Russian opti-
mism, because maybe I'm not going to meet anyone
again.

Kalyagin looked at the men from IBM. In four days
they'd be back in Britain. Did they realize that he
would have gone down on his knees begging to go
with them?

What had British security told them of him? Probably nothing. But if they did know, what would they
think? Traitor? Patriot? Worst of all, maybe they
wouldn't think anything.

They were led away down the corridor and out of
sight. One of the interpreters came up to him.

"I thought it went well, Comrade Secretary."

Kalyagin looked at the man with contempt.

"Went well?" he muttered. "How would you
know?"

◆

He returned to his office but he couldn't sit still.
Stretch out your hand, like a gun. That's the acid test.

Can you cope? Can you control it? His hand went out and the shake was there.

Kalyagin reached for his diary and scrawled a note in it, then sat back in the chair. Why bother? he thought suddenly, and his fist tightened. Think, think, think. Don't give in to the panic that's rising, threatening to break out. Don't give in. Take it slowly, step by step.

The message from the Englishman had been grade two. He was certain of that. Not a snap emergency but a warning of imminent betrayal. It meant there was some time, but maybe no more than a few hours. Still, that was something.

In any case, they would have to be careful when they came for him. It would be a small security operation, just a handful of people in the know. Maximum secrecy. They would probably follow tradition and come in the early hours of the morning. Careful. Oh so careful, for he was still one of the powerful.

Suddenly Kalyagin sat bolt upright. The time! Five minutes to four. My God! I might just make it. He buzzed his secretary and ordered the car sent around. All the way down Kalinin Prospekt and along Kutuzovsky he prayed he'd be in time to catch Zina Potapova.

◆

They were long days in the apartment, lonely days. But she didn't mind them. Zina Potapova felt sorry for the man who employed her, sorry that he had no wife or children, sorry that he shared a world of half-truths and deception. Her world.

The morning was for the cleaning, the afternoon for the laundry, and as darkness fell over the working city she threw on her winter coat and headed for the Central Committee store four blocks away. Clutching the special coupons, she purchased some beef fillets, lettuce, some oranges—and as an afterthought the Hungarian salami that Kalyagin enjoyed.

Even there the lines were long. The privileged class was stocking up for New Year festivities.

A merry-go-round of wining and feasting in prospect. And they kept it to themselves.

The day's sunshine had melted the pavement snow. And she joined the crowds shuffling through the slush. Two plainclothes security men nodded her in as she entered the apartment building and watched her until the elevator door had closed. There were those who said she could look quite attractive with a few minor adjustments. Like some new clothes, a hairdo, a little makeup. None of the things Potapova had ever wanted.

She had decided on a simple evening, no visiting, just thick vegetable soup beside the central-heating radiator, with her shoes and socks off and *Spartacus* televised live from the Kirov Ballet in Leningrad. It was good enough, she thought, putting away her shopping and hurrying back to the front door. In any case, what the hell else was there?

It was time to go.

The elevator was empty. Just four floors to the ground. She counted. As the door creaked open Kalyagin was standing there, and in that instant she caught the message from his eyes.

"Get back in," he mouthed, then loudly: "Good evening, good evening." And by then the door had slid shut behind them.

At the reception desk the security guards looked blankly at each other and went back to the sports pages.

Suddenly she felt the fear. The way animals feel it. Nothing to touch, nothing to hear, but fear carries its own aura and Dmitry Kalyagin had brought it with him.

"We have to talk, quickly," he told her. And now she could hear that his breathing was heavy.

"We may have been blown. I don't know how. I don't know any details. Have you seen anything? Anyone been here?"

She put her hands to her face. "Nothing. I've seen nothing."

The elevator door was opening. Kalyagin held her for an instant. "Just be quiet and follow me."

They emerged onto the landing. The camera on the left picked them up and stayed with them.

"I want you to find a shirt for me," he told her. "I won't keep you long." Voice normal. Too normal? But she couldn't judge. For Zina Potapova wanted very much to run and keep running. No safety here. Not in this building. With all of them.

Kalyagin had brought out his key and was opening the door. He ushered her in.

"Now if you'll just come through here with me."

He led her toward the main bedroom. He can't risk
it, she thought, the whole place is wired for sound.

"I've been looking for my dress shirt. Might need it
tomorrow," he prattled on. "Please have a look in the
cupboard or perhaps the laundry still has it."

"I will look."

Kalyagin was reaching for a piece of paper beside
the bed. They would have to get out. Now. No alter-
natives. Better to go separately, but where could
they meet?

He wrote two lines and handed the paper to her.
She hadn't moved.

"Ah yes, that's the one. Good that you found it. He
paused. "Now you may go. Thank you and good
night."

She didn't look at the paper. Her hands came out
in a gesture of appeal. Was there nothing more he
could do? Kalyagin shrugged his shoulders helplessly.
She turned away and he listened to her footsteps
down the corridor. The door banged shut and Dmitry Kalyagin was alone. He didn't know if Zina
Potapova would make it even to the rendezvous, still
less whether he would.

He sat down and his mind began to sort the information. There wasn't much. The grade two warning,
imminent not immediate. But the grades can
change. I know that. How old was the original message? How close was the KGB? What avenues, if any,
led out?

He could go to the British. Now, tonight. But the
embassy was guarded. At this hour documents would

be checked. And anyway, no one would know he was coming. There'd have to be a contact first. Somehow. And Potapova. That was another problem. Like it or not, there were two of them.

Kalyagin got up and felt in his pockets. Money. My God, he didn't have any money. Not a ruble on him. Why should he? The state gave him everything. He never had to pay. He hadn't spent anything for longer than he could remember.

But maybe in the kitchen. He hurried in, rummaging in the cupboards and jars. There had to be housekeeping money, something for extras. It had to be somewhere. He found it by the mineral water. Twelve rubles. Nothing. Quickly he began to fill his pockets with the things he might carry. A knife, some string. He looked in the refrigerator and pulled out the salami. It fitted into his coat pocket. From the bedroom he took an old woolen scarf, some extra gloves.

Now go down.

Don't ring first, don't order the car. They'll make excuses, say it can't be done, check with the security escort. Do it now, talk your way out. Use some authority.

He was opening the door when he remembered it. Hadn't thought about it for years. It was a wartime pistol—a Vostok—that he'd kept in his personal trunk. Memento from his father. Ammunition too. Old now, but better than nothing.

Kalyagin found it in his trunk, stuffed the gun in his waistband, the bullets in his pocket. Six rounds.

Enough to take someone. If it worked. He shut the
door of the apartment and called the elevator.

Zina Potapova put three streets between her and
the apartment block before stopping. She read the
piece of paper by the light of the streetlamp. It was
the last place she would have arranged a meeting.
She read it again. The final words had been under-
lined several times:

"Don't go home."

◆

"Please have my car sent around."

"At once, Comrade Secretary."

Kalyagin wasn't fooled. The desk security officer
was practiced and polished, but Kalyagin could see
the frown and knew he was making waves.

"Perhaps the Comrade Secretary would wish to
return to his apartment and we will advise him when
the car is ready. As you know, certain security arrangements have to be made."

First obstacle. Kalyagin upped the bidding.

"You will have the car here immediately as this is a
matter of national security."

"Of course, Comrade Secretary. And the destination?"

"You will be informed of that when I am on my
way." He noted that the man hadn't moved. "And
now let's see some action. Understood?" He raised
his voice.

That helped. The man reached for the telephone
and spoke to the car pool.

He was anxious now. Kalyagin could see it. The

questions forming in his mind, the departure from established rules. Poor bastard. They'd make him eat the book after this.

"You will appreciate, Comrade Secretary, that you may have to wait one moment while the security escort arrives. It's a busy time, so many coming back from the Kremlin. You understand, I'm sure."

"I understand your apparent inability to follow a simple command. I said now. I won't repeat myself."

He didn't need to, for the Zil had pulled in under the awning inside the courtyard. Kalyagin headed for the door.

He was a foot away from it when he heard the sirens. Don't wait, get in. The driver was holding open the door but a sudden compulsion made him look over his shoulder. The escort car came first, red and blue lights flashing on the roof. Behind it another Zil. And Kalyagin knew this one. The proud property of Ivan Kulakov, head of the KGB.

"Go now. Get on with it," he shouted at the driver. "Head for the Byelorussian station."

With painful slowness the man walked around and sat in the front. Kalyagin turned to see the escort car right behind them. Kulakov's Zil was pulling in beside it.

The driver faced him. "It must be our escort. A moment, Comrade Secretary."

"Now," bellowed Kalyagin. "Go now!"

This time there was no hesitation. Lurching, skidding, the great car screamed out through the main gates of the courtyard and turned across four lanes of traffic. There was an immediate clamor of horns. Brakes screeched. Close behind, the whistle of the militia. But now Kalyagin could feel the speed. It's not over, he thought. It's just starting.

For a moment Ivan Kulakov stood on the pavement, staring after the Zil. And his face took on a puzzled expression.

"Who was that leaving?" he asked the security man, who had rushed forward to open the main door.

"Comrade Kalyagin, Comrade Chairman."

Kulakov felt his jaw freeze. It was like the first time he'd tasted alcohol.

"Say that again. Is that Dmitry Kalyagin?" he asked.

"Indeed, Comrade Chairman." The man looked at Kulakov carefully. What was going on?

"And where is he going?"

"I'm sorry, Comrade Chairman, I don't know."

"But the security escort . . . ?" Kulakov stopped abruptly and looked into the wide, uncomprehending face. An old expression came into his mind. I'm talking to a wooden box, he thought. Why bother?

He hurried through the hall. Better to make the calls from his own apartment. He was hardly going to announce to the entire building that a member of the Politburo was on the run. For at that moment Kulakov had no doubt that that was exactly what was happening.

The driver swung the Zil into the center lane toward the Kalinin Bridge. Traffic controllers logged the car on the eastern riverbank and a snap warning was transmitted to the militia patrolling the route to the Kremlin.

The rush-hour lines parted for a half mile, right through to the Borovitsky Gate.

But without warning the car veered left along Revolution Square, circled it on the inside, and headed up Gorky Street before the police units could work out what was happening.

Kalyagin leaned forward. "If anyone tells you to stop," he shouted, "don't!"

But immediately the radiotelephone began buzzing, the tones long and insistent. He ignored it. Probably KGB protection or Kremlin security. Kalyagin didn't know. But he knew one thing. It was the worst possible luck to have been seen by Kulakov. Whatever head start he'd had was lost.

Suddenly he could see the green-and-white sprawl of the station.

"Take the underpass," he told the driver. "Stop at the main entrance."

"Comrade Secretary, you can't be serious." The man turned in his seat, gesturing to the crowds outside. "You're not going out there. It could be dangerous."

"Stop here," ordered Kalyagin. And then there was no time to think about it. He pushed open the door and hurried onto the pavement, the wind grasping for his face. He heard the driver yell something but he couldn't catch it, for he was already through a group of soldiers and into the departure hall. Now get out of here, he thought. Get out because they'll ring this area within five minutes and seal it.

He took a side exit and found himself in the flower market. All around him were gypsies and traders, mostly old women. Many held nothing but a single flower in their hands. The last produce of the day.

Crossing the road, he waved to a taxi but saw that it was full. To his amazement, the car pulled in to the curb.

"Kuda vam?—Where to?" asked the driver.

"Dmitrovskoye," he told the man.

"Squeeze in here. Go on, hurry up."

Kalyagin glanced quickly into the back. Two old women filled the seat, baskets on their laps. As they crossed Gorky Street he caught sight of a long line of cars and trucks racing up the center lane. He didn't know if they were for him. But it was a good bet.

On Prospekt Mira he took a bus, retracing some of the distance but cutting back toward the river. An old woman jabbed him in the back with her hand.

"Young man! Put your money in the slot. There're far too many people cheating the state."

He rounded on her angrily, but then smiled as a thought struck him. After twenty years on the power ladder, living in splendid and official isolation, he was back in Russia.

◆

Ivan Kulakov could have followed Kalyagin. Perhaps, he reflected angrily, he might have caught up with him. But what do you do then? You don't pull a Politburo member out of his car on a main street in full public view, handcuff his wrists, and then take statements from the two hundred witnesses who saw it. He shivered at the thought.

Soviet politics were different. If you had to remove a bad apple, you did it in a cultured way. *Kulturny*. You went for the man in the night when no one was around and you spirited him away. Quiet and clean. No blood on the floor.

But somehow, this time, he knew there would be no clean kill. Kalyagin had broken the rules. And the KGB would have to break them as well.

Inside his apartment he placed a call to the general. A second to the Kremlin. After ten minutes he replaced the receiver and wiped his face with a large white handkerchief. The militia would be in the area now, the rapid deployment teams, first set up during the Olympic Games in 1980 and then maintained to enhance the capital's security. They'd blanket the whole place, get witnesses, do what was needed on the spot. Clever to head for a station, thought Kulakov. But he didn't believe Kalyagin had taken a train. It was too obvious.

He called General Inozemtsev again. The teams had found nothing. They were taken off the case and ordered to leave the city without delay. Already they knew too much. For now, secrecy was as important as the man. Politburo members were like statues. You couldn't just go around losing them. You'd be a laughingstock.

Kulakov didn't feel like laughing. He stood up and went over to the window, looking out over Kutuzov-

sky Prospekt. He had always thought of himself as an
imaginative man. But he *couldn't* imagine why Kalyagin had betrayed the homeland. Of course life was
a struggle, but look at the benefits. He turned back to
the sitting room. Nothing here had been made in
Russia. The rugs were from India, the collection of
records was mainly from France, the desk was an
English antique, the paintings on permanent loan
from the Tretyakov Gallery. What more could you
want?

Everywhere you went there were people to drive
you, walk you, respect you, cook for you. And if you
played your cards right, they were there for life. All
the nonsense of multiparty politics had been removed years ago. What an odd man Kalyagin was to
have thrown it all away.

The KGB chairman plunged deep into his favorite
sofa, still wearing his coat and boots. There was a
strange irony to the situation, he believed. They
couldn't chase Kalyagin, but then the man had nowhere to go. He'd never made a friend, never traveled alone in Moscow, never stayed in a hotel, bought
from a shop, or stood in line. None of it—not for at
least ten years.

If he stays out, Kulakov consoled himself, he'll die
like a child alone in the snow.

◆

Despite the lateness Parker couldn't bring himself
to go home. As the hours passed he drew triangles on
his blotter and whistled tunelessly through his teeth.

For what he knew could not be said aloud. And there was no one to share it.

The rest of his department was long gone. Only the security guards manned the front desk and Farrar pored over his machines up in Communications. "Buzz if you get something," Parker had told him, but there had been no response.

He looked at his watch. He had expected a delay. Too much at stake, he thought bitterly, too many people out to dinner in the West End, too many gins to think clearly. He knew them all so well. They prided themselves on a twenty-four-hour, around-the-world intelligence service. But they were hopelessly undermanned. And about nine o'clock at night someone went out for pizza or Chinese takeout, at which point the rest of the world could go to the bloody dogs.

Parker had seen it happen.

As for Kalyagin, something small had been salvaged. The message had gotten through. The IBM man had said so, standing in the embassy courtyard, the wind blowing his hair across his face.

"Piece of cake," he had shouted to Parker.

"Did he say anything, react at all?"

"Not a thing."

"How did he look?"

"He looked fine."

Fine. He could just imagine what had passed through Dmitry Kalyagin's mind.

To escape the thought Parker donned his coat and made his way out into the embassy grounds, taking

the side route past the visa section and along toward
the doctor's office. A little British city, with a car
workshop, commissary, even a tennis court. He
kicked at the snow where the net should have been.
There were three, maybe four months of winter to
go, then the dry summer and back to the frost.

And yet they all respected the seasons—the only
things in Russia that came and went of their own
volition.

For apart from suffering the climate, being a foreigner in Moscow is not really to be there at all. You
don't shop with Russians, work with them, or share
the problems and pleasures of their lives. And even if
they wanted to, they are prevented from sharing
yours.

Soviet regulations prohibit them from giving you a
lift, putting you up for the night, or telling you anything that could come under the heading "professional information." In a clock factory, thought
Parker, that might mean telling you the time.

To the Russians, he mused, Westerners are a passing oddity. Like dancing bears, to be stared at for a
moment, then forgotten.

To the West they are a jigsaw puzzle that's lost
most of its pieces, a book with missing pages.

He stood still for a moment. Thirty feet away in the
bushes something was moving. He could hear the
sound. Slow, then fast, like an animal. A stoat, perhaps, or a badger. Or a man. He was going to move
closer, take a look, play it safe. But then who would

be hanging around on the British Embassy tennis court in the middle of the night?

Soon, he told himself, you'll start running from the moon.

◆

Farrar met him at the door.

"I think you should come up a moment, sir."

They trooped up the staircase silently, turning on lights as they went. Farrar collected a sheaf of papers from his office.

"Look, this is what I've got and it's bloody odd. Been going on for about two hours now. Very heavy traffic on some of the high-frequency bands, some of it scrambled, some not. Now normally these wavelengths are used for emergency signals. Anyway, there's also some unusual car-to-car stuff. I haven't broken it down yet, but you can see what I mean." He pushed a computer printout in Parker's direction. There was a coffee stain on one corner.

Parker glanced down and handed it back.

"Doesn't mean much to me, Jim, I'm afraid, bit after my course, this sort of thing."

Farrar grinned obsequiously. "One of these is the general secretary's car—either that or the chairman of the KGB. The Americans might have it a little clearer, but you don't want me to go round and ask, do you?"

"No, that's fine. See if you can make something of it."

Parker had ceased to be amazed by the advanced level of the technology. Years ago the Americans had admitted to bugging Brezhnev's own car. Now everyone could do it. With amazing accuracy they could tell which leader was where, whose plane was in flight, and on quiet days even whose wife went shopping where.

Secrets were what you kept in your head. Let them out and you might never know who would find them.

◆

Parker returned to his office and sat half watching the television news. The Soviet view of everything in the world—bleak, solemn, and unremittingly boring. Amazing how communism could take the fun out of life.

The program was nearly over, but as an Englishman he kept watching for the weather forecast. More than anything, it was habit. A Russian winter is a Russian winter. But suddenly he sat upright, his hands clasping the sides of the chair. The newscaster was reporting a police hunt for a man who'd escaped from a psychiatric hospital outside Moscow.

Parker had never heard an item like it. The escapee was described as fair-haired, in his late forties, and possibly dangerous. Any sightings were to be reported to the militia at once.

He sat back in his chair and swallowed hard. So Kalyagin was out and running. They could never announce that to their people. Instead they had set the scene for a manhunt. Some of the people would read between the lines, but most would simply keep their eyes open for strangers. Kalyagin would stick out wherever he went.

Carefully, Parker encoded a second message to London. It would only be a matter of time before the Russian tried to make contact.

◆

He was alone. Out on the streets with a thousand of his countrymen, and yet Dmitry Kalyagin felt quite alone. For longer than he could remember he had been shepherded, watched, guarded, fawned over. And now not a single person alive knew where he was.

It was hard going. His shoes had been made for receptions, not trekking the streets. But he walked with a lightness he had not thought possible. Fear had given way to purpose and even a sense of freedom. Maybe the hunters in Siberia felt it, or the nomads in Central Asia. But here in Moscow, where they scratch your name onto a thousand official files and log you throughout your Soviet life, it was a strange sensation. Moscow tells you where to work and where to rest. Only the choice of dying, he thought, belongs to you.

He had pulled his scarf over his mouth and kept his eyes on the ground. But he knew there were few who could recognize him. Soviet leaders are a remote, largely unapproachable breed, seldom in the public spotlight, and then only through choice. The proletariat would sooner expect to see a bug-eyed dragon wandering around than a member of the Politburo. On these streets he would be safe enough.

Kalyagin cut east through the city, passing within a thousand yards of the KGB headquarters on

Dzherzhinsky Square, before heading down to the Embankment. Another half hour, forty minutes, and he'd make the rendezvous.

◆

Zina Potapova was less sure. She had never expected to run. Not out of confidence or pride—it just hadn't seemed relevant. I'm Russian, she told herself. This is my country. But even as she said the words to herself, she knew they were no longer true.

Strange not to have a home. Something so final about being an outcast in this city—like a ghost lost between heaven and hell. If this system turns its back on you, you cease to exist.

Imagine! You don't have a trade union, a housing committee, a residence permit—a *propiska*. You might as well come from Mars!

For a moment her confusion gave way to fantasy. She imagined a little green man being stopped by a militiaman and asked for his visa and currency documents. Did he have leave of absence from his collective? Where was his permission, permission to come, permission to go? Why was his identity card not written in Russian? What was his ethnic origin? Was he a class enemy?

She could hear the voice. Under Section 16, Subsection 5c of the Criminal Code of the Russian Federation, he would have to accompany the officer to militia headquarters.

"What are you doing, woman, are you all right?" From a great distance Potapova felt her arm being tugged and she struggled to get away. But nothing happened. Slowly she opened her eyes to find herself sitting on a snow-covered bench near the Tomb of the Unknown Soldier.

A man was standing over her in the darkness. "Get up, you must. Can't stay here. They'll take you in. Have you been drinking?"

She peered into his face. He was young and officious and she decided instantly she didn't need him. Painfully, she eased herself to her feet and tore away from his grasp. What a place. No peace even for the dead and the dying.

"Can't you leave me alone?" she hissed.

He stood there in silhouette under the trees, uncomprehending, marveling at her lack of gratitude. Perhaps she was mad, he told himself, maybe from the mountains. They weren't normal, such people. Maybe he should tell the militia.

Potapova stumbled on toward the square, the cold and the anxiety taking their toll. She knew she would have to go inside soon, get some warmth, some hot food, some comfort. Otherwise it wouldn't matter anymore, any of it. She would lie down and let them come and get her.

Just a few more steps to St. Basil's—the back of it, that's what he'd told her, where all the buses park, just in the shadow of the clock tower on the Savior's Gate. She looked around her. He's not here. My God, he's not here. And the panic hit her and she felt herself spinning. I'm going to fall, she thought, and something inside her braced for the impact. But it

never came. For inches away from the ground a hand
caught her, an arm went around her waist, then a
second, and she was lifted lightly into the air. As her
eyes refocused she was looking into the face of Dmitry Kalyagin.

◆

He half carried her down toward the river and the
darkness. Not a rough grip but tender like a lover,
pulling her close, sharing the warmth.

As they looked at each other Kalyagin eased off a
glove and smoothed away the hair that hung down
from her hat onto her forehead. It was the first time
they had touched in the two years they had known
each other. Zina Potapova felt suddenly elated.

When they were under the bridge he broke away.
"Give me a moment to think."

She nodded, leaning back against the rough stone.
A car trundled past them, its headlights on full beam,
and Kalyagin stared at her. He didn't like what he
saw.

Little red blotches had begun to appear on her
face—the unmistakable signs of impending frostbite.
Russians are taught to look for such things. They pull
strangers out of crowds and rub their faces, hustling
them into the warmth of the nearest building. Kalyagin knew that Potapova would have to get out of
the cold soon or she'd be in serious trouble.

He took off his scarf and wrapped it around the
tiny cheeks, rubbing the pale skin as he did so, trying
to coax back the circulation.

It was clear there were few options. In an hour

they'd be caught in the void of late-night Moscow. Theaters and movie houses closed, restaurants pushing out their patrons, only the private parties or the special receptions in the "houses of culture" would still have guests—and those by invitation. Kalyagin well remembered his first visits in the sixties. They'd have to hurry.

The National Hotel has always been a special establishment. A much-prized people's property that occupies the corner spot at the bottom of Gorky Street and Revolution Square. Lenin once slumbered there, lending the place eternal recognition.

But there were other thoughts in Kalyagin's mind as he pushed open the door to the downstairs cafe.

An old doorman in white jacket and peaked cap shuffled toward him. "Closed, finished," he mumbled, "you'll get nothing tonight."

He gripped the man's arm tightly, so that the old fellow looked up, startled. "This is Party business, granddad. Get moving and none of your nonsense. I've an important guest with me and we require your manners and your food. Now get on with it."

And his other hand brought out the Party card with the red emblem that he had held in readiness. The card that locks and unlocks the Soviet Union, from Europe to the Far East.

The man didn't examine it. He tore his cap from his head and stood aside, bowing and shaking his head, scratching at the stubble on his chin. Nervously he began to hobble ahead of them, muttering to wait-

ers, clearing a path through the tables and the gawk-
ing patrons.

They brought the best they had—borscht, caviar,
some smoked salmon, a bottle of sweet champagne
from the Crimea. And then they brought the manager.

It had taken twenty minutes to locate Yuli Kirov.
They had looked in his office and checked the bar.
After that there was no choice but to search the vacant rooms. For Kirov liked to make use of them in
his spare time for a variety of purposes.

Sometimes he needed privacy for a caviar deal,
whereby something less than the full quantity would
go to the hotel, at other times he might wish to ac-
quaint himself with a new chambermaid to assure
her of his good intentions as an employer.

And so it was that evening. Kirov had retired to a
suite on the fourth floor, taking with him a young girl
from Kiev and a bottle of Armenian brandy. The
combination had given him much pleasure and the
laughter and merrymaking could be heard far down
the corridor.

Kirov had been less than delighted to hear his
name being called and to learn that a senior Party
official was even now in his dining room.

He stood beside the table for a full thirty seconds
before Kalyagin acknowledged him.

"Yes, what is it?" He looked up with an expression
of official disinterest. The squat, gray-haired figure
was rubbing his hands anxiously.

"Kirov, Comrade, Yuli Andreyevich, manager of the hotel."

He doesn't recognize me, thought Kalyagin, but that won't last. Buy time.

"Sit down, please, Comrade."

Kirov took a chair close to Potapova, bowing and gathering up her hand to kiss.

"We are here because of an unfortunate accident," Kalyagin began. "Our official car broke down along Gorky Street. A replacement has been ordered but it may take some time to arrive. We therefore need a room for a short while, somewhere for my assistant and myself to complete our work." He looked hard at Kirov to gauge his reaction. "I'm sure you understand what I mean? See to it, will you," he added, marking the end of the conversation. Kirov stood up hurriedly.

"At once, Comrade. I shall do it myself."

Zina Potapova watched him go. "How long do you think we have?"

"Not long. He'll call his friends in the district committee. They'll refer upward and then the word will get to Dzherzhinsky Square. But we may be lucky. People will be on their way home or still out to dinner. The weather's bad. We're all right for a while."

Potapova pushed away her plate. She looked better. The red blotches on her face were less angry.

"What happens after that?" She hadn't wanted to ask the question. You don't want to look too far ahead. It might not be a pleasant sight. Stick to now. It's safer, easier.

"I have to make a call," he replied, "then I'll know more."

She wasn't sure what made her remember it but she reached across the table and grabbed his arm.

"Maybe it's nothing, but a woman at work told me of an apartment, a sort of love nest, where she used to stay. Not anymore. The affair broke up. But the apartment might still be empty. It's worth trying."

He shrugged. "I agree. But let's leave the dogs something to follow."

They were shown to an office on the second floor. Kalyagin had no doubt that it was wired for sound. The hotel was considered a prime KGB target. The staff would be under almost as much surveillance as the guests.

A bowl of fruit and some flowers had been arranged on the desk. Beside them a box of Russian liqueur chocolates.

Kalyagin winked at Potapova and they began to talk rapidly in low voices.

◆

Two stories above, Yuli Kirov put down the phone and sat looking at it. What the hell was Dmitry Kalyagin doing? The man probably had three apartments, two dachas, and almost as many servants as the Czar. And here he was coming into the hotel and behaving like a clerk from the provinces. Damn him!

He got up and walked out into the corridor. Anyway, he'd done his bit. Passed it on to the local committee—an old friend from army days. Now they'd have to sort it out. All the same, it would be good to know a little more.

Kirov took the elevator to the ground floor, turned right through the cloakroom, and made his way down the back stairs. He knocked at an unmarked door and walked in. Along the far wall were a dozen banks of reel-to-reel tape recorders, four of them turning. Voice-activated, he assumed.

At a coffee table in the middle of the room two young men were reading magazines. They looked up as he entered.

"What's the matter, Yuli?" one of them sneered. "No leftovers tonight?"

Kirov regretted going down but there were certain things that went with the job. "Better keep an ear on 421," he said. "Might do yourself some good." One of the men got up and went over to the recorders.

"Don't forget who told you," said Kirov.

The man didn't answer.

As he slipped on the headphones he was just in time to catch a Russian voice. A man was telling someone that if they hurried they could make the Leningrad train. The American Consulate would look after them there and pass them on to Riga.

He didn't hesitate. With one hand he picked up the telephone, with the other he threw his magazine at his colleague.

◆

It was 1 A.M. when Kalyagin and Potapova reached the apartment, ringing the doorbell as long as they

dared, praying it was empty. Kalyagin broke the lock
with a single shove and they found themselves in a
warm, musty little hall with leopard-skin wallpaper.

For some reason Potapova wanted to laugh.

Chapter 19

DECEMBER 22

Sir David White normally took breakfast in his apartment at the embassy. Harriet called it their "cozy time," when she made the porridge sent out from London, strained the tea, and listened to the BBC world service. It was all just so and the childless couple loved it that way, with the engraved silver napkin rings, the Queen Anne chairs, and the Morlands sheepskin slippers. The little things that meant so much.

But not that morning. "Got to go and see my old chum Peter," he announced as they were getting dressed. "He's over at the Cosmos, just in town for a couple of days. I said I'd have breakfast with him. Mind if I take your car?"

Of course she hadn't minded, although it was a

little sudden. But then Peter's visits were always sudden. And what about the Rolls-Royce? She much preferred him to travel in that. After all, he was Her Majesty's ambassador, and well, with these people, you know, Communists, it didn't hurt to cut a bit of a dash.

She looked down at the three-day-old *Daily Telegraph* crossword and scanned the clues impatiently. Carefully she began copying the puzzle onto a plain sheet of paper. That way it wouldn't matter if she made mistakes. And David would be so pleased if she managed it all. He didn't really believe she could manage anything.

◆

The ambassador was in a bad mood when he sat down at the table. There had been a long line of Finnish tourists in front of him, and no one had the right money, and the whole self-service thing was a bit of a nightmare at the best of times.

Still, the pancakes looked all right and there was hot tea from the samovar and anyway it was just one morning.

Peter arrived just a minute later and Sir David brightened. After all, the fellow apologized profusely for being late and he was wearing the old school tie, the black with the pink stripe that none of them could ever bring themselves to throw away, even though it looked a bit stringy.

"How have you been?" asked Peter.

"Not too bad, you know how it is. A few ups and downs."

"I remember. Thank God I've been out of it for a while now. But it's not an easy job, not easy to keep everyone happy and pulling together." He sipped his tea thoughtfully. Sir David folded a layer of pancake and put it in his mouth.

"I always thought it was all right as long as you had good people under you," Peter went on. "You know what I mean—people who back you up, not too independent but polite and supportive."

Sir David looked across the table. He's aged a bit, he thought. Must be ten years since he got out of it all. And yet there was still a good head of gray hair, a trim waist, no shaky hand on the cup.

"Anyway, how are they all at the office?" Peter cut in.

"Don't suppose you'd know them. They're all about thirteen these days, barely out of nappies. And a lot of them quite cheeky with it."

"Who's head of chancery?"

"Fella called George Parker, but you wouldn't know him either. He's pretty young."

"And is he one of the cheeky ones?"

Sir David smiled. "I can handle it," he replied.

"I'm sure you can," he said soothingly. "I'm sure you can."

A waitress cleared away the plates and Sir David waited till she had gone. "I suppose I'm just a bit jumpy at the moment. Harriet hasn't been too well. And you know how much she looks forward to retiring in Wiltshire. I wouldn't want anything to get in the way of that."

"Of course not."

The ambassador looked at his watch. "My God, is that the time? I really ought to be going." They both stood up. "It's so nice to see an old friend," said Sir David, and shook his friend's hand warmly. "Thanks so much for the chat, and do give us a call when you're free again."

◆

The free-lance was stretched across three metal chairs. Neither young nor old, short nor tall, neat nor scruffy. He was a man to be forgotten, an inconsequential figure without charm or allure, trained to sit in back rows, to stand in shadows. A silent servant. Asleep now, but deadly.

The eyelids flickered as Perminev passed him in the corridor but they didn't open. He knocked on the general's door and went in.

"Your man"—the general motioned with a finger toward the corridor—"does he know what's required?"

"He knows only what he has to know. And afterward he will forget it. He has done so before. I have found his work to be completely satisfactory."

"See that it is this time." The general sighed. "What are the reports around the city?"

"We're watching the embassies, and they're watching us. They know something's going on. But there's no movement."

Perminev went over to the window, then turned to face the general. "It was so close at the National.

Just another couple of minutes and we would have had him. The men there did well."

"They screwed it up, Comrade, and you know it." The general jabbed a forefinger in Perminev's direction. "None of this crap about how well they did. The stupid shits would forget their names if they didn't carry identity cards."

The general sat down. "Do we know who's in charge of the MI6 station at the British Embassy?"

"We believe it's Parker, head of their political section."

"How do you know?"

"It's in the morning report."

The general shifted a pile of papers and began leafing through them.

"Look after Parker," he said. "He may be lonely. Give him some company. And let him see it." Perminev got up to leave. "And one more thing— send your bulldog in here. I want to make sure he understands what he's doing. Unlike everyone else."

An orderly shook the inert man but it wasn't necessary. At the first touch of his sleeve he swung lightly into a sitting position. There was no transition. He was fully awake.

When he walked it seemed for a moment as if his legs were stiff, but the general had seen that walk before. Not stiffness, but tautness, the peak of condition. Muscles toned and ready for action.

The man stood silent in the center of the room.

"Comrade Perminev has briefed you?"

There was a nod in reply.

"How many times have you worked with him?"

"Six, maybe eight times." The voice was surprisingly cultured. Unaccented Russian, thought the general, possibly from the Leningrad region.

"And how do you feel about him?"

"There is nothing to feel. He gives me orders and I carry them out."

"And if I give you orders?"

The question hung for a second unanswered.

"You are the senior officer, and I would obey you."

The general moved closer to the man but his face remained impassive. "When this is over I want you to kill Perminev, do you understand?"

"Yes, Comrade General."

"Now get out of here and follow your orders."

When the man had gone the general paced slowly around the room, his feet clicking noisily on the parquet floor. A tool of the trade, he told himself. A man like that is nothing more than a tool. We all need them. And yet there was something wrong with the creature. Available to the man with the most stripes. Where did he stop? Who could stop him? Who was to say that he wouldn't return one night with orders from someone else?

◆

Harrison stamped the last of the visa applications and closed the file. Another boring task. He had always been ambitious. As long as he could remember he had fought harder, worked later, risen earlier than his colleagues. It had stood out on his record.

That record had been open for fifteen years and had found a home in the end. That kind always did.

They had passed it from Oxford to London, and from then on less than a dozen people had known either of its existence or its contents. But it had fallen into a sealed archive in the Secret Intelligence Service along with a hundred others and had fallen out when it was wanted.

He was judged in stark silhouette, not kindly, but with an eye for detail. Good at sports, not a quick learner, but a thorough one. In his relationships he had been ardent if unromantic, heard to express the view that wives were mixed blessings. You either rose above them or they pulled you down. And it would never happen to him.

It happened soon after the Foreign Office accepted his application and set him to work in a room with high ceilings and little light. It looked out over Downing Street.

She was the daughter and sister of a banker, and nearly one herself, competent and businesslike at all times. Love had its place, which wasn't everywhere, and children were designated for "sometime in our late thirties if we must."

They had bought a Volvo with her father's wedding present, and a set of polyester and cotton sheets with his—and waited for the success they knew would come. In his case it was disguised as a posting to Moscow. After a long weekend of persuasion she agreed to mothball her pigskin briefcase, sell the home computer, and put the banking on ice.

A week later British Airways landed them in Moscow in a snowstorm.

A week later she found out that he was going to work in the consulate and not the chancery.

"How could you keep such a thing from me?"

"I didn't think it was important."

"Of course it's important. I thought you were going to be a diplomat, not a bloody form filler."

It had, he admitted to himself, been a rush job. None of the usual time to learn Russian, to adapt, to study. But they had wanted him quickly and he had gone.

And she did come around in the end. The ambassador's wife had spotted a kindred soul as soon as she heard the voice. And in Britain, where accent is still as important as rank, Mrs. Harrison was accepted, nay, pulled headfirst, into the Moscow of coffee mornings and interesting walks.

It was all right for the days. She even found time to glance at some of the old banking books. But in the evenings she had to rely on borrowed videotapes of wildlife documentaries and month-old news bulletins. And she would stretch them out to fill the gap between obligatory dinner parties and the late hours when her husband came home.

She had asked what kept him and he had told her he was trying to better himself. That was a laugh—pushing files in the consulate and stamping papers.

Harrison was feeling decidedly sorry for himself when the signal arrived calling him home.

◆

Warm and stifling. Like a million winter homes across Moscow. No open windows for six months.

Parker checked the overnight file and called Farrar. "Could you get over here please—as fast as possible?"

He was there within ten minutes.

"I can't find any response from London," he told him.

Farrar looked at Parker with curiosity.

"That's because there hasn't been one. Here, look at the sequence. You've got the standard acknowledgment for the two priority signals, and that's it."

Parker frowned. "I don't like it. We should have had a reply long ago."

"Want me to send a chaser?"

"If we haven't heard in an hour, send it."

He didn't like to leave the office. Each moment of absence seemed like a betrayal. First Unicorn, then Kalyagin, both reaching out across the city for a lifeline. But he needed to test the climate.

It took him five minutes to get ready and then he was out in the courtyard starting the car, coaxing it onto the Kamyenny Bridge, then west along Kropotkinskaya through the morning's straggling traffic. He parked in front of the main entrance to Gorky Park, next to a truant black Volga, its driver sprawled asleep on the front seat, the engine running. Half Moscow's gasoline was consumed by people who never had their eyes open.

Away from the traffic the frozen snow still smelled fresh and clean as Parker turned left past the giant

Ferris wheel, locked and motionless—a monument to the far-off days of summer. He didn't go the full circuit, but cut across in front of the pavilion and took the path to the Embankment. The wind was bitter.

By the time he reached the car his eyes were watering from the cold and his fingers seemed to have been injected with ice. He tore off his gloves and put his hands over the heating vents. The driver of the Volga was still asleep.

In all, the trip took just over an hour, and Parker knew it had been time well spent. Not only had he glimpsed two surveillance teams covering him, but something else had caught his eye—the eye that records without telling, that stores its memory close to the subconscious. You have to think to find it, think hard.

And Parker was back at the embassy staring at the compound wall when it came to him.

Yes, two teams. But they wanted to be seen, wanted to put pressure on him. They didn't dodge, didn't alternate positions, made no attempt to bracket him. One had been the standard Soviet chase car, the Volga with three inside. Two men and a woman because that looks normal.

And the other car—different. Just one face inside it, staying with him on the bridge, with him on the Gorky Street underpass. The face that carried the real threat.

Farrar stood awkwardly in the doorway. There was no reply from London, he announced. In fact, London had ceased altogether to acknowledge his signals.

♦

The room was still dark but Kalyagin knew that dawn had arrived. There are sounds that belong only to the day.

And yet as a child he had woken once with a start, dressed himself, and stood in the tiny hall of the flat in Tallinn, about to leave for school. Suddenly his mother had confronted him: "Dmitry, it's three o'clock in the morning. What are you doing?"

He could still hear the voice, still see the beautiful lady with the half-open eyes squinting at him. Mother, my mother.

For a moment he luxuriated in the strangeness around him. The empty love nest with its shabby walls, cracked plaster, the curtains each a different size—the seedy disorder that he had shaken off more than a generation ago to climb to the summit.

His coat lay across him as a blanket, his shirt had become his pajamas. Two miles away there was a wardrobe full of his clothes, but that was already history. He had what he needed. The gun lay under the cushion.

"Are you awake?"

Potapova had tiptoed in from the bedroom. She sat down on the floor beside the sofa. Kalyagin could see she was fully clothed but her hair was a mess.

"I wanted to go on sleeping," he told her, "but what does it matter?" He tried to smile. "Better to

get up early. After all, there's so much to do, so many
people to see. So many people who want to see us."

She looked at him blankly, ignoring the sarcasm.

He shrugged. "And then again, perhaps there's
nothing to do. Maybe nothing at all."

"I'll find some tea." She went into the kitchen,
opening the cupboards. The mood had changed. Last
night had been chase, excitement, a desperate thrill.
But now there were the old, familiar insecurities
brought by any morning and the new ones brought
by this morning. We should be doing something, she
thought, planning. And the inactivity lay all around
her.

She put his cup beside him on the floor. "You know
there is so much I've wanted to ask you." He looked
over to her, suddenly alarmed.

"We have never talked—do you realize that? Not
once in all this time. Oh yes, there was always some
nonsense about the weather, or sewing buttons, but
we never had a conversation. I barely know the
sound of your voice." She looked down into the
square face. Still a young face, she thought. This isn't
an old man.

"Let me think," he said. "Talk later." He tried to
turn away, but she sat down beside him on the sofa
and pulled at his arm.

"I want to talk . . . now. I must talk. We don't
know how long there is." She was crying suddenly,
and without thinking he reached across her, hugging
the stocky body to his coat. She pulled away. "I want
to know why we did this."

Kalyagin said nothing for a moment. Outside, a door banged and there were footsteps on the stairs. He waited till they had died away. When he spoke his voice was almost a whisper. "I have never thought of such questions, still less of answers to them. But perhaps you are right. Maybe I should, maybe we both should." He pulled himself up into a sitting position, the coat around his legs.

"You know what scares me," he said slowly. "You know I have enjoyed this life. First, it was communism. That was good. I was a believer. Believers like other believers, it gives you a team, something to belong to. But then I had something else as well. I had a group made up of people like you." Kalyagin paused and they looked at each other for a moment in silence.

"Your group gave me a secret side to my life—a dark side. And dark is always more seductive than light. You can go and hide in it, forget yourself in it, pretend there is everything you've ever wanted in its shadows. Most of all you can live twice when most people can't even live once. Who can refuse such things? I couldn't."

"Did they make promises to you? I mean, rewards?"

"No and they didn't need to. They were clever. They knew that. Oh, they could have said . . . We'll get you out, buy you a farm in Australia, a pension, dollars, women. Who knows what they could have offered? But I didn't want it. I had my two lives— truth and lies. I had it all. Me, Dmitry Kalyagin. Why would I have wanted to live in the West? I was sure it would go on and on"—he paused—"until it stopped."

"And now?"

"And now . . . now I'm losing my other life. I'm becoming like everyone else. I'm scared because there is nowhere to hide."

Potapova put out her hand and touched his. It was his turn to move away.

"Don't feel sorry for me. That's not why I tell you these things. I had the best this country could offer—the position, the power, the privileges—because those are the things that matter. You know what is strange? In some ways I'm a very good Communist. I never wanted six sheepskin coats, even though I could have had them. How many can you wear at the same time? I was never obsessed with material things. You can sit behind only one steering wheel at a time, even though Brezhnev tried to sit behind a dozen." He chuckled. "Look how much good it did him! No, it was the power, the responsibility. For me the double responsibility."

Potapova was listening spellbound.

Kalyagin shifted on the sofa and rubbed his eyes. He picked up the teacup and swallowed twice.

"They think of me now as a traitor and it's true, I have been. But I was more than that. I was good at what I did. I was a good manager, a good administrator. People brought me problems—I solved them. The nonsense of bureaucracy, the corruption, I cut through it. I knew the wolves from the chickens, I knew where to pull strings."

He must have wanted to talk, thought Potapova. It hadn't taken much to unlock his tongue. All those years of secrecy, all the triumphs applauded, all the failures forgotten. His eyes were alive, the memories were coming fast.

"They used to test us so carefully, you know. They'd test you one day and test you the next when you weren't expecting it. Little temptations, little offers—were you honest, were you loyal, were you too ambitious? If you had a chink, anything, a fault, a leaning, a tendency—they meant to find it. I remember early on in the *raikom*—the regional committee —I started getting thank-you letters from some of the people I'd helped. Nothing special—maybe someone who had needed a bigger apartment, a telephone, that sort of thing. And then gradually the money began arriving. Small rubles, large rubles— and in one case even some dollars. God only knows where they'd come from. But each time I gave the money to the *raikom* treasurer." He laughed bitterly. "Each time I reported it. And then years later I found out it had been just a test. Some idiot let it out at a New Year's party." He snorted contemptuously. "The same idiot that is still there in the *raikom*— while I went to Moscow."

She could see the arrogance, the confidence, dented now but not shattered. A man who had risen through the most competitive system in the world. No ordinary man. There were special talents, special stamina. The will to succeed. She watched him drain the last of the tea. We're not lost, she thought. Not yet.

◆

Wednesday. The turkeys arrived from London. A special day that always spells Christmas for the beleaguered British community in Moscow. The last act of generosity for the year from Her Majesty's government—an order of meat and poultry from Smithfields.

The manager of the commissary rang him direct. "It's here, Mr. Parker," she cooed. "Lovely-looking bird, and then there's the joint you wanted as well. . . ."

"Thank you, Mrs. Trippett, I'll get it all later."

" 'Ere,"—the telephone manner dropped for a moment—"if you hurry, there's a couple of extra sausages goin'. I'll put them by just for you 'cos I know you likes 'em."

"You're very kind. Thank you."

"Well, you need lookin' after, don't you? All this cold weather. You've got to stoke up a bit."

"Thank you so much."

Parker hadn't thought about Christmas for days. It hardly seemed relevant. Christmas, the birth of Christ, while all around Moscow people were dying. And London was sending turkeys instead of messages. He shook his head in disbelief.

And then it struck him and he wondered why he had missed it. They weren't planning to send a reply at all. The silence was the reply. They were cutting him loose. Cutting off the operation and Kalyagin because it was all going to blow. And they knew it.

Parker looked out over the courtyard. It was astounding to think of it. Kalyagin was the most important agent they'd ever had. And they were throwing him away. No operation to "exfiltrate" him, no recompense for his years of service.

The callousness of it shocked Parker. And yet, he reflected, it wasn't just the fate of the Russian that worried him.

If he, George Parker, couldn't find a way out of his mess, they'd cast him adrift as if they'd never known him.

◆

He barely heard the knock at the door, but there was no mistaking the smiling face. Harrison was dressed in a loud, light blue suit and crimson tie. Any other day, thought Parker, and I'd have laughed.

"Hallo, George, just thought I'd let you know I'm going to London today—just for twenty-four hours, shopping and a couple of other things. Anything you want?"

Parker shook his head. "Kind thought. Where you going to be staying?"

"Got a brother who lives in Hampstead. No problem there."

"Good," said Parker. "Well, have a nice time."

"Thanks, George. Let's get together when I'm back."

Let's not, thought Parker. He looked down at the desk and waited till Harrison had shut the door. Really, the man was becoming a complete pain in the rectum.

◆

Kalyagin was getting dressed when he found it, crumpled but still in the white manila envelope with the expensive and foreign watermark.

The English businessman had given it to him just before leaving the Kremlin—an invitation to cocktails at the British Embassy in honor of IBM. He had put it out of his mind in the same instant.

The card was standard enough. So, too, was the normal response—in the shredder. And yet, with the new general secretary in power, a few of the invitations were being accepted.

"We Russians must show the world that we can stand up with a drink in our hand and not fall over," he had told them after one of the Thursday meetings. And so the message had filtered back later through the bureaucracy, from the cabinet office to the secretariat: Go visit the Westerners in their embassies. Not every time, not for every party. Just once in a while.

And the Party apparatus, which scans group photographs for changes in policy, was beside itself with delight.

A return to the exciting days of Khrushchev, they all said, and sat back to wait for the revolution.

Kalyagin examined the card. In the dingy little apartment on Gruzinsky Alley, it stood out like a beacon.

◆

He called to Potapova.

"I have to go out."

She came in from the bedroom. "Go where? They're all over the city, searching."

"I don't think so. I'm certain only a few people are handling the case. They don't dare risk a full-scale hunt. The last thing they want is a big *shum*—a scandal."

Potapova was too tired to argue. She leaned back against the wall and closed her eyes.

"What do I do if someone comes?" she asked.

"They won't. Look at the place." He put out a hand and touched the sideboard. It came away covered in dust. "See, no one comes here."

She heard his footsteps on the stairs and then sat for a long time without moving, her eyes open and fixed on the floor, trying not to imagine the worst the day could bring her.

◆

When he put his mind to it Christopher Bodley was good at his job. At thirty he was bureau chief for Reuters news agency in Moscow, writing with a facility and humor that his colleagues envied.

But the humor was largely absent that morning as he emerged from the foreigners' block on Gruzinsky Alley, wincing in pain as the outer door slammed shut and the temperature plummeted eighty degrees.

In the dawn light he retrieved the ice scraper from his Volvo and began attacking the windows. Far too early to get up. And yet it was important to miss the

gaggle of foreign residents. In another hour they'd be
scurrying out to their cars, cranking their engines,
hoping for the morning miracle of technology over
climate. Someone might have noticed him, someone
might have guessed where he'd been. The foreigners' gossip was quite incessant.

He opened the door and tried the frozen engine. It
caught first time. Thank God. Driving out of the compound, Bodley glimpsed the guard through the observation window of his box. The telephone was in
his hand. So what? he thought. And yet for Jane, left
behind on the fourth floor, it was different. She was
married to a bore of a Swiss diplomat—at that very
moment investigating fish processing plants in Kare-
lia in the name of international cooperation.

Bodley had met her three weeks earlier during
dinner at the British minister's flat. She, twenty-
eight, plump with streaked hair; he, ginger with
beard and tortoise-shell glasses. It had, he reflected,
sort of happened. God knows one had to take refuge
somewhere. Anyway, what the hell? In six months
they'd probably be posted to Angola. Live while you
can.

Bodley smiled expansively at the street, thinking
of the small face on the king-size pillow, the just-
loved look that the eyes can never hide.

Turn left here. It's illegal but no one's there.
Quickly now. And he heard the thump on the passenger door and saw the figure at the same moment.
Christ! As the car skidded to a halt the man was in the
seat beside him. Bodley half turned, his fist raised

against a blow that didn't come. He knew the face the instant he saw it and his mouth opened wide in amazement.

"*Poyezhay*—drive," yelled Kalyagin. "Left here, quickly."

Bodley wrenched the steering wheel and the Volvo jerked, skidding crazily toward the intersection. The lights were changing to red. In the distance a policeman whistled, but they were already across the main road, careering wildly through the narrow streets off the inner ring.

"Pull in here." Kalyagin gestured to a cul-de-sac. "That's it. Now turn off the engine."

A shiver passed down from Bodley's neck to his spine.

"Come with me." Kalyagin got out and crossed the road.

For a moment Bodley stayed where he was. It's too fast, too ridiculous. Get out now, he told himself. They always said there might be trouble. Kalyagin was standing, beckoning. He looked around. The street was full of people on their way to work.

Bodley locked the car door and drew level with Kalyagin.

"What's going on, for God's sake? What do you want?"

"Keep your voice down." The Russian frowned at him. "People don't sit in foreign cars at six-thirty in the morning. They walk to work or take a bus. You can walk back to your car in a moment and go where you please." He turned and looked straight into

Bodley's eyes. "You don't ask who I am." It was a statement.

"I know who you are."

"You have the advantage then. Your registration number tells me you're a British correspondent, but I don't know your name."

Bodley didn't reply. He looked around again at the passers-by, searching for someone suspicious, some sign of a setup. Kalyagin took his arm like an old friend.

"I have one favor to ask of you," he said. "A simple thing. Deliver an invitation card to the British Embassy, not just to the embassy, to the head of the MI6 station."

Bodley snorted. "How would I know who that is?"

"You won't but they will. Give it to the senior political man and it'll find its way, I've no doubt."

"Why should I take anything from you? I could be arrested the moment you leave."

"You know who I am and that should be enough to tell you something. This isn't a joke. The Politburo doesn't walk the streets of Moscow at dawn playing games."

His grip tightened on Bodley's arm.

"Under the passenger seat of your car I have left an envelope. Deliver it as I ask and you will do something of service to your country. If that means nothing to you, then do it because your own personal safety may depend on it. I do not exaggerate."

Suddenly he was moving away into the crowd but he turned back to Bodley and gave him a friendly

wave. Two friends parting on their way to work. One
to an office, you might have thought, with his smart
coat and suit, the other perhaps to a bookshop or a
student library, there to further his knowledge and
learning in the cause of Soviet progress.

◆

Bodley delivered the envelope to George Parker
soon after nine o'clock that morning. In the Moscow
press corps current wisdom held that Parker was the
most likely spook. And Bodley was soon to discover
that they had chosen correctly.

By eleven he had been debriefed in the cage and
ordered, not requested, to sign a copy of the Official
Secrets Act. Further, he was advised to take a holiday
and not return to Moscow until contacted by the
Foreign Office.

On the whole, Bodley decided, for a fun-seeking
but tenacious reporter, it had been a lousy morning,
starting early and ending badly.

Alone in his office, Parker put the invitation under
his desk lamp. At first glance it seemed to be in its
original state. Only in the bottom right-hand corner
under the flowing "RSVP" were three words written
in a tiny, spidery hand: "Accepted with pleasure."

Dmitry Kalyagin was coming to a party.

◆

It took him an hour to reach the block on Gruzin-
ky.

Kalyagin no longer looked like a leader. He had
ipped the lining of his coat so that strands of it hung
down below the woolen fabric. Buttons had been

torn off his sleeves. His shirt was open at the neck and
the scarf had gone. A minor official, perhaps the dis-
patcher in a bus station. But not a successful one. A
man with his future behind him.

This Kalyagin had developed a limp, dragging his
right foot along behind him in the snow, slithering
and muttering to himself. Change the way you walk
if you want a real disguise. He hadn't forgotten that.
It's not your clothes that give you away. It's the
spring in your step or the dullness of your tread, or
the limp, or the stick. Your movements, not your
shape. And Kalyagin had chosen the limp.

As he approached the courtyard entrance he heard
shouting but his mind didn't take it in. Only as he
climbed the few steps to the ground floor did the
voice strike him.

For a moment he stood still in the corridor, frozen
against the wall, listening intently. Inside the flat
Potapova was shouting wildly, hysterically, threatening to call the militia. Something banged and a glass
object smashed.

Kalyagin didn't wait. He eased open the door and
crept inside. They were in the sitting room. He could
just see a man's back. Potapova was facing him. But
her eyes must have told the figure something, for he
turned unexpectedly and Kalyagin had to move fast.
As the man cried out he crossed the four feet between them and smashed his fist against the flabby
double chin. The stranger crumpled silently onto the
floor and lay without moving.

"What happened?" he breathed.

Potapova was standing by the wall. There were tears on her cheeks but she couldn't cry anymore.

"He came back, threatened to get the militia. Said it was his apartment. I was a thief. Then he said I could stay if I did what he wanted. He put his hands on me but I pushed the pig away."

Kalyagin bent down and listened to the man's breathing—a fat figure in an old blue parka. Maybe a caretaker. He wasn't hurt but he wouldn't want to forgive anyone when he woke up.

"Get your things together. We'll have to move out."

◆

Perminev had sent the free-lance on his way. A pointless mission to wait in Potapova's flat and search it. He already knew the bitch was gone and that was the end of it.

Registry had brought him Kalyagin's complete file but it had taken most of the morning. Those files, the top files, take time. You can't just have them brought up like a tray of coffee. He gritted his teeth at the memory. Eight phone calls, three signatures, and a note from the chairman himself. That's the way to stay in power, he told himself. Keep your records hidden and then it's almost impossible to bring you down.

Almost. He leafed through the early years, the commendations, the testimonies. All glowing. What was wrong with the man?

Check the index. It was a list of known contacts. Alphabetical order and dated. All the stars were there. The sportsmen and -women, the musicians, the actors. Soviet nobility. All well connected. But how do you know the lines of patronage? he wondered. How do you know who looks after whom? One false and hasty move could bring you up against a protégé of the general secretary. It had happened to others and Perminev knew they had lived to remember it.

He picked up the phone and began with the Moscow numbers.

In a country dedicated to restricting communications you can clear the channels fast and effectively. The government is bound by no procedure but its own, no committees but its own, no expedients but those it decides to employ. In short, the Soviet authorities can use their considerable power as they choose.

Within an hour Perminev had passed a word, which would become a rumor, then a fact—spread by the hierarchy through their friends and subordinates. Unfettered communications to all who needed to know. To many the unmarked black Volgas brought handwritten messages, to others came "eyes only" telegrams that required decoding. A few were summoned that morning to buildings that carried no sign or identification, to apartments with no numbers. By midmorning the word had reached its destination without aid from the press or from radio or television. More surely than that, the message had been passed.

◆

Deep in the vaults of the Lenin Library an old man, lined and bearded, took off his glasses, put the memo back in the envelope, and went over to the filing cabinet. It wasn't the first time. Over the last twenty years he had received many such instructions. Always the same form, the same stamp, the same issuing department.

He found Kalyagin's name and extracted the folder. No dust on it. His practiced eye picked that up immediately. Someone else had been reading this one.

The man took it over to his desk and switched on the lamp. From a drawer he extracted a magnifying glass. This would be a long process. Perhaps he would have to work all night. But by morning he would have listed every reference to Kalyagin in every current publication in the Soviet Union.

And then he would black them out, one by one, until no trace of the man remained, of his career, his achievements, not even of the imminent death that the old clerk assumed would be carefully arranged for him.

The man chuckled. It was like playing God, giving life and identity, then taking it away.

◆

They eased themselves into the phone booth and shut the door. In his hand Kalyagin held a small paper square, a list of numbers for the few real friends he had ever possessed.

He inserted a finger and dialed.

"Da, yes, who is it?" A woman answered.

"It's me, Dmitry. Tamara! How are things?"

He listened hard for any hesitation, a silence. But even through the static of a Moscow line he could hear the familiar gurgle of laughter rising from her stomach, breaking in her throat like a roar.

"You bastard, Dmitry . . ." She was giggling the way she always did. "It's been so long, my dear. Why don't you come around? Come now! I have nothing to do and all my friends are so boring. Come this minute, I insist."

He could imagine her standing in the hall, beside the window, the thick red hair bunched on her shoulders, probably lounging in a housecoat. So lazy. So lovable.

"Tamara, I have a friend with me."

"Anyone, as long as it's not a woman."

"It is."

"Bring her, too, if she's not dull. I'm learning to be liberal."

◆

Tamara's bodyguard rang from downstairs to announce them. A maid answered the door. And Kalyagin and Potapova stood for a moment in the paneled hall with the parquet floors, bathing in the heat.

Suddenly from the back of the apartment came a loud wail that became a shriek and finally a musical note. My God, thought Kalyagin, she's practicing.

Two minutes later, waving her sheet music, dressed in white knee-length socks, the number one star of Soviet pop music walked toward them, stopped in her tracks, and began laughing raucously.

"Dmitry! My Politburo member!" Tamara doubled up, her hands covering her face. "You look like a black marketeer. What's the matter, isn't there any respect anymore?" She turned to Potapova. "And you, my dear. You look like a frightened rat. Come in, come in. Have you just been to the zoo? Are the animals still in their cages?"

Giggling to herself, she led them into a vestibule. An ornate wooden bar had been carved into a corner. Behind it a young, unshaven figure in his early twenties appeared to be making cakes.

"Yuri—our visitors! Not the sort of class we're used to dealing with, but they're all we could get on a Wednesday."

Yuri coughed rudely, looked up in greeting, and looked down again.

"Sit down here, my little doves," cried Tamara. "Pay no attention to Yuri. He's written a poem and has depressed himself utterly. We shan't talk again until Saturday at least. He's often like that."

They squeezed themselves into a banquette upholstered in button-down vinyl.

"A kind gesture—" Dmitry began.

She put her hand out and touched his arm. "Crap," she interrupted. "Unless they've taken to having fancy dress balls in the Kremlin, you appear to be in trouble."

He loved her more than ever at that moment. . . . Tamara, you're so direct. Like a battering ram. Beautifully imperfect.

"We need somewhere to stay," he said. "For an

hour, maybe. Some time to think. I need a plan. I don't have one yet."

The telephone rang.

"Yes. . . . No, I'm busy. . . . Yes, Boris, I said busy. Now fuck off and leave me alone."

She turned to Dmitry. "That was Boris—another bore. So you need a plan." Her eyes narrowed suddenly. "But what have you done, my dear friend—stolen the Kremlin's caviar, lost the key to your lavatory? What is it?"

She got up. "I'll make some coffee. Seems to me you might drink it."

In the corner, Potapova's eyes seemed to be closing. She lolled lifelessly against a giant teddy bear. Kalyagin looked across at her. The animal seemed to be giving her some comfort. It was the kind of stylized toy that stars are supposed to buy and he assumed that was the reason Tamara had bought it.

She returned with cups. "Why don't you go out?" she asked Yuri. "You'll feel better. Take the metro—see Russia."

Yuri sniffed noisily and put down the pastry mix. "Give me your scarf and I'll go," he mumbled.

"Take it. What's mine is yours."

She began singing loudly in poor English. For Yuri it seemed like the final straw. He hurried along the corridor and slammed the front door.

"Such a child!" she called over to Kalyagin. "But what can I do with him? The son of my useless brother, who's in the embassy in Peking and may never come back. What choice do I have?"

She busied herself with a coffeepot, took a canister from the cupboard and peered inside it. "Perhaps there's a cake down there. Want some?" She looked up. "Your friend seems to have gone to sleep. Does she find us so tiresome?" Tamara grinned at Kalyagin. "At least we can be alone."

Kalyagin knew the flippancy was just a front. She had always been like that, incapable of being serious, afraid of what she might find inside her head. He remembered asking her once if she was happy. "That's not relevant," she had replied. And now? Now he didn't really care, couldn't care. Those days were long gone.

She edged close to him. "Well, how do I look? Wonderful? Fascinating? Beautiful? . . . Or am I old and raddled like a whore? Come on, Dmitry, say something. You're gone for a year. Then you just walk back in. What about a little affection? You could pretend if there isn't any."

"There is affection, more than that. You know there is. But I have a big problem." He shook his head. "No, not big—enormous. You must understand."

She took his hand. "I can try to help. Maybe I can talk to someone. You know I still see the Brezhnevs from time to time—the old man's widow and his son. The son might be able to put in a word."

"Brezhnev's son is a nobody." He rounded on her angrily. "Don't be a child, Tamara. I'm a member of he Politburo. You don't put in words for people like me. I'm either up there—or dead. There's nothing in between. And right now I'm close to dead."

Kalyagin's voice had cracked a little. They both noticed it. Losing my nerve, he told himself. Hang on. You'll work something out. Thank God for a friend.

◆

Kalyagin carried the limp Potapova through to the bedroom and laid her carefully on the Swiss duvet, and the birds on the flowery wallpaper were flying into a blue sky.

"How important is she?" asked Tamara.

"Very important. Maybe not in the way you think. But she is more than a colleague, more than a friend. We have shared our destinies and I won't desert her."

He played with the coffee cup. "We can't stay long. It could put you in danger if they know we've been here."

"That is not important. . . ."

"Sergei might think it was."

"Sergei and I are no longer married." She shrugged her shoulders.

"I'm sorry," said Kalyagin. "What happened?"

"You know, I'm still not sure. We had a row one night, went to bed without making up. At lunchtime we still weren't talking. I left in the afternoon for a rehearsal and when I came back in the evening he'd gone. A true artiste," she murmured. "Great performance, dramatic end. In truth, I haven't missed him but I've missed someone. Not the creeps, but someone who's something."

She looked at him, expecting a reply, but he was staring out the window.

"I can't say I understand your problem. I'm in the dark about politics. You know that. Party this, Party that, it never meant anything to me." She laughed. "You were a bit like that once."

Kalyagin seemed not to hear. All the years and all the plans, and now there wasn't one. Maybe that was the mind giving a signal of its own. Give up, lie down. It's over.

The phone rang. Tamara looked at it for a second without moving, then lifted the receiver.

"Yes. . . . Why, why now? Is it that urgent? . . . All right but no more than twenty minutes."

She hung up. Kalyagin noticed a frown he hadn't seen before. She put her hand in her bag and produced a key ring.

"Something is wrong, my dear. Badly wrong. Take these, the car is downstairs in the front, you know which one, take it and go. I believe someone is setting me up. I've been asked to go to my manager's house immediately, there is some problem with the band, it can't wait. This has never happened before, and I can only believe that they want me out of the way."

Kalyagin stood up suddenly. "I can't say anything. You know that. But I thank you with my whole heart."

Suddenly she was hugging him. He felt the thick, rough hair on his cheek, the full body against him. The last time, Tamara. We both know that.

He half carried Potapova into the hall, and in silence they put on their boots and coats. None of them said anything as they slipped out into the corridor. Kalyagin looked back just before the door closed. Tamara was smiling. If he hadn't known her better, he would have been convinced that she'd found something funny.

"Can you look after this for me?"

Kalyagin put the gun in Potapova's hand as the black Mercedes rolled down the hill onto the main road. He knew her strengths. There was a line of desperation in her. Cross it and she would do whatever had to be done.

She said nothing and they pulled away into the midmorning traffic, flanked by the trucks and buses transporting the patriotic citizens of Moscow to their legitimate destinations.

Abruptly Kalyagin pulled in front of a Zhiguli, turned left, and headed south to the river. A few cars honked angrily behind him. Why hadn't he thought of it before?

◆

Bitch, damn it. This bitch of all bitches. Perminev paced the hall, his boots clattering on the wood. If only it had been someone else, he'd have been able to kick them around, threaten them, even throw them into Petrovka. But not her—not Tamara Ryzhova. Not this one.

Perminev had taken a quick look at the file. Friend of the Brezhnevs, confidante of Gorbachev's wife, favorite of at least three other Politburo members who courted her favors but had so far failed to obtain them. Careful, go carefully with her. When this stinking affair is over there will still be Russia and you will have to live in it. Oh so careful.

"Would you come this way, Comrade?" She had approached him soundlessly. Perminev turned angrily to meet her.

"I've been expecting you." She raised her eyebrows and inclined her head. She was playing with him and he knew it.

They sat opposite each other. Perminev produced his notebook. Tamara saw that his collar was frayed and dirty. There was stubble on parts of his chin. This was a man who had slept little and badly.

"Comrade Ryzhova, I am to ask you certain questions and I would appreciate frank answers. We believe Dmitry Kalyagin was here this morning. Is that true?"

"True." She looked him straight in the eye.

"Was anyone with him?"

"A woman."

"What was her name?" Perminev's mouth tightened. Soon he would lose his temper.

"I don't know. We weren't introduced."

"Comrade Ryzhova, what precise information can you give me about this meeting?"

"Kalyagin rang, about ten o clock, brought his friend here for coffee. We chatted about old times and then he left."

"Where did he go?"

"He didn't tell me."

Perminev slammed his fist on the table, and then checked himself. He breathed deeply and laid his elbows on the table. He was inches from her.

"Perhaps I didn't make this clear, Comrade. My questions are part of a serious investigation that involves national security. I have the right to demand your cooperation. So enough of these one-word answers and evasions. You will tell me now exactly what passed between you this morning."

Tamara got up from the table, turned her back on him, and then walked around until she stood right behind his chair. It gave her the advantage she needed.

"Comrade Perminev, let me remind you of certain facts of life. I am Tamara Ryzhova, I am known to millions of citizens of the Soviet Union, I am an artiste of the Soviet Union, valued and entertained in the most important places in this country. You by contrast—" she paused for effect—"you are a grubby little agent of the security services who has no right to demand anything of me. I have given you all the information there is—now get out of here."

She moved to escort him to the door but Perminev remained seated. And his voice was so quiet she had to strain to hear it.

"You can throw me out this time, Comrade, and you can hide behind your powerful friends, and you can give your concerts and interviews to the Western press, and take flowers from your fans. But what will happen to you when you are old, and when you no longer sing, when the fans have forgotten you, and

your powerful friends are dead? Who will look after
Tamara Ryzhova during our long winters? Who will
hold her hand so that she doesn't fall on the ice? I
may not see you for some time, Comrade, but we will
meet again. Be certain of it."

He got up and walked past her into the hall. In the
silence she could hear her own breathing and the
thud of her heart in her temples.

◆

Mary Cross left her car on the street corner and
trudged toward the lights of the Yugoslav Embassy.
She considered it one of the supreme ironies that in
an atheist nation so many people took so much trouble to celebrate Christmas.

The Yugoslav party was one of the best and well
attended by the British community. For the Yugoslavs are often seen as the West's window on the East.
Communists, yes, but not men of Moscow. Mis-
guided, but still on the side of the angels.

Milo Lazarevic hijacked two glasses of champagne
as the tray floated past. He took Mary's hand, leading
her to a corner of the vast dining hall.

"You know there is one question Yugoslavs always
ask about Russians."

"And you're going to tell me."

"It is this. . . . What color would the river in Bel-
grade become if the Russian tanks invaded?"

"Tell me, Milo."

"Red, of course. But not with the blood of patriots.
It would be red from all the Party cards thrown into
the water."

He choked explosively over his champagne, spilling it on her arm.

"A thousand apologies, dear lady. You must excuse me. The end of a difficult year and the chance to let my hair down."

"You've done that once already, Milo." She raised an eyebrow and looked at him quizzically.

"Indeed." A sheepish look appeared. "I have not had the chance to apologize."

"Don't bother," she replied. "We both made a mistake."

But the sarcasm was lost and Lazarevic was grinning proudly. She could see all the gold teeth, gleaming inside the thin mouth like bars in a vault.

He was an odd sight at a Christmas party, she reflected. A bit like inviting a policeman to a murder. He was Montenegrin in origin. Fair but with tightly curled hair and a prominent cleft chin. She could imagine him tending sheep on a hillside, better still, stealing them in the valley. For he had the quick smile and the small furtive movements that belied his size. Six feet two, she decided, with clear blue eyes that held no emotion. This was not a bearer of gifts to children in stables. Milo Lazarevic would know nothing of the spirit of Christmas.

"Tell me"—he looked at her turquoise suit with admiration—"what are you doing for lunch?"

◆

It was after two when they arrived at the National Hotel—one of the few restaurants in Moscow that caters to spontaneous eaters.

And yet this meal was not spontaneous. Mary took in the cold *zakusky* already laid out—the cold meats and fish, the pickled vegetables, the potato salads piled high like lighthouses. This meal had been long in the making.

He waited until the plates had been cleared.

"You know I saw Sir David a few days ago."

"You mean our Sir David, the ambassador?" She was surprised and looked it.

"I don't know any others in this city. We had a brief chat."

"Indeed."

"How is he?"

"You tell me—you met him." She looked up disinterestedly.

"I don't know him well—but it struck me that he's changed. D'you know what I mean?"

She shook her head.

For a moment Lazarevic looked out the picture window, over toward Red Square. "He's nervous," he replied. "I haven't seen him like that before."

Mary Cross didn't return to the embassy until four. More important, she failed once again to submit the mandatory report on a meeting that involved non-NATO personnel.

And yet it probably wouldn't matter. After all, no invitation card had ever been sent, no phone call ever made. There was nothing to trace and no one to do it.

◆

For two hours George Parker had sat at his desk, barely moving. Not much to do now. It was the way that most operations arrived at their final phase. Quietly, no fanfare.

London had cut him off. Why? They had known the operation would end in a shambles. Maybe Dawling had finally let something slip. A changed fact, a new name, a smile. Show them a shadow on the wall and they would read it.

It must have happened back home. Arrogant old Dawling, spotlessly suited, former head of chancery in Moscow, present inmate of Parkhurst on the Isle of Wight, sometime diplomat, sometime spy, sometime traitor. He could have given them what they wanted —just for spite.

Too easy for London to inform Parker. Too easy to send out an alert and let the fox run into hiding. Solve two problems in one go. You lose an agent with his cover blown but you find a traitor. Somehow they would emerge together. Maybe smile at each other, perhaps even embrace. Or maybe just stab each other in the back the way it was meant to happen.

At any rate, leave it to Parker. Let him get his hands dirty and we'll keep ours clean. He got up angrily from the desk.

It wasn't going to happen by default. He wouldn't let it. He went over to the safe by the window. Old papers and coffee mugs were littered over the top of it. But inside were the station arms—three Smith & Wesson 9-mm semiautomatics sent out last year in the diplomatic pouch as replacements for the old

Brownings. Good pistols, a little on the bulky side. But each held nine rounds. Nine tries. Enough for occasional shooters.

He swung the door open and put his hand inside. A full half minute must have passed before he realized the package had gone.

◆

He didn't know if they had called his name or whether he had wakened by chance. But as Dawling rubbed his eyes and stared into the shadows, he could see the two men standing in the doorway of his cell.

"Get up, get dressed." It wasn't said unkindly.

"What's going on?"

They didn't answer.

He was barely awake, pulled into his overalls, a coat thrust over his shoulders and pushed through the corridors on a journey he had given up hope of ever making. The doors were being held open, *held open*, and then there was the wind and a light drizzle, a car with the engine running. Dawling glanced at the clock on the dashboard. Past midnight, and his first day out in three years. He sat back marveling at a view without bars.

◆

Five minutes later the car was exchanged for a helicopter, and then there were handcuffs. One man beside him, with his clean beige coat, the other in front with the driver. Beige again. Anonymous. The types, the colors, none of it ever changed.

And in a clearing, with the trees blowing hard and the moon covered by cloud, they ran with their heads down toward the police car, the rotor beating over them like the wings of a giant bird. To Dawling it seemed macabre, grotesque. Twenty minutes out of jail and he was in a different world.

They took the A3 north toward London, the four of them. Nothing was said. Dawling understood the pointlessness of questions. Besides, he told himself, I know you. I know the way you sit, the way you hold the steering wheel, the set of your eyes, the coolness, the practiced art. I learned it all in the same school. We're just the same, you and me. Except I took a turn, branched out. And who's to say I was wrong?

Oh my God, the road back into London, through the sprawl of Brixton, to Kennington, where he'd watched cricket, the Embankment now, the palace of Westminster. It's all there, just where I left it. And there's no traffic, not the way there used to be. Late, so late. Way past bedtime.

His pulse had quickened. And he knew why, didn't he? Passing Parliament Square, the Abbey, where he'd prayed every morning. As a child, as a student in that School for Spies. That's what the press had called it. Westminster School, with the pink football colors. And he wasn't the only spy to have passed through those sacred halls. Now was he?

No time to think back. And don't do it. It's not worth it. Don't think how it might have been different . . . long ago. Long ago. When you woke up listening to the chimes of Big Ben and truly believing the world ended in Victoria Street.

Hold those days before they fade, the summer

days, strolling home from the playing fields in Vincent Square, three pennyworth of chips in the newspaper. Muddy, wet, and the chips soggy with vinegar. Hold those days. Only he couldn't.

I don't know where we're headed, maybe a safe house, maybe a new house. But this isn't familiar. Up Kensington Church Street now. Why this way? Right at the top. And right again. And this is . . . it can't be . . . Embassy Row. The Soviet Chancery a little way down on the left, and the car was slowing to a halt. Christ almighty, what the hell are they doing?

The man on his right wound down the window and Dawling knew the face that peered in with the morning breeze.

"Morning, James, sorry to get you up so early."

Dawling looked at the man, incredulous.

"We thought we'd bring you here to pass a message, seeing as how you're so good at it." So innocent. So casual.

Dawling looked around. Dark. Bushes everywhere. And in the embassy, on the second floor, a single light. Over in the trees an owl or some other night bird.

His escort was getting out now, pulling him from the seat, extracting his keys, unlocking the handcuffs.

"You're on your own now, so get in there and do as you're told."

Quietly, Dawling turned to face him. "What is this?" he whispered. "What in God's name do you think you're doing?"

"Taking you to see your friends, old boy. Nothing

more, nothing less. Fact is"—the man leaned forward conspiratorially—"we're in a little spot of bother and we're ready to do a deal. You show yours, and we'll show ours, just like little boys and girls. You remember, James. Just the way it used to be played. And no one tells, do they?"

"S'posing I don't want to." The Dawling whine. "I mean, I don't know anyone in there, do I?"

"Don't give it another thought," the man said and smiled. "They know you, and they're looking forward to seeing you." He leaned against the car. "We'll wait here for you. Oh, and by the way . . ."

"What?"

"Don't be boring and try climbing out the lavatory. Can't be done. It's got bars on it." The man smiled. "Okay?"

◆

Dawling came out twenty minutes later. He was back home in his cell before dawn, before anyone knew he had gone.

◆

Harrison took the coffee cup and looked around for somewhere to put it. Out of the window he caught a glimpse of St. Paul's Cathedral, far down the river, deep in the city.

They had called and he had come, and now he'd find out why.

"We've offered the Russians a deal." It was the senior man who spoke. Harrison didn't know his name, but he'd seen the face. Thick jowls, bright red patches on the cheeks, bald but for two ginger mats around the ears.

"What deal? What do you mean?"

"We'll give them our man if they identify their's."

"I didn't even know we had one. Not after Dawling anyway."

"You didn't need to know." It was the sidekick who had chipped in. Much more suave, cocky. Charcoal-gray suit and the accent to go with it. Nose held high.

"So why the sacrifice now?" Harrison fixed the balding man with a stare.

"I thought I—" The younger man had begun speaking but he was cut off.

"That's enough, Nigel, let me do this. It's about time our friend knew a couple of things." He leaned back and studied Harrison through narrowed eyes.

"Fact is, we need to make a new start. The Dawling business damaged us beyond belief." He spread his hands and laid them on the desk. "It's still damaging us because it isn't over. Now we have to clean out the whole thing and rebuild from scratch." He pulled out a handkerchief and blew his nose, wiping carefully around the nostrils and the upper lip. Satisfied, he put the cloth back in his pocket.

"Look at it this way. All the old bets are off. The Russians are in a new era. There's movement, there's change, for the first time in decades people are starting to move up the ladder. That is fascinating. You follow me?" He paused and looked down at the desk. "Want to know something? We don't have anyone on that ladder. No one. Not a soul. Not an agent, not a

convert, not a sympathizer. No one. Oh, I expect the
Americans have a few. They always do. They pay
more. Maybe the Germans—they tend to offer the
world out of guilt. But we here, we haven't begun."
He peered in the direction of Harrison's coffee cup.
"Want some more?"

"No. I mean, no, thank you."

"We have a chance now to plant someone and let
him grow with the new order. Build a new network,
not for now, but for twenty years from now. But we
can't do it until the deadwood has been chopped
away."

"What are you saying?"

"I'm saying our embassy in Moscow is still contami-
nated. The dirt is in there somewhere. I want it out. I
don't care what we have to lose to get it."

"Even a high-level agent?"

"This high-level agent is blown anyway." The man
shook his head. "Besides, the new general secretary
will change them all around again in a year or two.
We want to start with someone lower down the scale.
In the end it'll be more valuable."

"So that's it?" Harrison looked up and his gaze took
in the two of them. He didn't like what he saw, what
he'd heard.

"Not quite." It was the younger man who spoke.
"We want you to go back and watch. After all, that's
been your job up till now. Make sure it all unravels,
make sure Parker's operation ends badly. Make sure
it all goes to hell and no one comes out of it." He

licked his lips. "Should happen by itself, the way things are going."

"Who's the traitor then?" Harrison stood up. "Who am I watching for?"

The older man answered. "That should become obvious pretty soon."

They didn't see him out, didn't help him with his bags, didn't drive him to the airport or wave good-bye. It served to remind Harrison that he was on his own.

◆

Winter creates its own hiding places, burying cars in snowdrifts, disguising the small wooden shacks outside the city, covering the firewood and bric-a-brac that litter the courtyards of Russian apartment buildings during the summer months.

Kalyagin looked at the inner suburbs for the first time, a lifetime of blinders removed. Of course they never brought the leadership out here—not without a couple of months warning, time to clean the area up, put a little more food in the shops, make sure no disgruntled, line-weary citizens started heckling or creating trouble.

He had known about it, just as they all did. But it had never been worth thinking about. After all, the Party knew what it was doing. The Party was the government. The Party was the people. Facts of life, like day and night.

It took half an hour to find. Neither of them spoke, but they both saw it at the same moment. The long, cylinder shape, covered over in a once-white tarpaulin. Probably an old Moskvich, he reckoned. Technology's sacrifice to the winter. A rotting lump, once loved passionately, now discarded.

Kalyagin stopped the car and looked around. Two women were steering a wheelchair into a neighboring street. He waited a moment and sprang out. Rapidly he untied the tarpaulin at both ends, then heaved it toward him, sending the piled snow and ice onto the road. Underneath, naked and unaccustomed to the sun, was a blue Moskvich, late fifties vintage, pitted with rust and not long for this Socialist world. Kalyagin folded the tarpaulin and slung it on the backseat of the Mercedes.

"Where now?" Potapova seemed to have thawed out a little. The catnap and the warm car had revived her.

"We must leave it somewhere near the embassy, where it won't stand out. They'll be looking for the car soon, probably started already."

Kalyagin found the spot in the maze of side streets beside the radio station, close to the Embankment. No one paid any attention as they covered up the Mercedes, hiding its license plates first, then pulling the tarpaulin across the roof. In the end it could have been anything, thought Potapova. Anyway, as long as it started the next day it didn't matter what it was. Just a means to an end, she decided. How true that sounded.

◆

They spent the afternoon at a movie house around the corner from Kalanchovskaya Street. Like many of the patrons, they watched it twice through, because it was cold outside and warm in the theater and their time no longer belonged to the state.

It was a rerun of an old favorite, *Moscow Doesn't Believe in Tears.* Both had seen it before. He, at a private showing for the regional committee in Tallinn. She, after lining up for two hours outside a Moscow theater six months after it had gone on general release.

This time, though, with their lives linked, they hunched close together out of warmth and fear. And when the second performance began Potapova threaded her arm through his and held it.

Hours later they made their way in darkness to the ring road and along to the main railway stations, joining the crowds and the traffic in the early rush hour. There would be no hotel to take them, no friend to accommodate them. Only the stations would give them shelter.

They had to stand for twenty minutes. And then a family vacated a space on the long bench seat and they dived in before others could snatch it. Again Potapova took his arm and this time there was an answering pressure. She looked up into the square face, topped with the thick fair hair, and for a moment the anxiety left her.

"Why did you never marry?" she asked after they had sat for an hour.

He looked at her and smiled. "How long have you been thinking up that question?"

"A year or two," she replied.

"Put simply, there was never time. But that's not really true. I had girlfriends, and when I was really busy I had girls. Some of them would have married me. You know the type that wants what goes with the job—the fur coats, the holidays, the cars—that sort of thing."

He yawned and rubbed his eyes with both hands. "I suppose I was looking for the other type. The girls who wanted Dmitry Kalyagin, Politburo or peasant." He shrugged. "But they didn't have much use for a man in the Party with his eyes on the Kremlin and his hands on his colleagues' throats."

"Is that the way it was?"

"Of course. What did you think?"

"That woman we met this morning—Ryzhova. Didn't you ever love her?"

"At one time very much."

"And . . . ?"

"And nothing. We would snatch an afternoon, maybe an evening every six months. She sent me flowers, I sent her flowers. That's not a basis for marriage."

He winced suddenly as a great bear of a man sat down beside him, black leather coat and fur hat. The fellow was as wide as a house.

Kalyagin turned back to Potapova. "Mind if I sleep for a little while? Long day tomorrow. Let's talk some more in the morning."

She watched his eyes close, the breathing steady, even as the night people of the station moved around him. At three, maybe four in the morning, someone called an ambulance. The sirens set off the fear again inside her. But for nothing. Two orderlies carried a stretcher and lifted a black bundle from a neighboring bench. Potapova couldn't see clearly, but the men weren't in a hurry. Not when they left. And she couldn't hear another siren.

A peasant woman with strange Russian and a colored scarf on her head jabbed Potapova in the ribs.

"Dead, they say. Old woman passed on in her sleep. Doesn't say much for the timetable, does it? Still, at least she doesn't have to wait any longer. Probably go the same way myself, I expect."

It's all here, thought Potapova. All Russia is here. Death, betrayal, and all the travelers' jokes the world has ever known. But what about hope? How much of that was there in the Kazan railway station as dawn broke over Moscow?

At 5:30 they reopened the self-service cafe and Kalyagin bought two glasses of tea. He sat down beside her, pulling up his coat collar. The night had left its chill behind and the day had brought a new one.

"I wanted to tell you . . ." He stopped for a moment. "No, I wanted to ask you so many things. You know—the background. Why you got involved, why I got involved. But this looks like the last day of our holiday." He smiled suddenly. "And now that we're this far, I don't think it matters anymore."

Chapter 20

DECEMBER 23

The old woman who swept the snow that morning at the Borovitsky Gate is lucky to be alive. For the car carrying the general secretary skidded wildly on a patch of ice under the arch and the front bumper scraped her right leg.

The Zil didn't stop because the bodyguards inside it have orders to stop for nothing. But the rear protection unit swerved to a halt and the driver inquired whether the shaken, yelping skeleton was hurt.

He was told sharply to mind his own business and get on with his work. If she could live through the German invasion, she told him, there was a chance she'd survive his driving.

It was the first unhappy encounter in the Kremlin that day. By ten o'clock there had been another.

The chairman of the KGB emerged into the courtyard outside the private apartments, his teeth chattering and his temper frayed. He hadn't enjoyed the
feel of the general secretary's forefinger in his solar
plexus, nor the accusations of incompetence, least of
all the fact that a classified signal from the embassy in
London had been hijacked by Kremlin security on its
way to his office. The bastards would pay for that
piece of treachery. They'd pay and go on paying.
He'd see to it personally.

The chairman climbed into his car. Like the others
in the courtyard, it had been left running. Overnight
the temperature had sunk to minus thirty, and if they
switched the engines off, they might never restart. As
the car passed through the Kremlin wall he caught
sight of a city still struggling to work.

Of course he hadn't been given a chance to speak.
He'd been told what to do like a schoolboy, told what
London had offered, told to respond. The British
wanted to end the game, lay down their cards, walk
away from the table. Maybe they were lying. Who
knew their motives? The general secretary had
paused for effect. Step up the search, he had ordered,
find Kalyagin and put an end to it our way. If that
fails, then go to the card table and deal. But keep a
card back, keep the ace in your pocket.

"But, Comrade . . ."

"But nothing . . ." The general secretary had insisted. "Take it or you leave here on foot."

The chairman clenched his fists. The worst of it all
was that Kremlin security would have been listening

to the whole thing. They'd have heard his humiliation, heard his protestations—heard them all and laughed. The chairman of the KGB transformed into a monkey before them. They'd all pay for that. In the meantime there were things to arrange.

He lifted the receiver on the radiotelephone and spoke rapidly into it.

◆

Perminev faced the desk. The general stood beside him. An unhappy couple, thought the chairman. Second-rate, nervous. He looked at them with distaste. Even on a cold day like this he could see they were sweating.

"Speak."

Perminev nodded. "It's clear now, Comrade Chairman, that the cleaning lady Potapova was an accomplice. She's missing too. There are signs that the boy Sasha Levin tried to warn her—some graffiti by her door. We don't think she ever saw it. The apartment is still being watched but she hasn't been back."

The chairman raised an eyebrow.

"How did Levin get to the apartment after leaving Petrovka?"

"Don't know. It's off the bus and metro route. Maybe he took a taxi, hitched a ride. . . ."

"What about traffic movements? Have you checked with the auto directorate?"

"Not yet." Perminev looked down at the floor. Damn, he should have thought of that. Often the traffic police jotted down car numbers at night, just to keep themselves awake.

The chairman got up and walked around to the other side of his desk. A gaunt figure, skeletal almost, his back curved like a question mark.

"You say the British have no leads?"

"Not yet. Parker goes around in circles. He knows he's followed, but he makes no attempt to break out."

The chairman took the general's arm and led him over to the window. He was perhaps a foot taller than the man and he bent low toward his ear, like a father confessor, intoning a blessing.

"Start mopping up." He said it so quietly. "Find the people who know about this, all of them, and clear up the mess."

"What if there are important people involved, you know what I mean, the *nomenklatura*?" The general turned his back to Perminev so he wouldn't hear.

"Makes no difference. The order is to mop up once and for all. Now get on with it."

Perminev watched them from the center of the room but he didn't see the general's thin smile or the quick nod of agreement from the chairman. He didn't know the shorthand of the forties and fifties and he wouldn't live long enough to learn it.

◆

George Parker gazed unlovingly at the head of embassy administration. More than ever he was convinced the man was an idiot.

"I don't care what you say to the doctor," he told

him, "but get him out of that place by five tonight. Him and his ghastly wife."

"I don't think I can do that. There's nothing in the rules that says he has to go." The administration officer looked down at his feet.

"Then make something up. Tell him there's a risk of high-level radiation and you have to investigate. There are plenty of empty flats because half the bloody embassy's gone home for Christmas." He glared over the table. Really, the man was being exceptionally obtuse and unhelpful. The administration officer got up to go.

"I'll see what I can do," he whined.

"You won't, you'll bloody well do it!"

Left alone, Parker reviewed the options. If Kalyagin made it unnoticed, the doctor's quarters would be ideal. They were inside the embassy grounds and reasonably private. Once he was there they could work on the details of an escape—probably forged passport, visa, hotel registration—maybe even some plastic surgery. There were always doctors coming in for medical conferences.

But if the Russian were spotted, they'd have no choice but to bring in the Foreign Office. The ambassador would open his own channels to the Soviets probably through the foreign minister, and who knew where that might lead? It would be messy and complicated.

Of course the continuing silence from London meant only one thing. London didn't believe he'd make it.

◆

Much of Moscow failed to reach work that morning
and most of it stayed away from school. In a handful
of outlying districts cars had been abandoned and
buses had broken down. Only essential services were
running and not all of them.

Even in the center the streets were largely deserted. A few dark figures slithered along the pave-
ments, keeping close to the walls. A skeleton contin-
gent of traffic policemen still braved the storm, each
with six layers of clothing, their bodies blanketed in
heavy sheepskin, scarves over their faces, boots half
an inch thick.

The free-lance was in his element, for the city was
his as never before. Everyone at home, everyone
where they should be. No surprises, no imponder-
ables.

He drove easily, skirting the snowdrifts, not hurrying, coaxing the four-wheel-drive Niva gently toward
the inner suburbs. The man had no need for bulky
clothes. They had equipped him with the lightest of
the Arctic insulation suits, tested near the North Pole
and on Everest. They never bothered with anything
but the best.

It was hard to see where the road ended and the
pavement began. He parked in a small courtyard
three blocks from the apartment building. A familiar
district, part business, part residential. For a man
who had worked for many years in Vietnam, it felt
good to be on home ground.

No one saw him take hold of the gutter, pull him-

self easily onto the first-floor ledge. Removing a glass
cutter from his tunic, he sliced four lines on the giant
frozen windowpane in front of him. With a sharp tap
to the bottom, it fell forward smoothly in an even
square into his gloved hand.

Taking the elevator to the sixth floor, he rang the
doorbell, half expecting to have to return later. But it
was Tamara Ryzhova who opened the door, her long
hair unkempt, her face clear of makeup, an ancient
dressing gown over her shoulders. Not a sight the
fans would have easily recognized, but to the free-
lance she was everything he wanted.

◆

Afterward Kalyagin didn't know why he'd done it.
Perhaps he had been searching for a final link to the
past. Maybe he just needed to be certain there was
no road back.

He had stood at the station wall, lifted the telephone, and listened for the long single tones. A number so easily remembered, so seldom used. A man
had answered, an elderly voice preceded by the
clearing of the throat. But he had recognized his
uncle's voice and the Estonian cadences that never
wore off.

A minute of hellos and then there was silence, as if
his uncle was awaiting inspiration.

"Where are you, Dmitry?"

"Here in the Soviet Union."

"Yes I know, but where . . . exactly? Maybe I
could come and get you."

And Kalyagin had put the phone down on the uncle, who didn't have a car and had never known how to drive. He tried to picture the man. There would probably be two of them with him. At least two. Numbers were important to apply pressure. Perhaps they had been waiting there for a couple of days, drinking the old man's coffee, eating his food, leafing through his books and papers to pass the time, and to remind him who they really were.

He lived near Sokolniki Park and rarely saw his nephew. Wary of the link to the Kremlin, the man had withdrawn into his veteran's apartment and tried to play it all down. Hard enough for a widower to find a friend, harder still if all the neighbors were scared of you. And they had been scared. Anxious not to play music too loud or hold too many parties—lest the old fellow complain to his nephew and bring the entire Soviet system down on their heads.

Now the two men would probably be shouting at him—accusing him of blowing the conversation on purpose. And maybe they wouldn't leave by themselves. Might they not take him with them, ignoring his cries, scuffing his shoes on the stone floor, dragging him across the corridor and out to the waiting Volga?

Kalyagin didn't know anymore, but he knew he would never find out.

He returned to Potapova.

"We have sixteen kopecks left."

"A fortune." She smiled. "Much healthier to walk."

He looked at his watch. "It's nearly two. The party begins at six-thirty. We should get going."

As they went out onto the street the sun broke through the snow clouds for an instant—a winter sun, already low in the sky, heading west.

◆

"There is a problem with your telephone."

"My telephone is working normally," she replied. But there was something in his eyes that made Tamara stand aside. And as he slid silently past her she took in the snowsuit and the absence of a tool bag, the light, careful stride of a professional.

He turned to face her and removed the woolen cap from his head. Below it a gray crew cut, a thin angular face, and a long nose that turned at the end. No marks, no expression. Tamara had never seen him before but she knew him.

"You're a few years too early, my friend."

"Is anyone else here?" he asked. So quiet, so calm.

She didn't want to tell him but the colorless eyes could see so well into her head. There was no point lying.

"My brother's boy—but he's asleep in the spare bedroom. Never hears anything."

Pause.

"Spare bedroom," he murmured to himself, for he hadn't seen many.

"Do you want to sit down?" he asked quietly.

"No, I'll stand."

"Better to sit," he urged. And she could see the hypodermic in his hand and the little black pocket case that had carried it.

"Wait," she told him. At least it seemed like her

voice. And then she felt a moment of extraordinary clarity. After years of confused thinking—such clear thought and such a bright light. She knew then that he hadn't waited after all, hadn't helped her, hadn't wanted to make it easier. And as she looked down at the thin steel spike in his hand, the hurt and the disappointment went with her.

◆

"They couldn't find her car." Perminev looked plaintively at the general.

"Who couldn't find it?"

"He couldn't."

"Odd. He seems to have managed everything else. . . ."

"He carried out his orders." Perminev's left eyelid began to twitch uncontrollably.

"I have no doubt. Anyway, we must assume that Kalyagin has the car. But why? It's a black Mercedes with Moscow plates and Ryzhova's own registration. Like driving around the city waving a flag. Everyone knows it's hers. What sort of use is that to him?"

"Maybe he'll use it only once."

"What do you mean?" The general sat upright in his chair.

"Let me check something." Perminev lifted the internal phone and put in a call to the Kremlin.

"His diary. I need to know what's in his diary for the next two days," he shouted. "Damn!"

He hung up. "They're checking. Kremlin security has already removed his possessions. Now we have to approach them formally."

"How long will that take?"

"Could be an hour or two. I'll get down there straightaway. Who knows? Kalyagin might have made some arrangement, hinted at something, anything."

The general didn't answer. He was staring out the window at the white rooftops. Perhaps the clouds were lifting. He couldn't be sure.

"Tell me," he asked quietly. "No problems at Ryzhova's apartment?"

"None. The nephew found her and called the ambulance. The doctors believe it was a heart attack."

The general shook his head. "Funny thing," he said. "My daughter likes her music. We've got some of the records at home. Nice cheerful tunes."

◆

The ambassador's secretary took the call with the kind of skeptical condescension that takes years to perfect. She belonged to the honored breed that types for no one but a head of mission, lies for no one but a head of mission, and is trained to erect an obstacle in anyone's path. All the same, the rudeness of the Soviet summons took even Judith Pilkington by surprise.

"I'll see if he's available," she told the caller.

"Do it."

She noted that the ambassador spent under twenty seconds on the call. Then he buzzed her, called for his car, and appeared, flushed and nervous, in the outer office.

"There's a flap on," he announced. "That was the

Second European Department at the Foreign Ministry. Apparently a Soviet diplomat in London has been seriously injured in a fight. Why doesn't London ever tell us anything?"

He hurried out the door before she could tell him, pulling his coat over his shoulders, the round fox hat clamped squarely on his head.

The two receptionists watched him on the television monitor as the wind whipped at his coat and the diminutive figure flung himself onto the backseat of the Rolls-Royce.

For a few minutes Judith Pilkington sat in her office contemplating Sir David's behavior. There was never very much she could do to help the poor lamb. God knows he was competent enough, although his wife wasn't much help. Bit provincial, at least for Miss Pilkington's taste. But it was just too bad if the Russians were giving him a hard time and London wasn't pulling its weight.

She looked hard at one of the two telephones with direct dial to London and then lifted the receiver. She was damned, *yes damned*, if she wasn't going to talk to a friend of hers in the Foreign Office and find out what all this nonsense was about.

And wouldn't Sir David be pleased with her? Wouldn't he commend her for using initiative?

She reached Mavis Bates just as the lady was on her way out to lunch. Mavis was a brick. Another head-of-mission secretary, filling in time on the Soviet desk before a posting to Sofia. Poor Mavis.

Never mind. She was so pleased and surprised to

hear from Judith Pilkington that she quite forgot about the open line. Of course she could rummage through all the day's files. It wouldn't take a moment. And it didn't. But try as she might Mavis Bates could find no evidence of a flap of any kind anywhere in Eastern Europe, and as far as she knew the entire staff of the Soviet Embassy in London were sound in body and limb. Irritatingly so.

All of which made Judith sit back in her chair and wonder what Sir David White was doing.

◆

Parker had no idea how it had arrived. The tiny parcel was gift wrapped in blue paper with bears running all over it. He picked it up off his desk and turned it upside down.

Inside, it all became clear. There were six little jars of Tiptree jam and marmalade and a Stilton in a jar. The handwriting on the torn-out diary page read, "With best wishes from Kevin Harrison. London is still standing."

Bugger! The man was back already. Now he'd have to go and thank him. And anyway, it was one of those last-minute, duty-free presents bought in the departure terminal. He lifted the wrapping paper and shook his head at the cavorting bears. Really, that said it all!

◆

It took the Moscow traffic police more than six hours to check their records. The computer had been down most of the morning with what they jokingly called "circuit amnesia." But by midafternoon the memory had been coaxed back to life. And the printout of the 206 cars logged on the night Sasha Levin had died, near the places he had visited, was on its way by messenger.

The records of the owners were cross-checked with Levin by a different, more reliable computer and at 4 P.M. the name of Marina Alexandrovna glared out from the screen. They ran the check again but there was no mistake. In fact, they considered, it all seemed to fit together rather well.

The free-lance was pleased too. All in all it had gone well so far. And he liked to prove himself. It was good to show the bosses that he still had a few tricks of his own, that experience still counted.

He was whistling happily to himself as he located the courtyard off Leninsky Prospekt and parked neatly among the array of Moskvitches and Zhigulis.

Marina's car was in the corner. He went up to it and touched the hood. Good, it was warm. She must have just gotten home.

The free-lance checked both ends of the courtyard but no one was approaching. Without any visible effort he slid underneath the car, a small metal object glinting in his hand. There was a jolt and he stood up and opened the hood. The work took him less than a minute, and being a tidy man, he kicked fresh snow under the car to cover the dark fluid.

Back on Leninsky, he headed north toward October Square and pulled into a side street four blocks down. From under the seat he took a portable radiotelephone. It communicated directly with KGB headquarters.

The free-lance requested connection with a Moscow number and settled back comfortably in the seat, the engine running, the heater at full blast.

"Hello, hello." He knew it was her. You developed a sense for these things. "Marina Alexandrovna?"

"Yes, this is she."

"You don't know me but I'm an old friend of Sasha Levin. We were at school together, haven't seen him for a little while. . . ."

"But Sasha has—"

"Look, I'm sorry to disturb you, but he told me to call if there was a problem. My little boy is badly ill, he's having convulsions. Only eight months old. High temperature. I can't get anyone to come."

"Where are you?" Marina had recovered her composure.

"Ulitsa Dimitrova 64, apartment 112, third entrance."

"I know it. It's not far from here. I'll come now."

The free-lance cut the transmission and edged the Niva forward a few inches. Now he could see a long stretch of Leninsky Prospekt as well as the building where the doctor lived. The position was perfect.

He didn't have long to wait and he knew immediately that Marina was in a hurry. The little orange car jerked out of the courtyard, snow flying from the front wheels, and onto the main road. She was in third gear before it had straightened out.

Easing off the hand brake, the free-lance snapped

shut the clasp of his seat harness. His eyes narrowed, measuring distance.

She was no more than thirty yards away when he revved out of the side road, turning directly into her path. Marina's foot hit the brake pedal but nothing happened, and there was barely time for her to register surprise. Her car smashed diagonally into the Niva and was flung upwards and sideways. No longer a car but a jagged metal slug, it slid a few feet on its side in the snow and stopped.

The free-lance got out and looked around. There was silence. The long street, normally bustling, was empty in both directions.

Quickly he strode over to the wrecked Zhiguli and looked inside. The front windshield had gone and the upturned vehicle was leaking gasoline onto the road. The engine had stalled but a wheel still spun soundlessly.

He didn't know if the doctor was clinically dead, and he couldn't have reached her to make certain. But if the crash hadn't killed her outright, the cold and the shock would finish it.

◆

It was a winter day of such high winds and chill factors that the residents of Moscow were to talk about it for months afterward. Many claimed they had seen it coming, others professed themselves totally perplexed by the sudden severity of it.

Those who reached work spent most of the day staring out office windows reminiscing about the cold days they had known as children, which led to talk

about the war, which led by and large to an entire
day of Socialist labor lost to the wind.

Kalyagin had stopped a black Volga only by racing
in front of it and tearing open the driver's door.

"Take us south to the Embankment," he yelled.

"Go to hell, bastard," screamed the driver. But
before he could slam his door Kalyagin had shouted
again.

"Twenty rubles if you do it. Twenty."

And without hesitating the fat, swarthy figure had
reached behind to unlock the passenger door.

He pushed Potapova in first, brushing the snow
from her hat. The driver was probably assigned to
one of the ministries, sent home early because of the
weather. Normally they cruised the streets looking
for easy money. But not today. Today was for survival.

The man ignored the traffic lights, for there was
now almost no one to enforce discipline on the
streets. At Traffic headquarters, on the Garden Ring,
the duty officers noted the violations, recorded by
static cameras at the main intersections. But many of
the devices had stopped working, and most no longer
responded to remote control.

In good weather the ride would have taken less
than fifteen minutes. In those conditions it was
nearer forty. The Volga crawled through the snow.
Once it stuck completely in a drift and Kalyagin had
to scramble out and push it free.

Of course he had no rubles to pay the driver, not a
single one. But most likely the man would just swear

at him. If it got nasty, he might have to threaten him. What the hell? It was the least of his worries.

They approached the radio station. "You can stop here, friend," he told the man.

"Give me the money," came the growl.

"I'm sorry. I've looked in my pockets. It must have fallen out. Take my watch instead."

The man turned himself awkwardly around.

"Don't want your stinking watch." He spat over the back of his seat onto the floor of the car. "You're going to pay what you owe me."

I'll have to hit him, thought Kalyagin. He could make trouble. But even as he prepared himself, the man's eyes widened in fear.

He turned sideways to see that Potapova had removed the gun from her bag and was pointing it at the seat, with the driver's stomach in direct line of fire.

"Animal," she hissed. "If there's another sound from you, you'll feel the wind in your fat belly. When we get out put your foot down and get out of the area as fast as possible. Otherwise there'll be trouble that you can't even imagine."

Kalyagin pulled her out and the wheels spun even before the door had slammed behind them. They watched the Volga skid down the street out of sight. In the stillness Kalyagin looked down at Potapova. I was right about you, he thought. You would use the gun if you had to. And you wouldn't think twice about it.

They walked the three blocks to the Mercedes in

silence. Several inches of snow had piled up on the tarpaulin. But as they shook it clear the black body of the car emerged sleek and clean into the evening light.

They loaded the cover into the trunk and climbed in. Kalyagin turned to Potapova.

"Let's see whether German cars are as good as they say."

He turned the key in the ignition.

◆

Judith Pilkington loved the party nights. The embassy would fill with all the beautiful and important people from the diplomatic world and she would peek out from her office into the hall with the teardrops in her eyes. That night was no exception.

"A long way from Epsom," she told herself, and gave the mauve dress a little squeeze.

But the worry wouldn't leave her. The ambassador still hadn't returned from his emergency meeting. Only half an hour before the guests arrived. Where was he? Lady White was in full flight, of course, dithering little woman, made up to the nines, buzzing to and fro telling everyone what to do. Miss Pilkington cringed in annoyance and took a step back into her office.

In the hall she could make out the slim build of George Parker. How nice that the head of chancery still followed tradition, welcoming the guests at the door while the rest of the embassy waited upstairs.

She liked Parker. A good-looking man, she decided. A little more class than some of the others.

And there was his wife. Lovely thing, really, but a bit on the frail side. Never joined in, never let her hair down. Come to think of it, not really one of the girls at all. Of course, Judith thought to herself, Mrs. Parker might feel herself a cut above all that. Married to head of chancery, fancy dinners every night, surrounded by maids and nannies. Gossip had it that the two of them hadn't been getting on so well lately since the boy's illness. Shame if it were true. On the other hand, it all added to the spice of things. She gave a little giggle. Perhaps she might even add George Parker's name to the list of available men. She'd be extra nice to him, she decided, and see what came of it.

◆

The city darkened around him as the messenger sped from the Kremlin to the security headquarters on Dzherzhinsky Square. His car was from the general secretary's own pool—a modified Volga fitted with bulletproof glass and light armor plating developed in West Germany. The engine had been taken from a Rover V-8 and nothing in Moscow could catch it.

Ten minutes after leaving the Central Committee the sealed package was in General Inozemtsev's hands.

Perminev watched him tear it open. The swine from the cabinet office had taken their time, running paperwork and protocol rings around them for most of the day, anything to prove superiority.

But it was there now—Kalyagin's black official di-

ary with the hammer and sickle in the bottom right-
hand corner.

"Let me see that." In his haste Perminev snatched
it from the general and leafed through the final
pages. Today is the twenty-third. December. He
pushed the book under the desk lamp.

"I don't believe it." He said it half to himself but
the general heard him.

Perminev knelt down beside the desk. "Kalyagin
must have made the entry before leaving his office."
He looked up and in that split second the general
could read his desperation—the lined forehead, the
dirty, frayed shirt collar, the dark circles around his
eyes. "It's a cocktail party," Perminev muttered.
"British Embassy six o'clock tonight. For the businessmen. . . . It's why he took the car!"

The general bit his lip until blood flowed from it in
a small stream. Angrily, he raised his forearm to wipe
it away.

"Get down there and stop him," he said. There was
silence for a second and he beckoned Perminev to
come closer. "If you fail, Comrade, I suggest you
begin running yourself."

The general pulled the telephone toward him and
dialed rapidly.

"Put me through, put me through." His finger
beat a rhythm on the desktop. "Hello. Yes, yes it is
It's all moving much faster. Too fast? I don't know
Anyway, the little bird has to get out. Now. It's vital
Make the arrangements and do it yourself."

◆

Mary Cross was in a hurry. On her bed were the three party dresses she owned and none of them were right. Too pink, too gaudy, too sexy—yes, far too sexy. That black thing with the bare back and the low front. They'd be groping her all evening and whispering, "Shouldn't this be worn the other way round, my dear?" She could just hear them.

Mary had just settled on the too-pink dress when the phone rang in the hall. The crackle and static were overpowering. But a million miles away, it seemed, there was the voice of a man.

"I can't hear you, you'll have to call back."

And then, as only Moscow telephones can do it, the line cleared for a second or two and the muffled voice fought through the interference.

"I want you to come over to the embassy for a little while. Something's come up. You might be interested."

Was it Milo? How silly! Who else would it be?

"Sorry, Milo. Can't be done. There's a thrash beginning at our place in about fifteen minutes and I'm going to be late as it is. Another time. Must dash . . ." She had been about to hang up when he said her name, not angrily, not shouted, but in a way that held her to the receiver waiting for his next words. A strong, insistent voice cutting through the electronic haze.

"I wouldn't ask you if it wasn't vital. You know that, Mary."

For a moment she didn't answer. But it was enough to tell him he'd won.

"I'll see you in twenty minutes, at the embassy."

Mary Cross left the party dresses where they were, reached into the wardrobe for her ski suit. Three zips later she was ready.

Halfway down the corridor she could hear her telephone ringing. She knew Milo was checking, making doubly sure. But she wasn't going back. It was done now. The decision had been made. She stepped into the elevator and felt quite calm.

◆

With a sprinkling of snow across its back, the dog stood quite still in the road as the headlights picked out its eyes. Half wolf, strong and arrogant. Potapova could see the two giant fangs in the open mouth.

Kalyagin brought the Mercedes to a halt just a foot in front of it. The dog stayed where it was, alert, the weight even on each paw.

Slowly the car inched forward but the animal refused to give way. Its head touched the hood and Kalyagin stopped again.

"Let's try something," he whispered, and leaned over to open the rear door. In an instant the dog had caught the movement, darted sideways, and sprung onto the backseat. A creature of the night—cold, wet, and black. Potapova shivered. Kalyagin looked at her and then back to the dog.

"I think we've found someone to help us," he said. The dog sat panting on the seat. Two minutes later they were rolling onto the Embankment.

On the left the tall square buildings, shuttered; on the right the river, frozen solid for more than a hundred miles. Supposing we stop, thought Kalyagin, turn around, run, head north into the Arctic. But it would always end this way. He knew that. They would always be there, ahead of them and behind.

The odds would get worse. It had to finish tonight.

"Open the windows," he ordered, and suddenly the wind was inside with them, the breath of Russia. Not long now.

Less than two hundred yards ahead was the embassy, a line of cars centered on it. Both main gates were open, two militiamen on each, but they were hurrying. No laborious checks, far too cold for them. Kalyagin's spirits leapt.

"They'll look for an invitation. That's if they haven't been warned in advance. I'll try a diversion with the dog. The moment you see an opening run for it and don't stop till you're in the building, whatever happens. They'll look after you then. For God's sake, don't use the gun."

She nodded.

Three cars ahead of them. Two. One. The militiaman was approaching on Kalyagin's side. Had he seen the registration? And then they heard the sirens closing on them, so near now, and the officer glanced up, bewildered.

The sudden noise must have frightened the dog, for it let out a loud wail and began barking. The guard leaned down to look in the car. Kalyagin saw a square face, blotched and reddened by the cold. "What the . . . ?" But the animal had lunged for the man's hand. Kalyagin heard a cry of pain. The dog wouldn't release him. His colleague was running around the front of the car to help and Potapova saw the gap. She flung open the door and began to run. Behind her a whistle blew but she ran on. And then a shot. Where was Kalyagin? She stopped and turned.

Twenty yards behind her he was half out of the car, slamming the door into the side of the second militia-man. But it wasn't hard enough. The big man caught his coat and tried to pull him back. There were shouts and suddenly she could hear the sound of boots running on hard snow.

"Quick," she yelled. "Dmitry!"

The officer had pulled Kalyagin to the ground but he had forgotten the dog. As she watched it released its first victim, jumped through the window, and leapt for the man's throat. His scream seemed to fill the courtyard. Kalyagin got to his knees, struggled to his feet.

But behind the car Potapova glimpsed the first of the soldiers. In an instant she took in the winter combat gear, the woolen hats. And he was running now as the first string of bullets tore into the snow beside him.

She stood on the steps willing him on. He was on the driveway now and the guests were scattering around him, some screaming. In the background she heard an order to cease fire. Ahead of her the embassy's main door had opened and a young man was beckoning her, both of them. They stumbled through into the strange, ornate hall and for a moment they looked around them, at the guests, the diplomats in their dark suits and elegant dresses, at the dark paintings on the walls—and there was silence. It was as if the entire building had frozen in shock.

◆

A soldier reversed the Mercedes out onto the street, past an armored car and three troop carriers. About twenty men took up positions just inside the main gate. Their faces were barely visible, just the slant of the eyes. These were men from the outposts in Central Asia, brought to Moscow by the KGB for local assignments. They didn't know the city, and therefore had no qualms or allegiances. They would do as they were told without scruples. They were violating British property and didn't care.

A handful of guests returned to their cars and drove off. Perminev conferred with the platoon commander. All around was the static hiss of field radios. No one heard the Rolls-Royce gliding slowly in behind them.

"What in heaven's name is going on?" Sir David White pulled himself out of the car and faced Perminev. In that instant he was aware that the squad behind him had come alert. The clatter of rifles placed in firing position has a distinctive sound and Sir David had heard it before.

Perminev turned angrily.

"It is we who should ask that question. Two criminals have forced their way into your embassy and appear to have been offered sanctuary. We have acted purely to protect the lives of innocent bystanders."

In the distance Sir David could hear a dog barking savagely.

Perminev closed the gap between them. "I ask you to order your staff to release these people into our custody. One of them is a former minister in our government."

"And I must ask you to withdraw your men. This is a flagrant violation—"

"Not before the criminals are handed over to us."

"I must protest in the strongest terms. I shall contact the Foreign Ministry immediately. . . ."

Perminev spat angrily on the ground. "Do what you have to do, Sir David. You know what that is. And let's waste no more time." He turned on his heel and strode over to the troops.

Beyond the fence the ambassador could see more heavy military trucks arriving. But even as he watched, a figure seemed to detach itself from the melee, beckoning him to the embassy gate. He took off his glasses and rubbed his eyes, but the man was in silhouette and he couldn't make him out.

The soldiers parted to let Sir David through, and as he reached the gate he gasped in surprise. For standing not three feet from him was his old friend Peter, from schooldays, from the university, as elegant as ever, fit, too, and with that thick head of gray hair just visible below the *shapka*.

"Good Lord, my friend, what are you doing here?"

The friend extended a gloved hand and pulled Sir David out into the street.

"My dear fellow, I was passing, saw the commotion, and thought I might be able to help."

Sir David felt himself being steered gently over the road and down the Embankment steps to the water's edge. Too cold, he kept thinking, we can't stay out long.

"Look here," said Peter reasonably, "anything I can do to help?"

"I'm not sure there is. . . . It's a complete mess. Some former government man has broken into the embassy and the authorities want him out. Look, I haven't even been inside myself yet. So I have no idea what's going on in there."

"I do understand. If I were you, I'd get back as quickly as possible, find out the lay of the land, and get this fellow back out again. Hand him over if necessary. In the circumstances I don't see how you can do anything else."

They climbed the steps and picked their way through the field trucks. A fresh platoon was arriving. Sir David could see the soldiers through the open flap of a troop carrier. Peter stopped at the embassy gate but the hand didn't let go.

"Don't mess it up, old chap." And the accent had hardened suddenly, the warmth gone. "Get the man out and quickly, otherwise you know what'll happen."

Sir David could feel his friend's eyes fixed on him as he made his way into the embassy.

◆

"*Iditye so mnoy*—Come with me." Parker had cleared a path through the astonished onlookers before anyone knew what was happening. He led them left down the corridor toward his office. Closing the door, he switched on the light and picked up the phone.

"Ask Farrar to get here as quickly as possible." And then he hung up, hardly daring to look across the desk. It was the moment he had planned for. Dreamed about. And now it seemed unreal.

They stood awkwardly, their clothes torn, Potapova still shivering. Parker took off his jacket and handed it to her.

"Here, I'm sorry, please sit down. I'm George Parker and I know who you are. Excuse me for a moment."

He reached for his pad and scribbled three lines, barely legible. His hand was shaking. God almighty, they made it. They made it!

Someone knocked at the door. Parker opened it Farrar stood there, uncertain, peering past him into the room.

"What's going on? I heard shots—"

Parker cut him off and thrust the message into his hand. "Send this top priority and wait for a return signal. Let me know immediately."

He turned back to face them. Kalyagin was bigger than he'd imagined. Younger, somehow. A full head of hair—a blond, almost Scandinavian look, with suntan ingrained from his youth. The woman? Har

to tell. Exhausted, bedraggled, clutching her handbag to her as if the world lay inside it. Ageless,
though. Like so many.

He cleared his throat nervously and coughed. "I
. . . I don't really know what to say to you—except
welcome—and thank God you made it. It's been such
a long journey, I mean, for both of you."

They were staring at him, faces drained of expression. They stood almost as though they had lost their
way in a storm and would, in a moment, continue
their journey. Kalyagin wiped his eyes. They were
moist. It's just the cold, thought Parker, coming inside after all that time.

"This isn't the place to talk," he told them. "Plenty
of opportunity later. But now we have to organize
things. The problem is that they know you're here, so
we're going to have to sort this out diplomatically."

They nodded without saying anything, but even as
he spoke Parker could sense their spirits falling. Kalyagin would know all about diplomatic methods, the
high risk of failure, the haggling over bodies. Parker
saw it in his eyes.

From outside the door he could hear Farrar calling
him.

"Come in," he said impatiently. "What is it?"

" 'Fraid it's bad news. I sent the signal but I don't
believe it got out, and I certainly don't believe London heard it."

"Why not?"

"We're jammed, old son. They've stuck up a whop-

ping great transmitter outside in the street. You can
see it a mile off. And at the moment it's aiming about
fifty thousand watts of junk in our direction. We can't
even pick up the local radio." He shook his head.
"Sorry, nothing I can do about it." He turned to go
but changed his mind. "Oh, another thing. They're
all over the place, these special troops they've got.
Outside in the grounds, round the back, everywhere.
Hope you've got something up your sleeve. Everyone's jolly frightened, you know."

Parker reached for the phone, listened, then threw
the receiver onto the desk. Quite useless. The line
had been cut.

Kalyagin was looking at him.

"They've begun," Kalyagin said softly. "The first
stage of pressure. They'll go on till they get what they
want. That's the way it is." Of course, he reflected,
they would follow all the old procedures, the prece-
dents, just as they always did. He could have written
the script for them. And that was its strength and its
weakness—that sluggish but inexorable machine of
Soviet government.

Hadn't he helped build it, shaped it into a blunt
instrument to be wielded over one sixth of the world
and anything else they could get? Didn't it always
remember those who served it and those who didn't?

Shots broke his thoughts, shattering the peace of
the city, echoing out over the river and the golden
cupolas of the Kremlin.

♦

The Yugoslav Embassy has one of the smartest addresses in town, Ulitsa Mosfilmovskaya, the kind of name that foreigners take a run at and trip on.

Mary Cross drove there quickly, in low gear to keep the car from slipping. But even the snow tires were useless. More than five inches of snow had fallen in the last hour. She knew she should have had chains.

There were no lights on the ground floor but the door was opened rapidly by a man in a pullover and slacks. She recognized him as one of the drivers who worked for Lazarevic.

"The embassy is closed," he said in poor Russian.

"I know. I'm expected."

"Your name?"

She sat in an anteroom off the main hall as the man spoke quietly into the telephone. Eastern Europe, she murmured to herself. Always a game. They knew her and she knew them. But they still had to play it.

"Please to wait," the man told her.

"Wait? How long? I'm in a hurry. Please tell Mr. Lazarevic."

The man raised his hand like a policeman stopping a car.

"Yes, yes, he know that. He say not to worry. He come down in moment."

She sat back uncomfortably and reached for a pile of newspapers. They were all Yugoslav and her anger mounted by the minute.

◆

The soldiers had shot out the two closed-circuit cameras, the first over the main door, the other along the side road. Parker peered out the window, surveying the damage.

"What is all this, Mr. Parker?"

He turned to find Jenkins, the night security guard, standing nervously, wringing his hands.

"I mean they've got a bit of a nerve, them Bolshies, haven't they?"

Parker smiled. "You're quite right," he told him. "Don't worry, it's not as bad as it looks."

"No, of course not, sir. Good thing the ambassador's back."

Alone in Parker's office, Kalyagin looked at Potapova, not daring to speak, immovable. It was she who broke the silence.

"Have you nothing to say, Dmitry? Such a long journey and nothing to say?"

He shook his head.

"I try to plan, but I see no routes ahead, no possibilities. I . . . I . . . ."

"There are no committees this time, my dear. No one to debate or convince. Just you and me," she whispered. "Which of us will decide?"

He reached out a hand and touched her. "I wondered how we'd feel when we got here. Like conquerors? Thieves? But it isn't like that." He looked around the room at the pale watercolors, the child's sketch of a black cat. "This isn't what we came for. Not this. Zina, I believe we've lost something. . . ."

He stopped suddenly and sat back in the armchair.

No way to explain. Outside was Russia, hostile and threatening but dominant, magnetic. Here, all around him, were foreigners, people he had never met, speaking a strange language.

Did I do it all for you? The quiet unspoken question.

"You know, the first race I ever ran at school—my brother, he was with me, way out in front, ahead of everyone. The boy could run like a horse. But suddenly, ten meters from the end, he stopped, turned around, and waited for me. And everyone ran past him, and he lost the prize, but it didn't matter. He suddenly realized that whatever was waiting for him at the finish line wasn't important. The race wasn't worth it. He found something more valuable along the way. Tonight, maybe, I know what he meant."

Potapova pulled the coat around her but she wasn't cold. She knew what she was hearing. The speech of a man who was winding down, closing the shutters, getting ready for the night. A man who had no intention of seeing the morning.

◆

Parker had reached the door but he never opened it. For a hand caught his arm with unexpected force and flung him around into the half-lit corridor.

For a moment Parker stood still in shock. The ambassador took a step back. His breathing was irregular, nervous.

"What's going on?" he demanded.

Parker's own voice came back to him, a hoarse whisper that he barely recognized.

"I don't believe this." He put out a hand to straighten his jacket. "You grab at me in a hallway and ask what I'm doing. Have you no idea what's happening here? One of the best agents we've ever had in Moscow has made a run for it. He's here now. In my office. The man is cold, frightened, and needs our help very badly. Something I'm sure even you could realize. And you ask what I'm doing?"

"I'm sorry." The ambassador shrugged his shoulders. "I'm just a little exercised by the presence of half the Soviet Army inside our grounds. You must see that surely. Look out the window! Look at them!"

"I think we can come up with something if we take this calmly, step by step. . . ."

Sir David looked at him sharply. "I'm sorry, I don't see what you mean. Are you suggesting that we try to keep the man here? Because if you are, that's out of the question. He goes back immediately and that's an end of it. Of course we shall try to ensure that he's properly treated. I'll make representations to the Foreign Ministry, but he can't stay here. That's government policy."

In the dim corridor Parker looked at the man with contempt. "I don't give a damn for government policy. This is a man who's risked twenty years for us, who's given us some of the best intelligence we've ever had, and you want to blow him away because it's a matter of policy." He turned toward the door. "Get out of here, Sir David, get out and tell the Russians he's not coming. Not tonight. Not any night." Parker stepped into his room and locked the door behind him.

◆

On the first floor the embassy staff had crowded to the windows, but there was little they could make out. For the troops had trained arc lights on the building, dazzling them, making it impossible to see the deployments below.

They had no idea that the ambassador had gone outside again, no idea that he was looking for a friend.

Perminev came out from behind a truck. He carried a megaphone.

"I trust you have settled this matter, Sir David."

"It's not that simple. Look, I want to see a friend of mine who was here a moment ago . . . you know . . ."

"I know who you mean, but he has had to go somewhere. He asked me to assist you in any way I could."

"I . . . I'm sorry, I need to talk to him. There are some things . . ."

"Perhaps you do not appreciate the urgency of this, Sir David, perhaps you think we are playing a game." Perminev's voice rose angrily, and his hand reached for the ambassador's lapel. He thought better of it.

"What, precisely, is the problem?"

"He's in a room with one of my staff. He will need to be persuaded. I must have more time."

"There is no more time. We cannot have half of Moscow treated to this kind of theater throughout the night. It must be finished and now. I ask you a final time. Will you deliver this man or not?"

"I must ask to see . . ."

"Very well, Sir David, we will do as you ask. I'm sorry you feel it necessary . . . but never mind." He turned around and three feet behind him stood a man the ambassador had not seen before. Not a soldier, not even a civilian. A man in battle fatigues, a loose khaki jacket over his shoulders. He didn't seem to notice the cold.

"This man will take you to your friend, Sir David, and let's dispose of this matter rapidly."

The free-lance bowed slightly and beckoned the ambassador to follow him. He walked briskly, skirting the embassy building, turning right into the shadowy side road. As he did so he removed the Colt pistol from his jacket, screwing the silencer to the barrel. He'd done it so many times he had no need to look. Sir David, of course, could see nothing but the man's back, so that when he turned, halfway down the road, and shot him in the middle of the forehead there was no time to cry out, no time to run. He died just a few yards from the doctor's clinic, although there was nothing the man could have done to help him.

◆

"We've a little bit of confusion." Parker stood in front of them, wringing his hands, trying to smile. Neither of them reacted.

"What we're going to try to do is get a message ou

to the American Embassy, make sure they know what's going on . . . and get some assistance."

"You can't win. . . ." Kalyagin barely opened his mouth.

"And then we should be able to force them off . . ." Parker caught himself suddenly. "I'm sorry, what did you say?"

"I said you can't win."

For a moment they looked at each other without speaking. Parker opened his mouth but the words wouldn't come. He turned back to the desk, turned away from them, didn't want them to see the hopelessness, didn't want them to read his eyes.

"There is nothing more you can do, dear sir." Kalyagin got up and walked to the window. "Please understand. I know how they work. It is . . . my way as well. They cannot just give up and go home, pretend it was all a mistake, send the soldiers back to barracks, and have a good laugh in the Kremlin." He laughed himself. "Really, it is not their way."

He turned back to the room. Parker took in the tattered overcoat, the shirt covered in filth, the two days of beard. A man who no longer had anything to hide. Twenty years in the underworld, twenty years of deception and power and fear. And now he stood in the little room with nothing to show for it.

Potapova took his hand and he sat down again beside her.

"You know I will tell you, just a little, and then we will do whatever we must. But I have tried to look back, tried to search for my reasons, for why we have come to this point." The voice was slowing, pausing for emphasis. Kalyagin wanted this to be remembered.

He smiled. "You tricked me. . . . No, no, it's true, all those years ago in Tallinn, I was burned by your network, your people. And I hated you for that. You wanted me, and you took me, the only way you knew how. It was a ruthless and cynical act." He shook his head, as if to confirm the gravity of the charge. "But you know as the years went by I began to admire your methods, your secrecy, your organization. I have to say, I never thought much about Britain, I never really thought about the evil of communism or the good of the West, or any of those things. I gave you information because . . . because it amused me." He looked hard at Parker, assessing his reaction.

"That surprises you?"

"Yes, I suppose I never really imagined . . ."

"Of course you didn't. You were a boy playing with sand castles. Besides, let me tell you a secret. The workings of your intelligence apparatus are exactly the same as ours. Don't think of the agent as a human being, don't imagine he has feelings, don't imagine he lives for anything except to serve your cause. For that is all that matters. Take the part of his life that interests you and shut out the rest. Isn't that right?"

Parker shrugged. "It's not far wrong."

"Good. Then at least we understand each other." He paused and wiped his mouth on his sleeve. "I tell you these things not because I regret them—how could I?—I did the job, knowing the conditions. In fact, in a strange way it seemed as though you were working for me. I supplied the information, you were forced to transmit it and analyze it. If I stopped, then you were without work. I began to control you." He sighed and smiled at Parker. "My friend, none of this matters much, a little diversion, a little case history, perhaps you will pass it on to your successor. Maybe I'll even become a name in a training exercise." He gestured with his hand, the reflex of a man once used to power, once used to obedience.

It was then that Parker heard the voice through the megaphone. And in the same moment all three of them looked to the window. George Parker, it called, come outside, George Parker, there is much to discuss and little time to do it. I demand your presence, George Parker.

He got up to leave but they didn't look at him. "I'll be back in a moment," he mumbled but they didn't respond. As he shut the door on them they were looking at each other and the message passed silently between them. Each, individually, had known it. Now the eyes had spoken.

◆

"You can't go out, sir, not like that, without a coat." It was Jenkins tugging at his arm.

A couple of them were there by the reception desk, crouching in the darkness. Parker recognized the man from Administration, the embassy doctor, one of the secretaries. Someone brought him a sheepskin coat and hat.

"Anyone seen the ambassador?"

"He must have gone out there half an hour ago. He's not back yet." Jenkins again. Christ, did no one else have a tongue in his head?

"Okay," he told them, "let's see what this is about."

Across the little driveway, down the few steps, straight to the middle of the grounds, and the soldiers had their rifles on him. No commands, no orders. Must have been given already.

Parker didn't know the man's name. It was enough that he carried the megaphone.

"Mr. Parker?"

"Yes, who are you?"

"I am in command here." The man's gaze took in the entire embassy.

"Where's the ambassador, Sir David White? I demand that you release him."

"He is not a prisoner, Mr. Parker. But let us not waste time on him. Sir David was not your man, he was ours, and we have terminated his employment. I don't think you can be surprised."

"You what?" Parker stammered. "My God."

But the man was no longer looking at him. His eyes had shifted to the embassy, and as Parker turned around he could see why. The door was opening and two figures were out on the driveway.

"Kalyagin," he yelled, "get back."

In the darkness it was unclear, but he could see the figure of Potapova behind, and there was something in her hand.

He remembered the single shot because it hung

there on its own, maybe for a second, maybe less, but then the soldiers must have been ordered to fire for the bullets began strafing the steps and the driveway. And in that moment he could no longer see Kalyagin or the woman, turning as he did, shutting his eyes against the noise and the killing.

The firing can have lasted no more than five seconds. And in the sudden stillness that followed he ran onto the steps. Kalyagin was lying on his back, an arm across his chest, his body motionless, Potapova facedown beside him.

A Russian in plainclothes bent down and examined the faces. Then he stood up and walked away toward the soldiers, still kneeling, still in firing position. Parker shouted at him but he took no notice.

It was Harrison who emerged to take his arm, pulling him gently into the embassy, muttering platitudes, shutting the main door behind him, closing out the city, leaving it to the quick and the dead.

It was Harrison who had watched the couple leave Parker's office, Harrison who had lighted the way to the door, opened it for them, noted their silent determination, released them into the night.

I've done well, he told himself bitterly. A watcher in the trenches, lying down till the war's over, coming out just to count the bodies and plant a cross.

Around the back of the embassy a dog began to bark—Kalyagin's dog—pounding the snow with its front paws, teeth bared with all the pent-up hatred for its lifetime of cruelty and mistreatment.

Dawn came before the noise died away.

◆

Mary Cross waited an hour at the Yugoslav Embassy before the thought came to her. She approached the driver who had let her in.

"He's not here, is he? I demand that you tell me."

"Please?" The man took a step backward.

"Where the hell is he?"

"Sorry . . . I know nothing."

That part, she reflected, was probably true. Lazarevic wasn't in the embassy, probably hadn't been there all day. The phone call could have been made anywhere. She clumped noisily to the front door and slammed it behind her. She was damned if he'd get away with that.

The Saab nosed its way through the ice tracks but the going was hard. The snowplows hadn't reached the Lenin Hills that night, and Mary cursed herself for taking that route instead of doubling back to the ring road, which was always cleared first.

Every time she skidded it seemed as if Moscow was trying to hold her back, divert her, delay her. Everywhere you looked a city of obstacles.

It took Mary almost half an hour to reach the compound on Dmitrovskoye Avenue. Entry was by a side road that curved away from the highway, slinking behind the long line of apartment buildings, each indistinguishable from the other. For a moment she lost her bearings. But ahead of her was the moon. And she turned into the parking lot behind the build ing, past the wire fence, past the guard, right up to the swings in the playground, half buried under the snow. She switched off the engine, leaned back, and shut her eyes. In this climate each completed journey was a triumph. Even to this place. Foreigners' Moscow. To Russians—the forbidden city.

She could see the light on the third floor and she knew Lazarevic was home. Really knew. Because it was clear the bastard had tricked her. A ruse to get her back to his apartment. A game. Nothing more. By God, she'd give *him* a game!

◆

Milo Lazarevic wasn't feigning sleep when he came to the door and he wasn't pleased at the banging. Nor were his neighbors, two of whom put their heads out of the window and yelled for silence in different languages.

Lazarevic was wearing his oldest pair of striped pajamas and a dressing gown with a string cord. So he clearly hadn't intended greeting visitors. Furthermore, he had an appalling headache and her shouting had made it worse.

She stopped suddenly and a look of realization came across her face. She put a hand on his shoulder.

"I'm sorry, Milo. Forgive me. We've both been mad."

Mary Cross was back in her apartment just over two hours after she had left it. Far too late to go to the embassy party. For a long time she sat on her bed wondering who had called her and why.

Seven hours later she had figured it out.

Chapter 21

DECEMBER 24

The first calls reached Parker at three in the morning. And then they kept coming. The newspapers, the radiomen, the TV. Please, George, give us a line, give us a quote. Had a spot of bother, haven't you? London wants to make it the lead. New York wants you live. No need to comb your hair, George. You look great like that.

And he'd learned his lines, hadn't he? The lines worked out with Perminev and cleared with London. The Russian had followed him back into the embassy, insisted on talking to him, setting the record straight, so there'd be no misunderstanding. And after an hour there hadn't been room for any. The body of Sir David White lay in a plastic bag beside the commissary freezer.

By dawn the jamming had ceased and London had told him to go ahead.

Only the first line was true. It had all been a terrible shock, he said, and it still was. Two drug traffickers from Central Asia had forced their way into the embassy shortly before the start of a cocktail party. Parker pursed his lips. With great regret, he said, I have to announce the death of Her Majesty's ambassador during a shoot-out with the intruders. Of course there had been nothing for it but to call in Soviet troops to restore order. During a brief siege the criminals had been shot dead.

Parker was authorized to offer his thanks to the Soviet government for its prompt action. Perminev had insisted on that.

Off the record Parker was prepared to tell the most trusted of the British journalists that nearly a quarter of a million pounds worth of heroin had been discovered in the drug pushers' car. That convinced the doubters and the story was sold.

The three wise men arrived that same afternoon on a connecting flight from Helsinki. Three investigators from MI6, aboard the last Western plane to reach Moscow before Christmas. The nickname was irresistible.

They wore jovial faces and brought brightly colored packages into the dark city. One of them had just had time to grab some mince pies and shortbread from the airport shop in London. Another brought a Santa Claus outfit. The third, a forensic scientist, carried chocolates for the embassy children.

Mary Cross, herself in shock, picked the men up,
cleared them through the airport's diplomatic chan-
nel, and settled them into their apartment. She returned to the embassy to comfort Sir David's wife.

Chapter 22

DECEMBER 25

As an act of collective catharsis they all attended morning service in the embassy. But their minds were elsewhere as the traveling Anglican priest with the largest parish in the world—from Finland to Vladivostok—attempted to bring them the Christmas message.

And then it all began.

◆

"Sorry, old boy."

"Sorry for what?"

George Parker looked at the bald man in the center with open hostility. They were crammed into the tight little cage with the trestle table and the green baize cloth.

"I'm sorry we couldn't tell you anything, sorry we had to cut you out."

Parker put his head in his hands and began to speak. He went on for nearly twenty minutes. At times he had to search for words. Once or twice he stumbled, his speech slurring, a glazed look across his eyes.

He told them about the loyalty of Sasha and Anatol, the motives of Kalyagin, the steely look of Zina Potapova's eyes; about an operation twenty years old that had first succeeded and finally failed; about an ambassador who had betrayed an elderly Russian Jew, a former agent. Former and dead.

As he spoke, they looked at him politely. But the hard information they knew already. The rest—they didn't want to know. The clutter, the background—it no longer had relevance.

Parker read their mood. They had come to sift and search, to disconnect the network once again and attempt to rebuild it. And there wouldn't be a place for George Parker because he had been the chief when it all went down the drain. He carried the mark of the beast.

"I think I should tell you I intend resigning from the service."

"I'm sorry to hear that," said the bald man. "You did a very nice job."

Flannel. English flannel. The compliment that masked the slur. The warm handshake with the cyanide pill in the palm, facedown. They never meant what they said, never did what they seemed to do. Just words. Parker went back to his office and wrote the letter.

◆

That night, long after everyone else had gone home, when the ambassador's wife had stopped crying, when the snow clearers had finished and Moscow sat peaceful, they ushered Harrison into the cage and quietly shut the door.

"Well?" they asked.

"Well, that's about it," he replied. "I watched old George and he did his best. Sir David was a surprise, though, I must say."

"Not to us."

"Why? What put you onto him?"

"Something Dawling said in his sleep." The oldest of the wise men took off his glasses, rubbed his eyes, and replaced the glasses.

"You mean you listen while he's asleep?"

"Of course. His type never gives up and neither can you. Sometimes it takes years, but they talk in the end. To us or to themselves. Funny, really. We played back the tapes and almost missed it. He doesn't know he gave it away."

"And now?" Harrison looked around at the three faces.

"You say it's over."

"Don't you agree?"

The oldest of the wise men stood up and patted Harrison on the back.

"You've done well," he told him. "Time to sleep."

Harrison stayed where he was.

"Come on," said the older man. "I think it's better this way. I really do."

Harrison gripped his arm. "What d'you mean 'better this way'?"

The man sighed. "Kalyagin was too hot. You must have known that. Did too well, got far too high up the ladder. He was about to be a major embarrassment." He shrugged. "Besides, we can't just take one of their top men. It broke the rules. They could have declared war over it—anything. It would have meant open season—like stealing Lenin from the mausoleum. Pie in the sky." He looked pityingly at Harrison. "Anyway, he was blown already." His forefinger shot out toward Harrison. "As I said," he added unpleasantly, "time to sleep."

They left the cage and in the darkness Harrison leaned against the wall to steady himself. He could just make them out, shuffling down the main stairs, one of them in carpet slippers. The three wise men, taking their wisdom with them.

◆

For some reason none of them were tired that night so they agreed to take a short walk in the embassy grounds. Just five or ten minutes. Time to freshen up. The business was almost complete. The main figures debriefed, the body of the ambassador examined by the forensic scientist, the Russian bullet located but not removed from his head.

Tomorrow they would interview Mary Cross, although that wouldn't take long. She hadn't been in the embassy at the crucial moment, and anyway she had belonged to the service for years. A good all-rounder, declared the bald man. Ideal for the new operation.

"Maybe we should clear her out as well," said the forensic scientist.

"So who do we have then to oversee the new network? We must have someone with experience."

"I still think we should clear the lot out."

"Oh don't be a bore, Gerald. You'll want to tear up the floorboards next."

At his desk in his private apartment the general secretary listened with mounting interest, stopped the tape, and then replayed the section for the third time.

It was a recording of a conversation between the chairman of the KGB and his senior general, made without their knowledge and hand-carried to the Kremlin an hour after it had taken place.

"Of course," the chairman was heard to say, "we now have a major gap in our British operation."

"A gap certainly, but not a major one." There was the noise of paper being shuffled.

"Explain."

"Well, we have plans to plug that gap before long." A pause. "If things go well for us."

"So you still have cards to play?" The chairman sounded animated.

"I'm thinking of one card, a new one. A queen, if you like, and every expectation that it will remain in he pack."

The general secretary switched off the tape. It was the first time he had smiled in a week.

◆

After two hours sleep Perminev was called to the general's office and ordered to take a week's leave. He was told he had acquitted himself well in the final analysis but too many mistakes had been made. His future would be discussed when he returned.

He picked up the free-lance, intending to drive the man home, and took the main Leningrad highway out of the city.

The two men hardly spoke to each other.

It's a bad time to travel. The roads are treacherous and so are the heavy trucks. Often the drivers are drunk, warding off the cold in their unheated cabins with vodka. They frequently cross the central boundary out of control and there are many fatal accidents.

Perminev's body was found halfway through the windshield. The car lay in a ditch facing the wrong way. The militia assumed he had been tired, fallen asleep over the wheel, and allowed the vehicle to stray over the road and take him to hell.

Such things had happened before.

They left the car where it was. In that weather there was nothing and nobody to shift it. Anyway, this was just another figure in the annual body count.

Chapter 23

DECEMBER 26

"Got it all now, haven't you?" Dawling spat at the man across the table. The prison guard watched impassively from a corner. "Well, it took you long enough, didn't it? Bunch of stupid queens pottering about as if you were on a Sunday drive."

"Pity you won't be going on one." Stuart smiled pleasantly.

Dawling stood up. "Don't draw any comfort from that, sunshine. What d'you think they've got waiting for you? Bloody great medal and a thank-you glass of sherry at Christmas? You'll be lucky. If you mess up, you could end the whole thing here, just like me. If you make it, they'll squirrel you away somewhere with five quid for a pension and luncheon vouchers. Idiot. Can't you see it?"

Chapter 24

DECEMBER 30

George Parker, Suzy Parker, and Steven Parker sat in the cafeteria at Sheremyetyevo airport. The London flight had been delayed an hour. Moscow's final gift to them—and they didn't want it. Steven had gone three times to the lavatory and they had prowled morosely through the souvenir shop. Suzy had bought a pair of hand-painted salad spoons.

"I just wanted to take something away with us." She looked embarrassed.

"I'd have thought we're taking away quite enough as it is." Parker frowned. "And you can throw that away for a start." He gestured to the tiny bunch of lilies that Judith Pilkington had thrust into Suzy's hands as they left the embassy that morning. "Anyway, they're half dead already."

She tried to smile. "Come on, George. Why don't we let them poison us one last time?"

They bought two coffees and a fruit juice with the last of their Russian coins.

"This tastes funny," Steven declared to the room at large, and spilled the remains of the juice on his trousers. Parker got up to buy him another. No one was serving. The waitress had given up.

"Nice-looking child."

The voice came from behind him and he turned around suddenly. Leaning against the bar was a man in his early sixties with thick gray hair, dark suit, fawn overcoat. Ex-guardsman, he assumed.

"Thank you. He's a good boy." Parker ordered the drink. "I said juice." He had to shout to get the cashier's attention.

The man nodded sympathetically. "Damn difficult to get served," he said. "Such a trying place in many ways."

Parker took the glass. "You on the London flight?"

The man looked startled. "Er . . . no. I mean not this one. Not today."

"Oh, I see. Been here long?"

"A little while, and you?"

Parker shrugged his shoulders. "We're just leaving, actually. I was with the embassy, but the tour's come to an end now."

"That's a coincidence. I had a chum who used to be there."

"What was his name?"

"He was the ambassador, Sir David—"

"I know who he was," Parker cut in. And then he saw something in the man's eyes, something he hadn't seen before. Sadness, maybe guilt. A newspaper picture—a headline so long ago. In that moment a cold shiver passed down his spine and he knew.

The pleasant facade of the man had gone, the smile with it. "It may sound strange to you, but I'm sorry it happened. Just for the record. I liked him, I really did. We went to the same school."

"You bastard—"

"Daddy, where's my drink?" Steven was shouting, and Parker turned for a moment, distracted by the shrill noise. Damn! Blast! Angrily he turned back to question the man again. But he wasn't there, wasn't on the stairs or the balustrade. Parker ran to the rail and looked down into the departure lounge. Nothing, not a trace. It was as if the man had never existed.

◆

The flight from Murmansk was noisy and crowded. Groups of sailors were heading home to Moscow for the New Year. Young men, cheerful, agile, and increasingly drunk.

By contrast, the last person to leave the plane did so quietly and in apparent pain. She was swathed in scarves, her skin the color and consistency of wax. A stewardess remarked that she didn't appear to have seen the sun for a long time. And she hadn't.

Lena Nikolayeva, daughter of Ira, friend of Sasha, was met by a member of her local housing committee who had received her instructions that morning by telephone. The woman was large and motherly, dressed in a dark green winter coat. There were fulsome words of welcome and friendship and a squeeze of sympathy.

It was dark by the time they cleared the terminal and the line for taxis seemed to stretch all the way into the city. But the woman took Lena's hand and her suitcase and led her to a small minibus in the parking lot. A driver greeted her and they set off across Moscow.

As they drove the woman recited her lines. Lena should know that the police had now arrested her mother's killer—a psychopath, a social misfit who had turned his back on the society that had nurtured him. Finally, then, it was safe for her to come home and she could resume her studies at the university. And who knew what might happen? The state often looked kindly on people who had suffered personal misfortune.

Lena let the words wash over her. After prolonged exposure to sedatives her mind was lazy, concentration short. It was a relief to arrive back in the suburb of Chertanovo, where the silky, sweet voice faded away.

Chapter 25

POSTSCRIPT

In the weeks that followed, Lena was to learn of Sasha's death. Heart trouble, they told her. He had always had a weak heart. A tragedy for someone so young and talented. And the lady with the green coat had visited again, holding out a large white handkerchief to catch the tears that Lena couldn't cry.

It struck her later that a handkerchief normally signified a cease-fire.

Gradually she learned to live alone, saturated herself in her studies, and was absorbed back into Soviet life. And almost a year passed before the letter arrived.

She had come home late one night from the university and seen it through the crack in the mailbox. A state money order in a light blue envelope. She assumed it was a mistake, put it in a drawer, and forgot about it.

Next month, on the same day, a similar order arrived for an amount backdated nearly twelve months. She took both envelopes to the savings bank in Chertanovo to seek guidance.

No mistake, she was told. The money was hers.

"But why?" she asked.

"How should I know?" answered the clerk crossly. "If you don't want it, give it to me."

Lena gasped and took the money. It amounted to 513 rubles a month, a small fortune.

She didn't know it was the state pension allotted to senior government officials. How could she? She had no idea that her true father had attained such heights, still less the circumstances of his fall. Try as she might she could find no explanation for the monthly check.

Sometimes she would think about it when she visited her mother's grave. She would sit there for an hour or two gazing out over the flatlands and the waste ground, daydreaming.

Her mother had never spoken of the past, of Tallinn, or a young Party man she had met. And now there was no one to speak for her. As Lena listened all she could hear was the wind, blowing snow in her face, freezing the tears.